"Jim, you're shaking," she said.

"I know," he admitted. "It's the dogs. It's like a phobia, it came out of nowhere. I only have to see a Snoopy poster and I break into a sweat."

He let her take the keys from him, and she guided him through into the main room and sat him on the threadbare old sofa. He'd been fine until the drive back, there simply hadn't been time to be scared, but now he could feel himself locking up tight like an overstrung violin. Linda went into the kitchen and came back a couple of minutes later with a tumbler half-filled with what must have been almost all of the remaining Glenfarclas malt.

"Here," she said, helping him to raise it to his lips. His hand was so unsteady that the glass rattled aginst his teeth.

"Better?" she said, and he nodded.

A couple of minutes later, he sat back. A couple of minutes after that, he was out.

Linda waited for a moment, and then spoke his name. He didn't react. She checked his pulse, which was strong, and then she went over to the doorway and switched the main room light on and off three times.

And then, having given the signal, she went through into the kitchen to clear the big table in readiness.

About the author

Stephen Gallagher lives with his wife and
daughter in North Lancashire's Ribble Valley.
He is the author of CHIMERA, FOLLOWER
and a number of short stories. VALLEY OF
LIGHTS, his highly acclaimed novel, was
published with great success and is currently
being filmed.

Oktober

Stephen Gallagher

NEW ENGLISH LIBRARY
Hodder and Stoughton

With thanks to Andrew Greenwood, Dr Philip Moorhouse, and Philippe Oriet for research advice and assistance

First published in Great Britain in 1988 by New English Library

New English Library Edition 1989

British Library C.I.P.

Gallagher, Steve
  Oktober.
  I. Title
  823'.914[F]

  ISBN 0 450 49178 1

Printed and bound in Great Britain for Hodder and Stoughton Paperbacks, a division of Hodder and Stoughton Ltd., Mill Road, Dunton Green, Sevenoaks, Kent TN13 2YA. (Editorial Office: 47 Bedford Square, London WC1B 3DP) by Cox & Wyman Ltd., Reading.

CONTENTS

PROLOGUE

A Ride on the Black Carousel

'Tis less the horror than the grace
Which turns the gazer's spirit into stone
– Shelley, 'On the Medusa in
a Florentine Gallery'

I don't know how you'd write about a winner if he wasn't a loser who'd prevailed.

— Warren Zevon

ONE

Seventeen was being a bitch, as usual.

If there was any irony in the thought, Bruno didn't see it. The dogs inside the pens always got jealous of the dogs that were still outside in the yard during the daily hosing-out, but he'd been noticing for some time now that the number seventeen animal took it worse than most. She'd lope back and forth from shelf to floor and back onto the shelf again, and the other five huskies in there with her would crowd back wherever they could to give her space. Two of them still had shaved patches and scars, souvenirs of their failure to get out of her way when Bruno had come within reach of the wire.

She hated him, it was as simple as that. She could read him in some way that the others couldn't, and she found plenty to be afraid of. Bruno leaned on his brush in the half-swept last pen of the row, and he listened to the even *bump-bump-bump* of her pacing on the other side of the rough wooden wall. Draining water lay like eels on the concrete floor, glistening in the light from the overhead fluorescents; the day never made it this far inside.

Down the row and around the corner, one of the dogs was crooning gently to itself. Only inches above Bruno's head – the ceiling was barely six feet high – there was an almost continuous scratching of claws on boards. The six bear-like Eskimo dogs in the roof space were getting restless, as if messages of tension were running along invisible lines.

The Siberian in the next pen paced from floor to shelf, from shelf to floor, on and on.

She hated him. "It's mutual," he said out loud, surprising himself with the sharpness of his voice in the cold air. The pacing continued without missing a beat, as rhythmic and as powerful as a steam-driven machine.

We'll need another dog for a lab sacrifice in a couple of weeks, he thought. *How'd you like to be the one to get it?*

Everything stopped.

The only sound was the slow drip from the hose coiled over its standpipe, halfway down the access passage and below the roof-space trapdoor. Even the animals in the yard outside had stopped their snuffling against the hatch.

Bruno waited, but still nothing moved.

"Four-footed bastards," he said, and carried on with his sweeping-down of the floor.

A couple of minutes later, he threw the broom out into the passageway. There was still some straw and ordure that he'd missed in the corners, but he'd had enough. Unslipping the juiced-up electric baton that he kept on a loop at his hip – better than any amount of affection when it came to guaranteeing obedience, in Bruno's experience – he winched up the hatch so that the dogs could come thundering back into their pen from the yard outside. They leapt onto their shelves or slunk into the enclosed dens beneath, and even before they were settled he let the hatch fall. They watched him, pig-eyed and glittering with malevolence, as he stepped out of the pen and secured the door behind him.

There was still a silence from number seventeen's enclosure.

Whoever had built the place had gone for solidity rather than finesse. The woodwork of the pens was like that of a log barn, and the door of each cell was held in place by double-bolted iron hinges. With the baton held easily by his side, Bruno put his face up to the wire mesh look-through alongside the frame.

It wasn't too light in there, but he registered nothing out of the ordinary. Three of the hulking Greenland dogs lay on the platform, and another could be seen half-in and half-out of the den underneath.

Bruno leaned closer to get a look into the corners.

An artillery shell of bone and muscle exploded in his face.

He took a fast step backwards, cattleprod held at the ready, but there was no way that the dog could get through to him. The Siberian was clawing and snarling and spitting, lips drawn right back and muzzle rammed up hard against the mesh with her eyes showing white rims of fury, but the wire was tough and it held. She fell away and jumped again. Now there were flecks of blood on the metal.

Bruno watched as she crashed against the mesh over and over, each impact a little less forceful than the one before. Dogs in the other pens were starting to growl, a low sound like a fleet of heavy trucks revving. Agitated skittering noises, claws on boards again, came from the roof space overhead. A couple more leaps, and then he'd reach out with the baton and stroke its live tip across the wire just as the dog was making contact. The burns would make her scream for an hour, if the shock didn't snap her in two.

On the next one. He tensed himself, ready.

"What the fuck do you *do* in this place?" the astonished voice of a stranger demanded out of nowhere.

Bruno turned around.

If there was one duty that Micheline Bauer disliked above all others, it was that of sitting up in the common room with a pair of binoculars and keeping an eye on the rich kids who turned up every now and again to borrow some of the sled dogs so that they could freak around on the glacier. But what could she say? Rochelle Genoud was the one who always brought them along, and Rochelle Genoud was the chairman's stepdaughter. There was nothing that the station staff could do other than to put up with their presence and hope that their visits would be short and that they'd keep their noses out of the research facilities.

She tried to focus the binoculars. These things always gave her a headache. It didn't help that her subjects were hardly more than specks in the blinding haze where the hard sunlight met the glacier. Beyond this were the mountains, razor-sharp and veined with ice against the sky.

There seemed to be somebody missing. There ought to be seven figures, but she could only count six.

Probably the heiress's bodyguard taking a break, Micheline told herself, and deciding that it was time she did the same she lowered the binoculars and rubbed at her eyes.

11

Not that the common room was much to look at, because its odd mix of tired old furniture and office throwouts gave it the air of a run-down youth hostel. The station was halfway up a Swiss mountain, a little-used railway stop on a line where thousands of ski nuts passed through but almost nobody ever got off. It had a staff of twenty, mostly Germans and French; it also had four good-sized labs, three operating theatres used mainly for postmortem dissection, a thousand or so rats, and about three dozen huskies that had been left over from the station's previous existence as a sled dog breeding centre. They used the dogs in tests sometimes, but generally their cold-weather metabolisms were so slow that they distorted the results. No original research was carried out at the station; it was strictly product pre-testing only, a continuous one-way processing of animal life into data for other minds to assess.

Johnny Tostevin wandered across the room behind her, heading for the coffeemaker. She wondered if he'd bring her a cup, or whether she'd have to ask.

She raised the binoculars again.

The glacier didn't seem so much like a slow-moving river of ice, more like a snow-filled basin with a gentle incline that was sheltered by the mountains above. It wasn't as safe as it appeared, and crevasse and avalanche danger meant that none of the ski runs from the higher resort even came close.

"What's going on now?" Johnny Tostevin said from just behind her. He hadn't brought her anything.

"They're only farting around," Micheline said.

"Did they stop for lunch?"

"They had champagne in the hamper. Now they're just running the sleds around in a circle."

Johnny gave a disgusted grunt. "Fucking chairman's daughter," he said. "I hope she breaks a leg.'

Rather than ask him for anything, Micheline set down the binoculars on the table by the window and went over to get her own coffee. Johnny picked them up to take a look at the distant scene, and started fiddling with the focus settings that Micheline had spent more than half an hour getting just right. Suddenly she hated this place, a surge of fury against the isolation and the company and the lack of social life and the lousy TV reception and the tattered magazines passed from hand to hand.

Over by the window, the internal phone buzzed. She didn't have to move because Johnny was already picking it up.

There was no more coffee. But the anger had all drained out of her now, leaving her bitter and spent. She had brains and she had ambition, more of each than a dozen Johnny Tostevins, and as soon as she'd put in an acceptable length of service on product research she'd be reaching for bigger and better things inside the organisation. Johnny, unlike her, had gone about as far as he would ever get. It annoyed her that she still seemed to dream about him at least once a week.

"You're kidding me," he said stonily into the phone, and immediately Micheline knew that there was some problem.

Johnny listened for a few seconds longer, and then he put down the receiver. "Trouble in the pens," he said, and he headed for the door. Her lookout duty forgotten, Micheline moved to follow him.

Trouble in the pens usually meant only one thing.

Bruno.

About half of the centre's staff were already down in the pens when Micheline arrived about five strides behind Johnny, everybody talking at once and trying to be heard over a background of howling dogs. They moved aside to let him through, and it was then that Micheline got sight of a figure lying on the bare concrete floor. It was a youngish man in Levis and a ski jacket, someone that she'd never seen before, and he was stretched out on his back with his jacket and his shirt ripped open to the waist while Chantal, one of the lab assistants, crouched over him and seemed to be listening to his heart.

"I can't hear anything," Chantal was saying desperately. "I can't hear anything at all!"

Johnny got down beside her and touched the man's throat, looking for a pulse. There wasn't much space here and everyone had to rearrange themselves around him, and as they moved Micheline got sight of Bruno. He was standing some way back from the others, arms folded and looking morose, and Micheline knew straight away that her first instinct had been right. She'd never liked Bruno much. He was tall and gangling, as unkempt as a polar explorer, and he had a habit of picking interesting little items out of his beard and inspecting them.

Johnny glanced up at Chantal. "Did you try resuscitation?"

"Right away."

"How long had he been out before you started?"

"I don't know. Not long. Ask Bruno."

But instead of asking Bruno, Johnny looked up at the others. "Let's get him out of this bearpit and into one of the treatment rooms," he said, almost having to shout because the racket from the distressed dogs all around them was so loud now. Four of them each took a corner of the man and hoisted him up like a battering-ram. Micheline, having been the last one through the door, now held it open as they carried him out.

"I could have been doing it wrong," Chantal was saying. "I only ever worked on dogs before."

They got him into treatment room number four, which was like a fully equipped operating theatre only three-quarter sized. When they knocked the straps out of the way and laid him on the table, his legs dangled over the end. Two of the men lifted him for as long as it took Johnny to get the ski jacket off. He threw this over to Micheline and said, "Go through the pockets, find out who he is." And then, to the others; "What happened to him? What exactly are we supposed to be dealing with here?"

The story didn't take as long to tell as it did to get a muzzle-mask fitted over the man's face. Johnny started heart massage while someone else worked the oxygen bag, and the man's chest started to rise and fall in a semblance of life. It was weird to see, and it looked all wrong. As she sorted through the cards and papers that she'd found in an inside pocket of the ski jacket, Micheline realised that she was already thinking of him as a dead man. If more than four minutes had gone by before Chantal had started work on him, they might as well send him down to the market to be with the rest of the vegetables.

He'd arrived with Rochelle Genoud's party, although nobody had ever seen him with the group before. Apparently he'd walked in from the glacier after taking a fall and wrenching his shoulder; Micheline thought it best not to mention that she'd seen nothing of this because she'd probably been messing around trying to adjust the field glasses at the time. Dagmar, the centre's housekeeper, had directed him to the first aid room, but he must have taken a wrong turn because he'd next appeared in the dog pens. Bruno's story was that he'd taken the intruder for a would-be thief or an industrial spy. His solution to the problem had been a quick *zap* between the eyes with the electric baton, and the man had dropped like a stone.

"He's English," Micheline said, looking at his passport. "James Harper." She had a little trouble pronouncing the *James*. "He's a teacher at one of the international schools in Gstaad."

Johnny looked up at her as she said this, but he didn't break his rhythm. "Just a teacher? Not one of the rich kids?"

"I've just been looking in his wallet. Definitely not one of the rich kids."

Johnny kept on going, beginning to tire, but now he was thinking hard as well. Micheline could almost read his mind.

Little Werner Risinger, Rochelle Genoud's half-brother, attended one of the international schools. They were small, expensive boarding schools specialising in intensive tuition for the likes of embassy children. Staff were usually recruited through agencies overseas and were often low-paid and unqualified, but in the vacations they'd get to move in circles that they'd otherwise only ever see in Martini ads. If James Harper was a teacher and only along for the ride, and if none of the party missed him . . .

"I'm still not getting any heartbeat," Chantal said. She'd brought in a cylindrical metal stethoscope from one of the other rooms and had put it against the pale skin of the

Englishman's side. Everybody else was watching with a sick kind of expression as the Englishman gave about as much response to the rescue efforts as a side of meat.

Someone else took over the heart massage, and another of the technicians brought over an ECG trolley and tried to make a decent guess about where best to put the electrodes. Johnny shone lights into the Englishman's eyes but it was obvious that he only had a vague idea about what he was doing. The ECG monitor, when started, gave a hopeful-looking blip every time the heart muscle was put under pressure, but when the massage was stopped for a moment the screen showed nothing more than a flat line.

"Any suggestions?" Johnny said to the mute crowd around him.

"Shot of adrenaline, directly into the heart muscle," someone offered.

"Is there any adrenaline in the building?"

But this time the best that anybody could do was to give a shrug.

Micheline said, "What about the new EPL formula?"

Johnny looked at her. "What about it?"

EPL was the name of the reformulated drug that Micheline had been running tests on for more than six weeks now. "It's a stimulant," she said. "The formula doesn't resemble adrenaline, but it has some of the same properties. Look at him. What are we going to lose?"

Everybody looked at the Englishman, white as a broken dove under the operating light.

"Get it," Johnny said.

She ran up to her own lab and broke out two phials of EPL and the longest, toughest hypo needle that she could find. On her way back she glimpsed Bruno at the end of the treatment room corridor; he seemed to be hanging around trying to pick up some idea of what was going on without wanting to get too close, and when he saw her he drifted away like some kind of wraith.

They parted to let her through. Nothing on the table had changed. The six weeks of tests had told her very little about EPL that could be extrapolated into the case of a human subject, and it went without saying that they were on dangerous ground here.

Looking at Johnny, she said, "If this works, then we're okay. But if it doesn't, and someone spots the puncture site . . ."

"Try to disguise it," Johnny said. "Find a freckle, or something."

She studied the Englishman's skin for a moment. "No freckles," she said. "I'll go in through the nipple."

Not even Johnny could bring himself to watch.

They worked on him for another half-hour, but by then it had become obvious that they were wasting their time. Everybody had taken a turn either on the oxygen bag or at chest massage, and the only time that the steady line of the ECG monitor had seemed to waver independently had been when someone had tripped over the wire.

Finally, Johnny reached up and switched off the operating light.

"Everybody listen to this," he said. "I'm going to go upstairs and call Basle. I'll tell them the problem and we'll see how they want to handle it."

"What about the police?" Chantal said.

'That's not going to be my decision," Johnny said. "Until we get told otherwise, none of this has happened. We're all going back to our jobs and we're going to carry on as normal. If anybody's asked about a schoolteacher, no-one knows anything. Somebody find Bruno and make sure he gets that into his head. For now I'm going to lock this room and hold onto the key."

They filed out into the corridor, silent in the aftermath of disaster. The passageway ran almost the length of the chalet and had glass bricks for windows which let in a pale, rainwashed-looking light without images. Micheline stayed to watch as Johnny locked the door behind them.

The Englishman lay as they'd left him, his arms and legs still overhanging the sides of the undersized table.

Micheline had used his ski jacket to cover his face.

Johnny was gone for most of the evening, and didn't get back until well after twelve. A team from Special Projects had arrived in a Mercedes four-wheel-drive after a hazardous climb on ploughed tracks, and they'd taken away both Johnny and something that a stranger might have guessed to be a weighted sack wrapped in sheet plastic. Rochelle Genoud and her friends had departed a couple of hours before. None of them even seemed to have noticed that one of their number was missing; apparently the Englishman wasn't a much-valued member of their set.

Bruno at least had the sense to stay out of everybody's way. He kept himself down in the pens and probably spent the time wondering about his future; deep questions like, whether he was going to *have* any future when the company had finished with him.

It was almost one in the morning when Micheline found Johnny, exhausted-looking and slumped on one of the threadbare old sofas in the common room. The eyes that looked up at her were dark-ringed, but they didn't have the bleak no-hope message that she'd been half-expecting.

"It's fixed?" she said.

"It's a long story. I'm going to call a meeting in here and tell it to everybody in the morning."

"I'm the one who put the needle in, remember," she said. "I want to know now."

He sighed and closed his eyes for a moment, but he was too beat even to argue.

"We took him back to his school," he said. "There are about five or six staff on the premises right now, nobody else. We waited until the housekeeper left and the others all got into the school minibus to go down into Gstaad, and then we broke in. We got the body stripped and put it into bed, put the reading light on and left a book open by him, made it look as if he might have had some kind of seizure in his sleep."

"So they'll do a post-mortem, and they'll find the EPL in him. They might even find the puncture wound in his heart and the shock-burn on his skin. What then?"

"We left a load of stuff at the back of his underwear drawer – speed, cannabis, cocaine, you name it. Nobody's going to start puzzling over an EPL fingerprint on the chromatograph with so much junk close to hand. Anything

18

they can't explain, they're going to assume it was self-administered. The rest of it, we'll just have to take a chance. You did a good job on the point of entry. We wiped off one drop of blood and then nothing showed."

"And that's *it*? No report to the police, nothing to explain?"

Johnny looked at the floor, and rubbed at the side of his face as if it had begun to go numb. "The expression used was that we're going to 'keep this one in the family'. But I don't think that means it will stop here."

"Meaning what?" Micheline said, warily.

"Meaning that there's going to be an internal enquiry, the present staff will be dispersed to new jobs, and the centre may even be closed down."

Johnny looked anything but happy at the idea. As head of the facility, he was probably going to find himself carrying the weight for the disaster even though it had been Bruno who'd wielded the overjuiced baton. Wherever he went after this, it was bound to be downhill. For the first time ever, Micheline put a sympathetic hand over his; and, almost absently, he turned his own hand over and gave hers a return squeeze.

But Micheline hardly noticed. Johnny Tostevin was now yesterday's news, her gesture hardly more than a reflex.

Micheline was already beginning to think about tomorrow.

And almost at that same moment, on the outskirts of one of the most fashionable of Swiss winter resorts, a Volkswagen minibus was crunching to a halt on the turning-circle in front of an empty chalet school. Its doors opened and three young men climbed out, their heads pleasantly buzzing with good times and imported beers.

"Hey," one of them said. "Jimbo's back," and the others both looked up to where a single light burned in a window under the eaves.

"Let's go see if he scored with an heiress," one of the others said, and so laden down with cans of Stella Artois from the back of the van they clanked and stumbled their way into the building.

There had been four of them when they set out but Dieter, the young maths graduate from Mainz, had managed to pass himself off as a ski instructor and had been taken on to a party somewhere by a couple of American girls. Of those remaining, one was an Australian physics dropout and the other two were recruits who'd come to the international school via the same agency as Jim Harper. There wasn't a single formal teaching qualification between any of them, but they got on well with the boys and the school's end-of-year results were always good.

They made their noisy way up the back stairs past the empty dormitory level, burping and calling out Jim Harper's name as they went.

"Shit," the Australian said suddenly as he stepped onto the upper landing where the staff bedrooms were all situated. There was a loud crash as every can that he was carrying hit the boards. He leapt forward, his head instantly clear.

Jim Harper lay halfway down the landing, his body twisted in around the bedsheet that had dragged along behind him. The rest of his bedding made a trail back to the open doorway of his room, evidence of his slow and tortured progress towards the pay phone at the landing's end. He'd made it about two-thirds of the way, but he wasn't moving now. One hand was reaching out, braced hard against the boards like the pale claw of a fallen statue.

The Australian, who'd worked two summers as a life-guard in a public pool, rolled Jim onto his side and, after checking that his airway was clear, started to put him into the recovery position.

He looked up at the other two men, who were gawking helplessly.

"One of you get on the phone, quick," he said. "Call for an ambulance. He's hardly breathing."

PART ONE

The Caretaker

Two

"It's always pissing with rain around here," Bob McAndrew said, and his voice echoed up through three storeys of empty rooms and peeling wallpaper. "I should have bought a boat instead of a house."

Not the most encouraging start, but this was Jim Harper's first real job in a year and he didn't want to blow it on the first day, so he said nothing. He shivered, and wondered if the dusty grate would take a fire. He could find out as soon as the McAndrews were out of the way, although he didn't have much hope; the house didn't seem to have been occupied for years, and the flues were probably blocked with soot and old birds' nests.

McAndrew stood in the large bay window, the most impressive single feature in the place. One of the panes had been cracked and repaired with tape, and the rain-jewelled glass now gave a view of the town and the sea beyond which was like a slashed painting. Jim waited, but McAndrew didn't move. A momentary darkness seemed to be passing through him somewhere deep inside as he stared out into the soft afternoon light. In the shadows on the far side of the room, McAndrew's wife stood wrapped in a bear-hug of expensive white fur. She hadn't spoken since Jim, their new caretaker, had arrived, but she watched McAndrew as a lioness might watch her last surviving cub.

"Bob?" she said, softly.

McAndrew heard. He seemed to give himself a shake, and then he turned his back on the town. He looked at Jim and said, "Now, what do you need to know?"

"How do I get paid?" Jim said promptly.

"At the bank in town, every Thursday. Just show up and prove who you are, they'll know what to do."

"Oh."

"Something wrong with that?"

"No, it's just that I'll have nothing to live on for nearly a week."

"What about your last Giro?"

"I spent all of that to get myself here."

McAndrew looked at the ceiling, and sighed. His self-image was obviously that of a hard-nuts businessman, hotter than shit from a phoenix, and somebody whose world turned more slowly or with less organisation was an obstacle that he couldn't understand.

Lynne McAndrew said, "You can call the bank in the morning, can't you, Bob?"

McAndrew frowned. "That's hardly a business arrangement."

"Oh, come on." The voice from the shadows was gentle, persuasive, and apparently effective. It was a relief for Jim to find that somebody was on his side. He knew that he wasn't exactly a confidence-inspiring sight; he hadn't been able to shave since the day before, and the hand-me-down overcoat that he wore over a splitting leather flying jacket had originally been bought for somebody a couple of sizes larger. On the bare floorboards beside him, his suitcase was leaking out some of the water that it had absorbed on the long walk up to the Cliff House.

"All right," McAndrew said, after enough of a pause to suggest that this was his own decision. "I'll authorise them to release the first payment early. But the other cheques stay on schedule – as far as I'm concerned we've got a contract, and that's my side of it. I expect you to stick to yours."

"What exactly will you want me to do?"

"Just sit tight and keep the squatters and the gypsies out until the spring. I've nailed up all the windows and put new locks on all the doors. Use them every time you go out, even if it's only for five minutes. No animals and no visitors. A local agent will be calling around every now and again with builders to look the place over. Nobody else is to get in. Understood?"

It sounded to Jim as if he was going to be living in constant danger of siege. He said, "Should I expect someone to try?"

"There are three or four empty places along the cliffs. They're all targets for kids and tramps. Just make sure everybody knows this one's lived in." McAndrew took out his wallet and sorted through a fan of business cards; he removed one and held it out. "Any trouble," he said, "tell the agent."

Jim took the card. It gave no address, just a telephone number. He said, "Is there a phone in the house?"

"No. And there's no power on the upstairs floors, either. Water supply's usable in the kitchen only, unless you've got a taste for lead."

Lynne McAndrew said, "Tell him about the floor," but McAndrew shrugged as if it was a matter of no real importance.

"Some of the boards have rotted, that's all. You go for a wander in the bedrooms in the dark and you're liable to end up in the cellar with two broken legs and an arse full of splinters. If I were you I'd just forget the upstairs altogether." He breathed in deeply and looked around, as if the cold, damp air of the house might remind him of something that he'd missed. Jim was trying to imagine what it was going to cost to make the place decently livable again, but he was beginning to lose track of the zeros as McAndrew turned to his wife and said, "I'm going to make sure I got all the windows. Take him through and give him the keys, will you?"

Jim picked up his case, and followed Lynne McAndrew into the kitchen. The floor was covered in old lino and the walls were gloss-painted, and overhead a hundred-watt bulb hung without a shade. Most of the floor space was taken up by a family-sized table with three unmatched chairs around it, and this was backed up against an off-yellow electric cooker that looked big enough and old enough to double as a sacrificial furnace.

"Quite a place," Jim said, he hoped diplomatically.

"Quite a dump," Lynne McAndrew corrected as she walked around to the head of the table, where a cardboard Chivas Regal box overshadowed two keys on a tag. "The way Bob goes on, you'd think he owned it."

"Doesn't he?"

"Bob's an undischarged bankrupt, he doesn't own a thing. All this is in my name."

Jim set down his suitcase. "You don't seem very keen."

"I'm not. It's a grim old house in a dead town. He's failed here once, and I just know he's going to do it again. Now he thinks he's got something to prove." She held up the two keys. "One for the front door, one for the back. But if you ask me, nobody in their right mind would ever want to break in." But she smiled as she said it. She was dark-haired and pale even against the white of the fur, and seen close-up she was neither as old nor anything like as brittle as Jim might have expected.

"Hey," he said, "don't knock it, it's work."

"I'm only sorry we couldn't fix you up with anything better."

"This is fine. It's not as if you owed me anything."

"Perhaps not. But we owe Doctor Franks, and that's something else." Her face turned serious. "When Bob was doing well I was getting through a bottle of Pernod every other day until it nearly poisoned me. Alan Franks dried me out and wound me up and set me going again. Then when Bob's business started to fold, I was suddenly all right. Don't you think that's strange? I can't take it when he's successful, but when he's on the skids there's no problem. I don't touch the stuff any more, but I haven't turned into an evangelist about it." She indicated the cardboard box. "You'll find the odd bottle in here, along with an electric heater and one or two other things which should make life a little easier."

"Thanks," Jim said. Somewhere far-off in the house, a hammering started.

Lynne McAndrew looked around, and said, "I hope this works out all right. For you, I mean. I heard all about the bad year you've been having."

"I'll be fine. Anywhere that isn't a hospital already has a lot going for it."

"That won't last. Go down into the town and get to know some people. Throw parties. You could hardly damage the place, could you?"

"But your husband said . . ."

"He's just afraid of his creditors finding out about the house and trying to get it attached. What I'm telling you is, live a little. Put it all behind you, do you hear?"

McAndrew returned then, so Jim didn't get a chance to reply. McAndrew was carrying a hammer which was so new that it still had an orange price tag stuck to its handle.

His wife said, "I've just been suggesting to our new caretaker that he should fill the house with women and throw wild parties."

"Very funny," McAndrew said, and he turned to Jim. "The fuse box is in the hall and the water shutoff's under a plate in the front garden. Is there anything else you want to ask?"

"I don't think so."

"Right." McAndrew pocketed the hammer. "We've got to pack and catch a plane."

They moved out into the yard, which was enclosed by disused outbuildings on two sides and a fence with a double gate on the third. The roof overhang of the former stables made a covered walkway against the house, and as McAndrew turned up his collar and ran out into the rain to unlock the BMW, his wife and the new caretaker stayed in its shelter.

"Nice motor," Jim said.

"Rented," Lynne McAndrew said, keeping her voice low. "Unlike the villa we're heading for, which is borrowed." McAndrew slid across the inside of the car to unlock the passenger door, and it was time to go. She said, "Take care . . . what is it? James? Jim?"

"My friends used to call me Jimbo," Jim Harper said.

THREE

Wet slate, and mist.

These were the two over-riding impressions that stayed in Jim's mind as he spent most of that first week exploring the small town that was to be his home for the winter. The house was about a mile out along the coast and way up on the cliffs, and when Jim stood in the bay window of the main room he could look down and see most of the seafront in a single sweep. There was a fairly wide beach, and at the far end of town a cast-iron pier that had become so dangerous that they'd had to close it ten years before; beyond that lay a headland, and beyond the headland lay the rest of the world that Jim had been missing for too long.

He'd straightened things out with the bank on the second day, helped by a fair and bookish girl with a nameplate that read *Miss K Pryor*. He spent the rest of that afternoon wondering what the *K* might stand for, and buying in cans and packets of stuff to begin stocking his kitchen. Later in the evening, in the grainy twilit hour before the darkness, he went down into the town again. Wherever he wandered, he always seemed to arrive back at the iron gates of the pier.

Not that there was much elsewhere to keep him away; the row of big Edwardian hotels with their private gardens overlooking the promenade were all closed for the off-season, and life in the town seemed to have slowed to the faintest of heartbeats. Many of the shops were behind bars and canvas, and arcades in the promenade arches had been shuttered with plywood. There were no hands on the pavilion theatre clock, and the pavilion box-office windows were pasted several layers deep with posters for last year's rock venues in bigger towns far away.

The streets were grey, and steep, and empty. And most of them seemed to lead him back to the pier.

Exactly why, he couldn't say. He tried to work it out as he leaned on the seaward railing of the promenade. The iron structure out over the sand seemed to be beached and long-legged as it waited for the tide to come in and restore its proportions, but it was the peeling wood fantasy-tower structure right out at the far end that drew him more than anything else. Part of it seemed to have been burned away in some old accident; there was scaffolding around the damage, but no sign of any repair work. The access gates had been padlocked and topped with wire.

Well, Jim, he thought . . . I don't know what this is. But Gstaad, it ain't.

He'd had two brief letters from the Australian, who'd last been heard of heading for home via Bali and who'd written to Jim care of the hospital. From these he learned that Rochelle Genoud, referred to as 'the adorable and untouchable', was now in Paris and getting a hard dose of reality as she served out a lowly apprenticeship with one of the fashion houses there. Of his current journey, he wrote 'lots of agony, not much ecstasy', and wrapped it up with some good wishes for Jim's continued recovery. He carefully mentioned nothing of the circumstances of the night on which they'd found him.

As far as Jim was concerned, the whole thing was just a haze with some *very* scary patches in it. He was lucky that the others had checked his room and flushed the drugs cache they'd found down the toilet, or else he might have been walking straight out of medical care and into jail; but as to how the drugs came to be there, or what had happened to him, or even what he'd been doing for the previous couple of weeks, he had no ideas at all. His return to health had been slow, and marked in the early stages by a series of nightmares more vivid and detailed than he'd ever have believed possible. But these had faded and so had the partial paralysis, leaving him with a dull no-sensation area in his left hand and a loss of peripheral vision on the same side; and even this wasn't something that he'd been aware of until the tests had shown it up, because without even knowing it he'd simply become used to turning his head a little more than usual to compensate.

And now this. Caretaker in a house where even squatters would form a line to get out, sleeping on a folding bed in the kitchen of a wind-strafed icebox on the cliffs because he was unqualified and, in his present state at least, probably otherwise unemployable. He'd already formed a theory as to why McAndrew wanted to renovate and move in here, and it was linked to the bay window view from the main room; Jim believed that he wanted to stand there looking down as he had on that first afternoon, one step nearer to heaven than the town where he'd failed. When Jim stood in the same place, watching as the tide slowly crept in to drown the glazed mudflats of the shore, he found that his attention

29

was drawn not to the town but, again, to that cut-price Chinese palace that stood out over the rolling grey sea.

Perhaps he'd write something about it in the mostly-neglected diary that Doctor Franks had urged him to keep.

Perhaps later.

His home set-up was embarrassingly sparse; his clothes, a few books, a *Dark Knight* poster, and an old Bang and Olufsen radio held together with elastic bands. He also had a six-month supply of each of his prescription tablets, but he was doing his best to wean himself away from them without telling Doctor Franks. He'd already collected a sizeable backlog in a plastic carrier bag, and he'd yet to feel any adverse effects.

Now, the winter stretched ahead. The idea was beginning to scare him a little.

During all of the time in which he'd been shunted from Swiss hospital to British hospital to out-patient clinic, his one obsession had been to get back out and to start up some kind of new life as soon as possible. But now, faced with the reality of his surroundings, he was beginning to wonder what he'd let himself in for. It was easy enough for Lynne McAndrew to encourage him to be social. You could be more social in a morgue. There were people to talk to in a morgue, even if they didn't answer back.

New life? If this was going to be it, then he'd gone seriously wrong somewhere.

But everything changed from the day that he found the wallet.

FOUR

It was a three-storey building with gabled attic windows at the far end of the town. There were four separate buzzers and four mailboxes under the red-tiled porch, each with apartment numbers but no names. Jim was still thinking over what to do, when the front door was opened from the inside.

She stopped in surprise. She wasn't the girl whose photograph was on the out-dated security pass that he'd found in the wallet. She said, "Are you looking for someone?"

"Somebody called Linda McKay." Jim said. "Am I in the right place?"

"Top-floor flat. But she isn't in."

"Any idea when she'll be back?"

"No, but I know where you can find her now. Come on, I'll show you." And she pulled the door until it clicked shut behind her, gave a hard shove to test it, and beckoned for Jim to follow her down the short garden path and into the street.

She was moving at speed, and he had to scramble to catch up. She said, "Have you found your way around yet?"

"Just about," he said. "It didn't take me long." And then, belatedly, he realised that he'd seen her before. He said, "Don't you work at the bank?"

"Yeah," she said. "And would you believe that it's the most exciting prospect I could find around here? We're not exactly talking boom town."

They turned a corner into a residential road that would take them downhill and into the centre. Some of the houses had been subdivided into holiday flatlets, others were showing sale boards.

"I've been keeping my eyes peeled for any detectable trace of social life," Jim said. "Am I wrong, or isn't there any?"

"Pretty close," the girl with the *Miss K Pryor* nameplate said. "There used to be the pier dances, but the pier burned down. And then there used to be the cricket club, but that closed when Bob McAndrew's place went bust. Now there's only Spencer's."

"What's that?"

"You're going there. Espresso bar and Jesus junkshop. It found its style in nineteen fifty-eight and hasn't changed since."

They came to a four-way junction where a butcher's van with a holed exhaust was inching over the line against a red traffic light. She took Jim's elbow, and guided him around to where he'd be able to see. "Down there," she said, pointing. "Under the awning and about halfway along."

The lights changed, the van surged impatiently forward and stalled. Jim was looking at a slate-grey row of shops whose pavement walk was protected by a conservatory-style overhang supported by iron pillars. He'd sheltered there the day before when he'd come down to check on the books in the second-hand shop. The shop had been closed, the rain had been falling, and he'd eyed the small café a couple of doors along. He hadn't gone in.

He said, "I know the place you mean."

"Well, you'll find Linda in there. In fact, when it's raining and the library's closed, you've got a good chance of finding *anybody* in there." She started to move away, tugged by the soundless call of her job. "See you around."

"Right," he said. "And thanks."

It was strange, but already he felt as if he was losing the only ally that he'd made so far in this town. He called after her, "What does the *K* stand for?"

But without even breaking her stride, she only turned, and waved, and walked on.

The 'Jesus junkshop' part of the café was a sales window stocked with plastic saints and day-glo copies of famous religious scenes. They were crowded up behind the steamy glass like headstones in a Parisian cemetery, blurred relics and bleeding hearts and papal reading lamps. Nothing was priced, everything was dusty. Jim went inside.

He spotted Linda McKay straight away.

He'd found her wallet that morning, on the path into town where it descended the rock face in zigzags. It was the square kind which fastened with a tag and a clip, the kind used by both men and women, and when he opened it out he saw that there was money inside. There were also two library tickets in her name, a watch repair ticket that had given him her address, and the security pass carrying the Polaroid shot from which he recognised her now. She was three or four years older than her photograph, and her hair was shorter. She was alone, and there was an open magazine on the table before her. She seemed to be staring straight through it, her mind taking a walk in another country far away.

She wasn't even aware when he stood beside her.

"Excuse me," he said. "I think this is yours."

She stared at it blankly for a moment, and then recognition clicked into place like a ball in a roulette wheel.

"Christ, yes!" she said, but then she quickly caught herself and looked around in case the café owner might have overheard; there was no reaction from the other side of the service hatch, and so she looked up at Jim. He saw eyes that were blue shading almost into violet. "Where did you find it?" she said.

Who cares? he thought. *I think I'm in love.* But all that he did was to tell her about the cliff path.

"You should have been a detective," she told him with a half-smile that was kind of wary of him as a stranger without actually shutting him out completely; like she was saying, I don't know you but you look okay so you can step into the garden, but one false move and I'm running for the house and locking all the doors. At first he thought that she reminded him of somebody. Then he decided that she probably didn't.

He spun out the story for so long that a quarter of an hour later he was still sitting with her, and when she insisted on getting them a pot of what she called Spencer's famous old stewed-pennies tea he put up only token resistance. While she was gone, he shrugged out of his overcoat and let it fall onto the back of his chair, and then he unzipped his flying jacket most of the way. The well-beaten leather had a fair chance of making him look like a renegade or a freedom fighter, while the overcoat only made him look like an oversized orphan.

He had himself back in check by now. For as long as he could remember he'd reacted to certain types of new company in the same kind of way; it had been the Australian who'd had a phrase for it, telling him that he had a dick like a compass needle with any blue-eyed woman standing in for due north. Totally untrue, of

33

course . . . although he *had* fallen flat-out for Rochelle Genoud after only ten minutes of watching her playing tennis from the library of the Risinger house.

And look how *that* had turned out.

While Linda McKay was still over at the counter, he looked at the magazine that she'd been reading. It was open at a Situations Vacant page. Some of the job ads had pencilled queries alongside their boxes, but the magazine itself was at least a couple of weeks old and the marking-up had the look of an ingrained habit.

She came back with a rattling tray bearing a chrome-plated teapot and mismatched crockery. As she set it all down he took the chance to study her again, his first since he'd walked in and spotted her; she had an oval face with delicate features, framed by hair that had been cut almost as a ragged Joan-of-Arc. She wore no rings, but that didn't necessarily mean anything these days.

She also didn't seem in any hurry for Jim to move on, which suited him fine. "Where are you staying?" she said, and so he told her about his job and the Cliff House. She'd heard of McAndrew – apparently you couldn't spend any length of time in this town *without* hearing of him – and she remembered seeing the house when she'd been out walking the evening before.

"You're actually living in that place?" she said incredulously, and Jim could understand what she meant. In its present state the house looked less like a home and more like a mausoleum.

He said, "I'm kind of camping out in the kitchen."

"What's it like?"

"At nights, it's bloody cold."

"I can imagine. What were you doing before?"

But instead of talking about the hospitals, he managed to change the subject.

Jim found that Spencer's tea outdid its reputation, having the taste and appeal of boiled goldfish shit, but he didn't want to say anything to break up the party. When he finally got to glance at his watch without making it obvious, he almost couldn't believe that more than an hour had gone by. The café's clientele showed almost no turnover since he'd arrived; the homely teenaged girls in punk makeup were still by the window, and the old man reading a bodice-ripper paperback had yet to get any further than the page that he'd been studying when Jim had first walked in. This was going to have to end soon, he knew ... but how to make sure that it didn't end completely? She'd seemed interested in McAndrew buying the Cliff House, maybe she'd like to see the inside of the place.

"I think I've seen enough of Spencer's for one day," she said before he could put the idea into words. "Feel like a walk down to the pavilion, or have you got things to do?"

"Nothing I can't get around," he said casually.

He found out more about her as they walked along, both of them hunched slightly against the cold breeze that was coming in from the sea.

Her mother died young, her father lived in Cornwall. She'd worked for an airline and then for a computer firm that had gone bankrupt. She'd been in town for only a few weeks, moving here and renting a flat on the promise of a job in a solicitor's office that had then fallen through. Now she'd become one of the seaside unemployed, and already she was being pressured to move on or lose benefit on the assumption that she was living the good life at the taxpayers' expense.

"I don't know where these people get their ideas about the world," she said. "Or maybe I'm living somewhere else."

She said that she planned to stay for a while. Even if they stopped her money she had some savings that nobody knew about, and it was ludicrous to think that you could jobhunt with any degree of seriousness when you had to uproot and drift on every couple of months.

He learned other things, too. He learned that the girl who worked at the bank was named Kim, and that despite appearances it *was* possible to meet new people and to make new friends even in a place as bleak as this town seemed to be. And by next summer, there would be work in the hotels and on the arcades; it wasn't living the way most people understood it, but it was better than going under.

He wanted to tell her something interesting, something that might impress her. He wondered about using the old ski instructor line, but somehow it hardly seemed appropriate to their surroundings.

And then something happened which put the notion out of his mind.

"Oh, no," she said under her breath. "Not again."

An ancient-looking van which had passed them only moments before was making a U-turn about a hundred yards further on.

Linda said, with some urgency, "Listen, Jim, do something for me. Pretend we've known each other for ages and go along with anything I say. I'll explain why later."

And then he felt her hand slipping into the crook of his arm as the van came to a halt level with them.

The man who got out from behind the wheel was about Jim's age, but a couple of inches taller and a few pounds heavier. He was wearing a dark blue seaman's jacket and jeans, and his hair had been cut a little closer than suited him. In spite of the rough clothes he didn't really look like a workman, more like a student who'd overstayed his time.

"Meet Stephen Fedak," Linda said to Jim. "Steve, this is Jim Harper. I've known him absolutely ages and I can't *believe* that he just walked into Spencer's and found me there."

Fedak looked at them both with eyes that had the dull glitter of marbles, and Jim knew then that Linda wasn't going to have to explain a thing that he couldn't already read from the situation.

Ignoring him almost completely, Fedak said, "I was hoping we could talk."

"We already did," Linda said with a hint of darkness and warning in her voice, and Jim felt her grip on his arm tighten just a little. "Listen," she said, "about tonight. Kim says she can't make it, but is it okay if I bring Jim along?"

Fedak looked as if he'd rather shake hands with a proctologist. But after a moment he seemed to make a conscious effort to loosen up.

"Yeah," he said. "Why not?"

"Jim's working for Bob McAndrew now," she added, and this time Fedak looked at him with actual interest.

"Is that right?" he said, and his face cracked into a pleasant expression that looked about as deep as a paper mask. "Well, I'll see you at seven."

"In the van?" Linda said, but Fedak shook his head.

"I'm taking the van along to Terry's so we can start stripping it down," he said. "I'll get hold of the Beetle instead."

They watched as the van spluttered and coughed into another U-turn, heading away from them along the promenade road. Linda's grip on him relaxed at last, and he felt her hand drop away from his arm.

She said, "I'm sorry for throwing you in at the deep end like that."

"Don't apologise," he said.

"I suppose you got the general idea."

"Enough to get by. Do I take tonight to be an invitation, or what?"

She smiled, sheepishly. "If you can bring yourself to overlook the circumstances it was issued under."

"I can overlook almost anything," he said, "but at least tell me where I'm supposed to be going."

"Nothing much . . . just a couple of pubs out on the moors to make a change of scene from the City of the Living Dead."

Jim thought of the limited nature of his wardrobe, and the even more limited nature of his funds. He said, "It won't be too . . . upmarket, will it?"

"You mean expensive," she said, "and the answer is no. It'll be strictly poverty row and come-as-you-are."

Was he a fast worker, or what was he? The only faint cloud on Jim's new horizon, he considered as he ascended the cliff path which was his shortcut home, was that he'd done something right but he was damned if he could work out what it was. Ahead of him the Cliff House loomed, no longer his prison but just three storeys and a high arch of roof with the stained cream of the outside walls beginning to shed like a skin.

However it had happened, it was about time. His one real social outing of the last few months had taken place when he'd let one of the junior doctors persuade him to go along on a double date with a couple of nurses. He'd suspected that Franks had set the whole thing up, but he'd let it pass. The two nurses had spent the evening drinking halves of lager and telling stories of their experiences in the 'special' clinic, an in-house euphemism for twice-weekly VD treatment sessions. Jim thought he'd done rather well, but the young houseman had ended the evening in a decidedly glassy state.

He needed this. He felt as if he'd been running on half-power for too long, and he'd been starting to get used to it.

Who'd have believed it?

The world could still be good, after all.

And as Jim was letting himself into the Cliff House to find that, surprise surprise, nobody had broken in to make off with his radio or the wallpaper or the rotten old floorboards, Linda McKay was drawing the curtains in her attic apartment even though it wouldn't yet be dark for several hours. She'd fed the meter for a tank of hot water, but it would take at least half an hour before she'd be able to get a bath out of it. Atalanta Pryor had subdivided the building when her husband had died, and now she and her daughter Kim lived on the ground floor while the rest was offered to let. The space available for Linda's flat made it hardly more than a glorified bedsit, but unassuming digs with private-line telephones weren't easy to come by.

By the light of her bedside lamp, she undressed slowly and put on a soft robe that was almost threadbare in places. She'd had others, but this one she'd never thrown away. She supposed that it represented continuity, of a kind. It had her name on it, hand-stitched – how long ago? Back in more innocent days when she'd considered such things worth doing, anyway.

She was thinking about Jim Harper. How at last, he'd found the item that she'd gone to such trouble to drop on the path close to where he was living.

And it was about time. She'd been beginning to wonder what a girl had to do to get herself noticed, around here.

FIVE

Jim got to the rendezvous well before time. It was a Victorian designer's idea of a garden pagoda, green-painted and graffiti-covered, at the seaward corner of the pavilion lawns. Rain and the occasional wind-spray from the highest breakers lashed across almost as far as the low wall between the promenade and the gardens. Jim stood in the dryest part that he could find under the roof overhang, and he shivered. The shelter stank of wet newspapers and of something else that was even less pleasant.

Linda McKay joined him about five minutes later.

"We really picked a night for it," she said breathlessly as she shook out her folding umbrella. "I thought I'd better get here early to look after you, since you hardly know Steve and you don't know Terry at all."

She was referring to Terry Sacks, Stephen Fedak's business partner, co-owner of the van they'd seen that afternoon, and so-far unseen fourth member of the evening's group. Jim wasn't entirely easy with the situation here, and hoped that he'd be able to read it better as the evening went on. He tried to tell himself that however it went, it wouldn't really matter. What did he have to lose, after all?

Linda said, "Here's Terry."

He was approaching at a run with his shoulders hunched against the weather. His denim jacket was a size too small and the black pullover underneath it was a size too big, and as he ploughed through the standing puddles of the promenade his training shoes couldn't have been any protection at all. He seemed small and delicate and as hairy as an ape.

Raindrops glistened like jewels in his dark shoulder-length hair as Linda made the introductions. Terry Sacks was like a pocket Frank Zappa with large, innocent eyes. His handshake was brief and almost without pressure.

Linda asked him about the van.

"It'll be off the road for a week, at least," he said. "Special parts order."

"What about the business?"

He shrugged. "We're stuck until we can move the gear. I'll do some phoning around tomorrow."

The double-pip of an underpowered car horn drifted across the gardens. "That's Steve," Linda said, and the three of them waited for the wind to drop a little before they moved out, leaving the shelter to the spiders and the ghosts of old men with nowhere more interesting to go.

Fedak and their transport were waiting in the pavilion's staff parking lot, a ten-car space that had once been kept empty by a guard-chain and which was now kept empty by an absence of staff. The car was a ten-year-old Volkswagen Beetle, home-sprayed a dark, metallic green and fitted with wide wheels. Patches of primer and lines of filler seemed to indicate that somebody had lost heart for the conversion about halfway through, and now the rust was starting to show.

They climbed inside, Linda first, then Jim, and finally Terry Sacks in the front. Fedak was as grey as a stone under the streetlights, staring straight ahead and with the radio playing too loud. Terry Sacks had to raise his voice when he turned and said, "What about Kim?"

"She's getting a call from her boyfriend in Germany around nine," Linda told him, and he nodded and faced forward again.

Fedak brought the Volkswagen around in a tight circle, and they moved out. There was too much music to allow conversation, but without it the noise of the engine would have done the job just as well. Linda was pushed so close in the narrow seat that Jim could feel her breathing against his side.

They were on the coast road and heading out of town in the opposite direction to the Cliff House; Jim recognised it as the route taken by the bus that had brought him into town. It was a stretch of land where the beaches got wider and the fields levelled out to meet the sea, and within a few minutes they'd passed five or six roadside boards indicating the entrances to trailer sites and caravan parks. One sign had been covered with a tarpaulin, but most of the others relied on locked gates to keep off-season interest away.

The radio signal began to fade, but Fedak found another. They left the coast and followed a smaller road, up onto the inland moors.

They got to the first pub after about a half-hour of driving. It was a low stone building with a walled yard that had been opened up for cars and which was lit by a single overhead floodlight. Beyond the boundary was an endless sea of wind-driven heather that disappeared when Fedak cut the Beetle's headlamps. They all crawled out and shook themselves and made for the pub's sheltered entrance. There were no other lights on the moor for as far as Jim could make out.

Five minutes later, at a table by the big open fire in the main bar, he was staring into his Guinness and trying to think of something to say. Linda had gone hunting through the converted farmhouse for a powder room, leaving him in alien company. If Fedak started to ask him anything about his and Linda's supposed long-standing friendship then he'd be sunk, so he said, "What line of business are you in?"

"Steam cleaning," Terry Sacks said. He was closest to the fire, and he was giving off some steam himself. "We pooled our severance pay to buy the gear and the van."

"You mean car engines, that kind of thing?"

"Hotel kitchens," Fedak said, seeming to make a conscious effort to unwind a notch. "You get so much shit building up in all the little grooves and corners that you need high-pressure steam and detergent to move it, or else you get the health inspectors threatening to close you down. Off-season's the only time to do it; we go in and strip all the fittings out and clean them off. It's filthy work."

"And it pays you?"

"Barely. Either the gear breaks down or the van doesn't

run, and without it we can't shift the big tanks and the compressor."

The two of them, it appeared, had both been employees of Bob McAndrew's latest failed company. He'd originally started the first all-video amusement arcades along that part of the coast when the video game had still been regarded as an expensive and unpromising gimmick, and over five years he'd financed himself into original design and manufacture on an almost cottage-industry scale before losing everything to Japanese competition in a six-month slide. For some strange reason, his failure seemed to have increased most people's respect for his abilities; bad times had turned him into a hero.

"When the plant was open," Fedak said, "he was employing nearly a hundred and twenty people. Now most of them have moved away. You could go down the promenade on a fine day last summer, and if you spotted anyone under sixty it was worth making a note of."

Linda reappeared, and Fedak hitched his chair aside to let her pass. He went on, "Nothing's been the same since. The local council set up an enterprise board. Three weeks back, they announced that they'd be deferring all their grants until next year because all of their budget had gone on administration."

"We were down for a new van," Terry Sacks said morosely, watching the bubbles rise in his glass. He'd asked for a lager with a shot of blackcurrant juice, but he hadn't touched it yet. Somehow, Jim couldn't blame him.

"It's frustrating," Fedak said, warming to his theme, "because we were really going somewhere and now we're right back down at the bottom of the heap. Six months more and we might have made it through on our own. We had this little software sideline going that McAndrew didn't know anything about, but he folded before we could get anything finished."

"I never heard about this," Linda said.

"We've had to keep quiet about it," Terry said. "Mostly because half the stuff we were writing was illegal."

"Illegal how?"

42

"Like *Deus*," Fedak said. "Short for *Deus X*. It was going to be the ultimate hacker program. There's no way we could have sold it over the counter, so we were going to do private deals with businesses for one-off usage. They pay a fee, we set *Deus* to work on their competitors' databanks. It was brilliant, Terry wrote most of it."

"You can actually do that?" Linda said.

"Most hackers in big systems tend to work for the people they're ripping off," Fedak said, "and then when they get found out you don't hear about it. Outsiders have a tougher time because the links are along private rented lines that don't connect to the telephone net. Get into one of those, and you introduce a little democracy into the system. Terry wrote a thing called *Maggie*, you sent this one in and it just messed everything up. And then we were working on a video game, we called it *Snuff* . . ."

After a while the bar started to fill with sports jackets and cravats and Friday-night furs, and Linda suggested that it was time either to re-order or to move on.

When they reached the door it was raining harder, so hard that there was no way that it could last for long. Fedak sprinted for the Volkswagen, now lost amongst Volvos and Saabs, and the rest of them waited in the porch.

Jim had been aware that Linda hadn't said much in all the time that they'd been inside. But now she said quietly to Terry Sacks, "Has Steve already been drinking?"

"You mean, before we set out?" Terry shrugged, but there was an element of evasion in it that he couldn't completely disguise. "Search me."

The Beetle braked hard on the gravel before them, sliding the last couple of yards with its wheels locked and the grit spraying. Fedak was showing no lights; he snapped them on a moment after the car had stopped.

Everybody piled in, the doors slammed. They were on their way again before Jim could even get his breath.

"Sorry about this," Fedak said, looking around as the others stepped through the double-doors behind him.

It had been a fair-sized coaching-house, a staging post on the edge of a moorland village, but it seemed that the owning brewery had brought its designers in. Now it was a Disney artist's bad dream of Olde England.

It was more crowded than the last place, but the clientele was interchangeable. Fedak squeezed his way through to the bar as Jim, Linda, and Terry Sacks bagged a table that had just been vacated in a buttoned-velvet alcove alongside the entrance.

Jim watched to see if Stephen Fedak needed any help. As far as he could make out, Fedak had just managed to catch the attention of one of the counter staff and had jumped the queue by about five places. Nobody around him spoke up, and Jim could sense why; Fedak was beginning to exude a faint but unmistakable aura of danger as the evening went on. The more he loosened up, the more freely he talked and the worse it seemed to get.

Linda was asking Terry Sacks about a job interview that he'd been called to about a week before; a six-hour train ride to a twenty-minute chat ending in a weak handshake that told him he hadn't got it. Jim tuned them out, his eyes still on Fedak. He was leaving the bar now, somehow managing all four glasses at once although he had to stop at a table halfway over to adjust his grip. He was moving again after a couple of seconds, but not before Jim had seen a glint of light on the silver hipflask that he'd used to top up his own glass.

Seated again, he turned his attention to Jim.

"You're in the cliff place, then," he said. "What led you into a job like that?"

"I used to be a teacher overseas. But it didn't last."

"What went wrong?"

"Nothing went wrong. It finished, that's all."

It was quickly becoming clear that Fedak had decided that he wanted to hear something which would make him feel better than he did. And right now, it seemed that the only thing that might improve his mood would be some unhappy piece of news about Jim Harper.

"Being a caretaker," he said. "Isn't that a big step down?"

"No more than being a cleaner is for you," Jim said.

"Steve," Linda said, and there was such a sharp note of warning in her voice that all three of them looked at her.

She went on, with a distinctiveness that carried her words to the tables on either side, "You're being a prick."

Silence all around.

Fedak stared at Linda, and he didn't know how to reply. And then something deep inside him quietly broke, and he lowered his head to stare into his half-emptied glass.

The evening was dying on its feet. Their pool of money ran out, their empty glasses were cleared away, and they had no choice but to go.

They left in single file, threading their way through crowds and copper-topped tables. Just as they got to the door, Jim felt a hand on his arm. Terry Sacks held him back, saying nothing.

The door eased itself shut; Linda and Fedak were already outside. The sky had rained itself clear and the parking lot was glistening wet under amber lights. Two shadows paused on the tarmac, words were exchanged. The taller of the shadows turned and walked away; the other lingered for a moment before following.

Terry Sacks relaxed, and released Jim's arm. He hadn't spoken or looked at him once.

They went outside.

They'd had to leave the Beetle on the road outside the crowded car park, half on and half off the grass verge with the solid darkness of the moors beyond. Jim was trailing behind a little when they reached the car, but Fedak was only just getting the doors open.

"Well, boys and girls," he said with a brightness that was obviously forced, "the night's still young and we haven't got a bean between us. Any suggestions as to how we proceed?"

Nobody had, because nobody could think of anything that they could do which wouldn't cost money. Fedak seemed deliberately to be avoiding looking at Linda now.

So Jim said, "Anybody want to see McAndrew's new house?"

"For what? A little ghost-hunting? Tap the walls for secret panels and look for skeletons behind the brickwork? Or maybe we could just count the woodworm holes until we fall asleep."

"I've got a bottle."

"Ah," Fedak said. "Now, that is more *like* a suggestion."

So they went through their Beetle-cramming act again, and started out on the drive back to the coast. It was mostly downhill, and on the first long slope Fedak cut the engine and freewheeled to save fuel.

Linda was leaning forward immediately. "I've told you before," she said, "you either keep the engine running or I'll walk home, Steve. I mean it."

Fedak complied. He didn't speak again for the rest of the journey.

Jim had only approached the house by road once before, and that had been on his first day before he'd known that there was a path. The road climbed in a series of near-hairpins, a couple of them actually overhanging the sea. If he was expecting some bravado driving display from Fedak, he didn't get it.

They stopped, not in the kitchen yard, but on the more impressive circular drive at the front of the house. As Jim was opening up, Fedak saw the new locks and said. "That's a lot of security."

"And for nothing much," Terry Sacks added. "What's the idea?"

"He's scared of squatters," Jim said, stepping inside and groping for the lightswitch. "That's the only reason why I'm here."

The light was unshaded, the large hall uncarpeted; some of the plaster had fallen from the ceiling and exposed the laths. Fedak said, "A squatter would have more taste. Where's the booze?"

"In the kitchen."

"Then that's the place to be."

He set off into the house with a real sense of purpose and a slightly worried-looking Terry Sacks close behind; Jim wondered how long the two-thirds bottle of Glenfarclas that Bob McAndrew had unwittingly donated was going to last. He was about to follow, but this time it was Linda who held him back. "Wait a minute, please," she said.

Down at the far end of the hall, Fedak stopped.

"Jim's going to show me the rest of the house," she told him. "Carry on, and we'll join you."

Fedak looked for a moment longer. Then he abruptly turned, and shouldered his way through the service door that led towards the back rooms.

"There's no power upstairs," Jim started to say, "and the floors aren't too safe," but Linda stopped him. Another door slammed somewhere deeper in the house as Fedak looked for the kitchen.

She said, "That doesn't matter. I just wanted to say that I'm sorry."

"For what?"

"Steve's been playing up, and it's my fault. I shouldn't have involved you the way that I have."

"Don't worry about it."

"He's pretty decent, really. You're just not seeing him at his best."

"I know. Don't worry about it, I'm having a good time. Shall we join the party?"

She didn't say anything. She stood in the bare hallway with her arms folded against the chill, and she started to smile at him. One glance from those eyes, he thought, and gold would melt.

Or maybe the Australian hadn't been so far wrong about him, after all.

They made their way through the house, following the trail of switched-on lights that marked Fedak's search. He'd finally found the kitchen, and he was sitting with one of the chairs tilted back against the cooker while Terry Sacks sat on the table. Both were holding china cups from the rack over the sink; the Glenfarclas bottle stood between them, its level down by two inches or more.

Fedak rocked his chair around to face Jim. "We've been talking about you, Jimmy boy," he said, a little too loudly. "We think you're being improperly serviced, and we're going to do something about it."

Jim glanced at Terry Sacks. Terry's face was a blank, with loyalty cancelling out anything else that might have been written there. Jim said, "Like, what?"

"We're going to fix you up with some furniture. Make the place a bit more like home."

Now Linda's eyes were on Terry, and he said, "Don't look at me. I don't know what he's talking about."

"You don't have to *know*," Fedak said, leaning forward so that the raised legs of the chair thumped back onto the floor. He stood up. "All you have to do is watch. Come on, everybody back in the car."

Linda wasn't exactly happy, but Jim was ready to go along with any scheme that meant that he could stay in her company a while longer without, after all, having to sit in an empty house watching Stephen Fedak drinking himself into a depression.

As Jim was locking up behind them, he heard her say, "Steve, are you okay for driving?"

"If I wasn't okay," Fedak said, "I wouldn't drive."

He narrowly missed clipping the stone pillar at the end of the Cliff House approach.

They were heading away from the town and further out along the cliffs. Linda said, "I thought this road didn't lead anywhere."

Terry Sacks turned to look at her. "It's about five miles to the old lighthouse, and then a dead end."

"Now, now, boys and girls," Fedak said, gripping the wheel tightly and watching the narrow road unrolling under his lights. "No speculating. Just wait."

So they stayed silent for almost ten minutes, waiting to see what Fedak had in mind. The tall hedges on either side of the road crowded in even closer, and they made it impossible to get any idea of distance or direction. Fedak seemed to know where he was going, though, and he finally stopped and reversed the car into the open entrance to a field. Then he switched off the engine and got out, and the others followed.

The sky had cleared a little more, and now there was even some starlight and a thin sliver of moon high above the clouds. The shadow of a house could be seen against the skyline, and a few yards further down the lane were a couple of overgrown gateposts with no gates. Fedak started out toward these.

"Hey, come on, Steve," Linda said. "What's the idea?"

"The Moynahan place," Fedak said, turning toward them but making no effort to lower his voice. "It's been tied up because of the will for nearly a year, and it's full of stuff that nobody's using. We'll liberate a few sticks for Jimmy boy."

"You can't just break in and help yourself!"

But Fedak was already on his way. "Let him try," Jim said quietly. "He probably won't even get in."

"What if he does?"

"Then there's no way of taking any stuff back."

She was doubtful, but she went along with it. Jim was right; there wasn't even the extra space in the Beetle to carry a table lamp. Terry was still silent as they walked up the driveway behind Fedak, but he seemed relieved now that he knew the excursion couldn't come to anything.

Fedak was almost at the house, and barely visible in the darkness. It was a big double-fronted Victorian place; Jim was thinking that it didn't look unlike the Addams Family home, and then a moment later he was wishing that he hadn't. Linda was staying close to him. He felt her reach out and touch his arm for reassurance as they moved through the night toward the pool of deeper shadow where Fedak was trying to open a window.

Jim was starting to get more than a little nervous. He told himself that the place was empty and that Fedak was soon going to have to give up and walk away, but he couldn't argue his way around a deeper conviction that the reality might prove to be different. Fedak, it seemed, was on some kind of face-saving exercise that was aimed more at impressing himself than anybody else.

There was a squeak, a momentary hint of moonlight on glass. Fedak had managed to raise the lower sash of the window about six inches, and then it had jammed. He put his arm through, and tried to lift the sash further by forcing it with his shoulder.

Jim looked around. Terry Sacks' denims and dark hair made him hard to see, and it was a surprise when his voice came drifting back from some distance ahead. He was whispering and it was impossible to make out what he was saying, but Fedak cut him short and obviously didn't want to hear it.

This was about as close as Jim cared to get. He and Linda had reached the stone-chip forecourt that linked the house to the double garage alongside, and here they stopped.

She'd taken a nervous handful of his overcoat, and she wasn't letting go. She leaned close to his ear and said quietly, "I'm starting to think that this whole party was a mistake."

"Only this part," Jim said. "Why don't we tell him there's somebody around? We could say we'd seen a car in the garage."

There was a long silence.

Then Linda said, "There *is* a car in the garage."

From over at the house came a crash of breaking glass. Fedak had thought of another way around his problem.

"Oh, shit," Jim said bleakly.

Upper floor lights started to come on straight away. Even worse, dogs were barking – at least two of them, loud and deep and in no way playful. Jim turned Linda around, and they started to run.

Within a couple of yards they were stumbling over a raised edge of turf where stone chips gave way to grass, but they both managed to keep their balance by holding onto each other. Behind them, the house was suddenly haloed with the brilliance of yard lights around the back and out of sight. The dogs were out, and coming their way.

Two shadows darted past, Fedak and Terry Sacks with salt on their tails. They were running all-out, straight down the centre of the drive. Jim hustled Linda into the angled shelter of the garage side just as the two animals appeared at the far corner of the house. They were leggy and loping, the biggest Dobermans he'd ever seen.

"We can't outrun them," he whispered fiercely as Linda tried to pull away from him, and even as he spoke the two dogs flashed by. They didn't even seem to be trying too hard, and they'd already closed up half of the distance between themselves and the prey ahead. *This is absolutely the last thing I need*, Jim thought, and he looked around.

There was enough light spilling over from the house for

50

him to see that they were in a brick-floored yard formed by the meeting of the garage wall and the boundary hedge. There was an open wire incinerator for trash and garden debris, and alongside this was a split-wood pen containing a row of four dustbins. There wasn't any way out.

Somebody whistled from the upper storey. Halfway down the drive, one of the dogs made a wide turn and started back.

"Come on," Jim said, and he pushed Linda toward the incinerator. It was no more than a free-standing cage, and it tipped over with a loud crash and a cloud of bitter ashes. Linda scrambled onto the platform it made, and Jim got up alongside her. He didn't have to look back to know that the Doberman was arrowing toward them; he grabbed hold of Linda and heaved her onto the top of the hedge alongside.

The dog came skidding into the brick yard, thrown for a moment by this unexpected move. It looked eager. This was the best thing that had happened to it in months. Linda was crashing down through the hedge to the ground on the other side, and the Doberman's jaws snapped in the air like a sprung trap as Jim dived after her and rolled over.

The hedge was woven as tough as a fence, and it almost held him and didn't let him fall. Then it gave with a tearing sound, and it dumped him into the wet grass alongside Linda without too much force.

The dog wasn't happy. It paced back and forth on the other side of the hawthorn, looking for a way through and seeing none. They could hear it panting hard, almost muttering to itself only a couple of feet away.

Linda was helping Jim to his feet. "The car's in this field," she said.

They set out to follow the line of the hedge. On the other side, the dog stayed with them.

The going here was soft, almost marshy. If there was a gap or a space anywhere and the Doberman got through, they wouldn't be able to run at all. They'd go down fast, and stay down. Linda missed her footing, and Jim put an arm around her to hold her up. The Beetle was just a glint of moonlight on metal in the gateway a thousand miles ahead.

Something was coming through the hedge before them.

It squeezed out into the night and stood up, and was followed by another shape that fell against it heavily. Sacks and Fedak, bramble-scratched and almost exhausted. A third shape started to force its way through after.

It growled and snarled as they beat it back, going for their clothes, their fingers, anything that moved. Sacks had managed to break a bough downwards just as Jim and Linda came level, and he jammed it into the breach where it caught and barred the way so that the Doberman couldn't push any further. As the four of them set out to cover the final distance to the car, both dogs were starting to dig.

The doors were unlocked and the keys were inside. Everybody dived in without bothering which way they were facing or how they were arranged, because they'd all heard a second whistle from the house. Jim didn't need to be told that it wasn't a recall.

The engine turned over once, and then again. Terry Sacks got himself into the passenger seat and slammed the door just as the dogs appeared in front of the car. They were going so fast and so hard that they could barely stop; one of them bounded from the bonnet-hood onto the roof and slid down across the rear window with a startled yelp, shaking the car and making Terry Sacks cross himself quickly.

Fedak got the engine started, and he crashed the gears twice. The car took off like a stone out of a sling.

Apart from Fedak, nobody moved for a while. Linda was crammed in a corner, Jim was lying with one foot still caught in the passenger seatbelt, Terry Sacks was half on the floor. It was Terry who was the first to speak.

He said, "Is that your idea of nobody home?"

Fedak didn't answer. Nobody else spoke until they pulled in by the Cliff House.

Terry made way so that Jim could get out, and Linda followed him. The Beetle's engine was still running, and Fedak hadn't turned into the drive. He sat with his hands on the wheel, staring straight ahead much as he had when Jim had first seen him at the start of the evening.

Jim said, hollowly, "Well, thanks for the ride."

Linda stood behind him. "You can carry on down," she said to Terry. She didn't even look at Fedak.

"Listen, Linda," Terry Sacks began, but she shook her head.

"It's okay, Terry," she said, only now she sounded just a shade less unforgiving. "We've got some old times to talk about, here. I'll see you tomorrow."

He was going to say something else, but then he changed his mind and simply nodded. He got back into the car.

Stephen Fedak looked once at Jim. His eyes held no more expression than a lizard's. Then he crashed the gears again and drove away. One of the Volkswagen's tail lights wasn't working.

Far out to sea, a lightship winked like a fallen star. Linda touched Jim's arm. "I'm sorry the evening turned out this way," she began, but then she frowned.

"Jim, you're shaking," she said.

"I know," he admitted. "It's the dogs. It's like a phobia, it came out of nowhere. I only have to see a Snoopy poster and I break out into a sweat."

He let her take the keys from him, and she guided him through into the main room and sat him on the threadbare old sofa. He'd been fine until the drive back, there simply hadn't been the time to be scared, but now he could feel himself locking up tight like an overstrung violin. Linda went into the kitchen and came back a couple of minutes later with a tumbler half-filled with what must have been almost all of the remaining Glenfarclas malt.

"Here," she said, helping him to raise it to his lips. His hand was so unsteady that the glass rattled against his teeth.

"Better?" she said, and he nodded.

A couple of minutes later, he sat back. A couple of minutes after that, he was out.

Linda waited for a moment, and then spoke his name. He didn't react. She checked his pulse, which was strong, and then she went over to the doorway and switched the main room light on and off three times.

And then, having given the signal, she went through into the kitchen to clear the big table in readiness.

SIX

They backed the van into the yard so that its doors were almost up against the entrance to the kitchen, and then they came around and started to unload most of the high-tech equipment that they'd brought. Some of the pieces were so big that they came in on self-contained wheeled trolleys, and within minutes the kitchen was becoming too crowded for any standing around. A rubber sheet had been spread on the table and a man-sized anglepoise light was being swung into position over it as Alan Franks guided Linda back into the main room.

"They know what they're doing," he said after he'd introduced himself. "We'll be better off out of the way."

They came through for Harper, two of them expertly lifting him from the sofa and carrying his slack form back through the doorway to lay him under the lights. Linda saw his head rock forward as they sat him up to take off his jacket and shirt, and she turned away so that she wouldn't have to watch.

Franks said, "You kept us waiting long enough. What was the delay?"

"The evening took a couple of unexpected turns," Linda said. "This was the first chance I had to get him alone."

Franks nodded, obviously not wanting to make anything of it. "This won't take long," he said, and although he was talking to Linda a fair-sized chunk of his attention was being drawn back to the scene in the kitchen. He added, "I hear you were having some trouble with one of the locals."

"It seems I did too good a job of getting myself set up amongst them, that's all," Linda said. "It's nothing I won't be able to handle."

Franks shrugged. It wasn't his problem. He was tall and dark and in his early forties, and he was starting to lose his hair. Either he'd taken a holiday in the last few weeks, or else he had the regular use of a solarium. He said, "What's your brief on this?"

"Observe and report only. As far as the company's concerned, the show's all yours. They haven't even told me the half of what you're planning, yet."

She glanced back over her shoulder. Jim Harper was being rolled onto his side so that a line of electrodes could be taped along his spine, his arm falling loosely as he was turned. Franks was right, his people were fast; already they'd taken a fair-sized blood-sample and a selection of scrapings and smears, and one of them held a catheter ready to draw off urine as soon as the body lay still again.

Franks said, "Well, now you've met him. What do you think?"

"Considering that I only met him this afternoon, it's a little early to say. But so far, he seems okay."

"I know," Franks agreed, "but he's wide open. He trusts *everybody*." He gave her a sideways glance. "I'll bet he opened up to you straight away."

"We got along," she said uncomfortably.

Franks didn't seem to feel that his staff needed close supervision, and after he'd watched them for a while he wandered over to look out of the cracked bay window. Linda kept her back to the doorway, but she could hear them moving around.

She'd been sent over only three weeks before, pulled from a steady staff job at the main company office in Basle and given barely enough time to check over her apartment for a long absence. There were a number of Britishers in-house or on the Special Projects payroll, many of them with better degrees or longer service or with experience in the field that she couldn't offer, and she didn't really know why she'd been chosen over them for this particular assignment. Her section head had made some wry joke about the colour of her eyes making her perfect for the job, but he'd seemed to avoid giving her any serious reason for her selection.

An avoidance of detail had been characteristic of her involvement in the case so far. Apparently Franks had recruited amongst his patients for control-group volunteers in a clinical study grant-aided by Risinger-Genoud's pharmaceuticals division, and when Harper's name had been reported in with all the others it had flashed up a double-security coding on the mainframe's screens. This meant that there was a classified file on him with limited password access, but sight of the file hadn't been included in Linda's briefing. All that she knew was that there had been a product-related incident at some time, and that until Harper had resurfaced the case had been considered closed.

What the hell, she thought. It wouldn't hurt to do a spot of fishing. She said, "Have you had a look at the file, at all?"

"They've only let me have access to the sections with the clinical data so far," Franks said. "They promised me more but I don't know the hows and the whys yet. All I *do* know for sure is that a group of fit and healthy slants out in South-East Asia somewhere got a mis-labelled batch of the same preparation, but they didn't take it anything like as well as he did."

She was about to push him a little further, but as she started to speak she was distracted by a sound from the room behind her. It had been a noise resembling a brief shot of compressed air, low-level and over in less than a second, and when she turned to look into the kitchen one of Franks' staff was just moving across her field of view. As the man stepped clear Harper was revealed again; the electrodes had been stripped away and Harper was being eased over to lie on his back as before. He was looking deathly and almost sheet-white under the lights.

"Just a vitamin shot," Franks said. "I think we've got everything we need, now. Where does he sleep?"

"He says that he camps out in the kitchen," Linda said.

She stayed out of the way as the temporary examination area was quickly converted into an ordinary room again, the lights and the gear being taken out and stowed into the back of the van. Harper's folding bed was set up and Harper was lifted over onto it, dressed in the old shorts and T-shirt that they found tangled up in his duvet. Not one of the crew had spoken to Linda or even appeared to notice her.

Franks said, "He's all yours, again. We should have first results in a week and then analysis some time after that. Will you be wanting a copy?"

"I'll want copies of everything," Linda said.

Five minutes later they were gone, taking every trace of their presence with them.

Linda checked on Jim, but he seemed to be out of the sedation that she'd given to him and sleeping normally. He wasn't likely to wake for several hours yet, but all the same she moved quietly as she set the room back as it had been when they'd first arrived. She then pulled out one of the dining chairs and sat watching him for a while. About fifteen minutes later she stood, replaced the chair, and let herself out without a sound.

After a few minutes alone in the empty house, Jim turned over stiffly in his sleep.

It was then that his nightmares began again.

SEVEN

When Jim woke up in the morning his head hurt and his back ached terribly, and it was a big effort to slide out from under the duvet to switch on the rings on the electric cooker in order to warm the place up a little. No question about it, he was going to have to find some better alternative to the camp bed even if it was only an old mattress from somewhere, laid down on the floor. Right now he was feeling as if he'd been stabbed between the shoulders with a hot needle.

It burned a little when he went upstairs to pee, as well, and he groaned aloud at the thought of the wreck that he was letting himself become. He'd been pretty fit, once, but in the past few months regular exercise had joined the long list of things that he'd been promising himself for the indeterminate 'better times' that were surely coming. For now he was making do with half an hour daily of squeezing a soft rubber ball in his left hand to keep up the muscle tone in the areas that he could no longer feel. He'd scared himself once by neglecting this therapy for almost a week; his hand had started to draw itself up into a claw, and he'd had to prise it open before he could begin working on it again.

Better times on the way. He didn't care to face the possibility that this might be as good as it was ever going to get.

It wasn't until he sat down to his breakfast that he realised that a significant piece of the last evening appeared to be missing from his memory.

He rubbed at his eyes and then at his temple, disturbed. Surely it would come back to him. He could run through everything up to the point where Fedak and Terry Sacks had driven away leaving Linda at the house, but from then onward it was like a recurrence of that entire week leading up to his 'accident' – no blurs, no hard-to-grasp shadows, just a seamless continuity as if time itself had been edited somehow.

There was a muffled tap on the outside door. He wasn't expecting anybody; he wondered if it might be the agent with some builders to look over the house. He slid out of his chair to open up.

The morning air was so clear that it was almost brittle. Linda was standing there with both arms wrapped around a cut-down cardboard box. It was just big enough to be awkward, and she didn't wait to be invited in.

"What's all this?" Jim said as he stepped back to let her pass.

She dumped the box on the kitchen table, making his radio jump. She said, "Something that I noticed you don't have much of," and she flipped open the untaped lid and reached inside.

"You name it, I don't have much of it," Jim said as he closed the door. Linda was wearing tight cord jeans and a nip-waisted tweed jacket over a rollnecked sweater.

Looking at her, Jim had a powerful feeling that he was rediscovering something already familiar. She was making a stack of paperbacks on the table.

He saw *Magic, Sharp Practice, Rosemary's Baby*; there were a couple of John Steinbecks and more than half a dozen Leslie Charteris titles in yellow covers that had to be thirty years old at least. She added *Great Expectations* as he was reading his way down the stack. "I don't know how well I chose them," she said, "but there's hundreds more down in a place near Spencer's."

"I know the one you mean. I looked in through the window, but it wasn't open."

"It never is. You have to go across the road and get the key. I'll show you where."

"I appreciate this. Thanks."

"I'll show you now, if you like," Linda hinted patiently. "Unless you had something else planned."

Jim had a whole winter with nothing else planned, so he grabbed his overcoat and they went out.

Far below, the tide was starting to unroll its way down the beach. A night frost had firmed-up the path, but still they took it slowly. He told her about Bob McAndrew, about how he'd gone tiptoeing about on the rotten boards upstairs like Maxwell with his silver hammer, and about how he'd stood in the bay window staring down at the town, wanting to play emperor even as he took himself away into exile. But even as he was telling the story, Jim's thoughts kept on straying to the troublesome blank of the previous night.

Linda said, "What will you do when all this is over? Start teaching again?"

"No," Jim said. "That whole thing was a fluke. I'm not even qualified for it."

And then as they descended, he began to tell her the story of his short-lived career and its abrupt, inexplicable ending. He told her about Rochelle Genoud, the chairman's stepdaughter, and how he'd written to her in Paris twice only to see his letters return unopened. He didn't think that Rochelle could have seen them, let alone have had a chance to read them. He even told Linda about the

59

drugs that they'd found in his room, something that he hadn't ever admitted to Alan Franks in any of their long afternoon sessions.

"I'm not a mental case, or anything," he added quickly. "Franks ran all the psychiatric tests and I came out okay. He more or less says that I'm damaged goods, now, and I'll have to learn to live with it. I don't have the kind of money to go over and get the other side of the story from Rochelle, so I suppose he's right."

Linda said, "You really trust him, don't you?"

"Of course," Jim said. "If you can't trust a doctor, who can you?"

The end of the cliff path met the end of the promenade in a kind of unfinished no-man's-land where the headland ran out and the town began. Concrete patches on the flat showed where shelters and benches had stood in another time. The pier was still some distance ahead, the cross-ties and pillars of its understructure lacy with weeds. They'd been uncovered by a falling sea that would soon move in to drown them again. When Jim had last taken a look down onto the pier from the house he'd almost been able to imagine that it was made out of bones, with the damaged pavilion at its end a clubbed-in skull. But it was a relic, nothing more, and he wondered why he should keep on getting these ideas.

They paused at the rail, looking out together at the dark sky and the pewter sea, and Linda said, "What kind of bad dreams do you mean?"

And Jim was silent for a moment, because one small missing piece of the previous night had just fallen back into place for him.

Then he said, "It's always through a doorway. In the very early ones it would stay closed and I'd just hear sounds coming through from the other side, but later on it would start to open and there would always be something different waiting there for me." He leaned forward on the salt-eaten rail that fronted the promenade. Gulls were circling out over the swell, crying aloud over something interesting they'd found. "Being operated on in a cellar somewhere without an anaesthetic. Drowning in a box.

Burning alive. Being skinned and being eaten. Blind men with nothing but whites to their eyes. Anything with dogs in it would be twice as bad and I don't know why, because I always used to *like* dogs, couldn't even watch somebody being cruel to one."

Linda said, tentatively, "But they've stopped for good, now?"

But Jim didn't answer, his attention caught by something out across the water. He said, "It looks like something's been dumped off the pier."

"Where?" Linda said, and he pointed.

The gulls dived and turned. For a moment there was nothing to see, but then the tide went swilling back and uncovered the upward-pointing nose of a green Volkswagen Beetle.

EIGHT

There was a concrete ramp some way ahead that would lead them down to the sand. It was chained off, and guarded by a broken-down beach truck that stood on four flats and hadn't moved in at least as many years; they were running by the time they reached the chain, and racing by the time they'd reached the lower level. From there on, however hard they tried, the sand slowed them down to a walk.

Jim's hopes that they'd made some kind of mistake over a rock or an odd piece of driftwood lasted for just as long as it took the sea to recede and uncover the car yet again. It seemed to have been jammed down into the sand at an angle, and only the highest of the high rollers covered it completely; as the sea drained away, a full two-thirds of the Beetle were left sticking into the air.

They reached the edge of the water. The car was another twenty yards out, and Jim started in toward it. Linda stayed back.

Most of what they couldn't see must have been buried in the sand, because when Jim got level he was no deeper in than his knees. The water was so cold that he'd lost any sensation of it after a couple of seconds. Pinhole jets were spurting out of the bodywork under pressure; the car was a tank full of seawater, green and milky.

He turned and shouted back to Linda, "I can't see anybody inside." But he had the irrational feeling that not only were Stephen Fedak and Terry Sacks still inside, but that they were also alive. Linda probably couldn't hear him over the thunder of the sea, just as he couldn't make out what she was calling to him; he looked around in time to see the rolling wall of another high wave, and he ducked into the shelter of the car as it broke over the roof. He was almost drenched, but the force of it had missed him. The sand boiled and foamed and dragged at his legs as he ploughed around to the side of the car to try the doors.

The first was either locked, or else it had jammed. Jim could barely see the line of the steering wheel inside, and that was all. He splashed around to pull at the passenger door, but he couldn't make it move. As he was straining, he saw a dark shape drift by on the other side of the glass. It might have been a hand. He guessed that it was.

Another big one was gathering, starting its final run from the far end of the pier. There was nothing he could do. He floundered back toward the beach, soaking himself even more.

"What can we do?" Linda shouted desperately as he got within earshot, her face wet with salt spray and tears.

The wave broke behind Jim, shaking the car but not moving it. "We need a telephone," he said, and then the wash was around him. It plucked at him harmlessly, making weak pleas for him to return, but he fought his way on to where Linda was standing ankle-deep and unaware. "Come on," he said, but she didn't seem to want to move. "Come *on*, Linda," he insisted, and he grabbed her arm and started to pull her back up onto the sand. After a few unwilling steps, she took over for herself.

They were both shivering and wet on the promenade when the police Range Rover arrived a few minutes later.

There was only one man inside, a thirty-five-year-old constable who had all of the town and most of the surrounding farms included in his patch. The blue light on the Rover's roof turned noisily on a dry bearing, but he left it running as he came around to take a look at them. He didn't introduce himself.

Down on the beach, the tide had washed back far enough to leave the Beetle uncovered in the middle of a still pool. Jim was wondering how long they'd have, and wishing that he'd taken more notice of the movement of the sea over the last few days. He couldn't be sure, but he thought they'd have two hours or less before the tide returned.

The constable went around the back of the Range Rover and opened up. He dug around under some traffic cones and brought out a set of waders and a light shovel with its blade in a clean plastic bag. Sitting in the open hatchback to pull the waders on, he looked at Linda and said, "Do you want to sit in the car?"

Linda shook her head. "No," she said. "I want to come."

"If anybody's inside," he told her, "you won't like it," but Linda seemed determined.

Jim tried to explain. "We think we know who's in there," he said.

The constable looked him over – wet, shivering, almost wasted-looking in the cold. "What about you? Are you fit?"

"As long as I keep moving, I'm okay."

So the three of them set out across the flats, leaving the Rover with its squeaking blue light to mark the place where they left the promenade. The constable's lapel radio was turned low, an odd intrusion of life elsewhere into the dead world of the sands. He said, "Who is it, then?"

"Last time we saw the car," Jim said, "Stephen Fedak and Terry Sacks were in it. They were driving down from the cliffs on the old lighthouse road."

"But there could be nobody," Linda suggested lamely, and it was obvious that she didn't really believe it. Jim was watching the policeman, looking for some reaction that might indicate that he was making a link between the car and some complaint of the night before. But the constable was giving nothing away.

He walked along the edge of the sandbar, inspecting the Beetle from a changing angle. Its windshield faced up to the sky, and its wheels hung like the legs of a treed cat; both headlamps had been smashed out and the metal around them scraped clean.

"This one's been through a barrier," he said finally. "We've had cars go off that road before, but I've never seen one fetch up as far along as this. Most of these bugs are nearly airtight, they drift before they sink."

He waded out to the car, stirring up a trail of underwater mud as he moved. He tried the doors but they still wouldn't give, so then he peered in through the side-windows. He didn't seem to be able to make out any more than Jim had. Jim knew that he ought to turn Linda around and walk back with her to the town, but he only turned up the collar of his overcoat against the wind and tried not to shake. Linda was as pale as new snow.

The constable was splashing toward them, shaking his head. "No good," he said, raising his voice to reach. "We'll have to winch it out before the tide turns."

As he came level, Jim said, "Can't you cut it open?"

"No point. We can't do a thing for the poor buggers inside, and we'll need the car in one piece to see what happened."

The gulls were still turning and calling overhead as the policeman unclipped his radio and moved aside. He was the town's only officer in the low season, but he could bring in local reserves from their day jobs and he was owed enough favours to call on extra manpower when special skills were needed. This one would take at least a breakdown truck.

Now the pool around the car was draining slowly, and after fifteen minutes it was worth trying to make a start with the shovel. Jim took a turn and dug around under the doors, but almost as fast as he spaded the sand away, the sides of the hole would melt back in. The first of the half-dozen reserves started to arrive as he worked, ordinary-looking men from the shops and council offices, and those that had brought shovels with them started to dig the sand away on every side of the Beetle.

Jim kept at it, harder than he knew he should. It was driving the chill away, and it saved him from being drawn to look into the car's pond-green windows. He glanced once at Linda, standing alone on the sandbar; he knew that the closeness they'd been starting to feel had gone, perhaps for good.

It was useless, like trying to dig around in a can of paint; after half an hour of effort they'd made no more than a gentle depression around the car. The weight of its rear-mounted engine had held it down, and the mud-sand mixture had flowed around it like honey under the pressure of the tide. The arrival of the breakdown wagon was the only excuse that they needed to ram their shovels in a picket line on the sandbar and wait by them, breathing hard.

It was a deep-blue Transit recovery van with RAC plates and red-amber accident lights. The back had been cut away to mount an electric winch and sling, and it came with a three-man crew; they unhooked the guard chain at the top of the concrete ramp before driving down and about fifty yards onto the beach. There the van stopped, and one of the men got out and walked the rest of the distance.

He was wearing oily jeans and a dark blue pullover that had been oiled-down into the same condition. As the constable stepped out to meet him, he glanced back toward his van and said, "This is as close as we can get. The sand's too soft."

"Have you got any boards you can lay?"

"Not enough."

The constable looked back at the Beetle. Jim could see that he wasn't looking forward to handling what was inside, but a delay was still a frustration. The Beetle continued to stare blindly at the overcast sky.

"Make a start, anyway," the policeman said, and he unexpectedly put a hand on Jim's shoulder as the driver-mechanic headed back toward his van. "Come on," he said in a quieter voice that had a trace of sympathy in it. "Better get your girlfriend somewhere warm."

Linda returned to the promenade with the two of them. She said nothing until they reached the top of the ramp, where she looked up and found herself face-to-face with Terry Sacks.

He was wearing a yellow zippered anorak over his denims, and a look of total incomprehension on his face. And this was all that Jim had the chance to see; the constable had come up with an idea, and Jim was suddenly needed.

"Run down and get the chain-cutters from that van," the constable told him, "and meet me at the pier entrance."

He tried to run, but he was beginning to feel as if he was a machine made out of cheap parts that were all on the point of wearing out together. His head was beginning to ache, the dull sensation between his shoulders was turning into a hot knifepoint again, and he was so cold that it was no longer possible to tell where the no-sensation zone in his hand began.

He got the chain-cutters, and made for the long stairway by the pier. Looking up through its understructure, he could see weeds and corroded iron and slung catwalks running through the darkness. Patchy wire netting had been wrapped around the support pillars to prevent anybody from climbing. It was a piece of derelict architecture, nothing more; a raised wooden deck with a long arcade leading to an old music hall out over the sea. So why did this glimpse of its slimy underside bring back all of the apprehension that he'd felt when he'd first looked along it from the shore?

It took the two of them to cut through the gate padlock, although Jim wasn't able to add much in the way of strength. The gate squealed as they pushed it back and stepped through onto the boardwalk. He still didn't know what they were supposed to be doing.

The decking ran clear and wide for a hundred yards or more before the first low buildings of the superstructure began. From there on it was a jumble of Eastern styles piled one on top of another, towers and pillars and minarets and, capping everything, the half-destroyed Taj Mahal dome that had reminded Jim so much of a beaten-in skull. It was an empty pleasure city where the gates had been locked whilst inside the pleasures had begun to go slyly wrong.

If they were going to have to make their way inside for any reason, that would be it. Jim knew that he couldn't do it.

The constable stepped out ahead, waders flapping as his footsteps echoed on the boards. He reached a stack of something that had been roped under tarpaulin against the side-rail, and he beckoned to Jim to help him drag the covers off.

Deckchairs.

If this was all, if he could help with the deckchairs and get off the pier, then he could probably manage it. Jim could see almost immediately what the constable had in mind; a canvas track that could be laid across the sand and which could get the breakdown truck close enough to the Beetle for a winch to be attached.

They got some of the chairs free, and then the constable stood at the rail and gave a loud two-fingered whistle to get the attention of his reserves. Some of them were making another attempt to dig out the car, but they all came toward the pier when they realised that they were needed.

No more than a dozen chairs had gone over the rail when they realised that they were wasting their time. The wood and the canvas were rotten. They weren't even surviving the fall to the beach. The constable cursed once, loudly, and then he made a wide *forget it* signal. Down below and across the sand, the reserves started to turn back.

The policeman punched the tarpaulin in frustration. Dust wheezed out at the dull smack, and something skittered around deep inside.

"We're not going to manage it," he said to Jim. "We'd better try to get your friend out of there."

Jim could see the reason for his pessimism as they descended again to the beach. The tide had begun to turn.

The second try at digging-out had got them no further than the first. If anything, the Beetle seemed to have sunk deeper. Jim stood amongst the reserves on the sandbar, all of them watching the constable as he took his spade and circled around the car to look for the best footing. Jim thought that he'd caught himself swaying unsteadily, but he couldn't be sure; one of the reserves might have spoken to him but he couldn't be certain of that, either. It was only just beginning to occur to him that he'd pushed himself too far and too hard. He'd been soaked through and running around in freezing winds for more than an hour, and for what? If Fedak was still inside the car, he was dead. End of story, and no thanks to Jim Harper for doing his best to follow. His back was giving him real pain now, and he seemed to be seeing everything through a dull haze.

Tentative first shallows of the returning sea were beginning to run across the flats as the constable found his footholds in the wheel-arch and sill. He hoisted himself up and stood braced as he inserted the blade of his shovel under the windshield's rubber seal. He banged it home with a single blow, and the windshield popped free without cracking.

There must have been gas pressure underneath. The glass lifted whole and spun into the air, and Fedak came out after it and made a jack-in-the-box grab for his rescuer.

The policeman lost his footing and fell back heavily onto the sand. Fedak, his last energy spent, flopped face-down onto the Volkswagen's bonnet. He was as pale and as bloated as a catfish, not even recognisably human anymore; he'd been too many hours in the sea, and he'd started to change into something that belonged there. Someone behind Jim started to be sick on the sandbar. Jim was thinking how strange it was that such a sea-fattened shape could ever have fitted into those tight clothes.

"Christ, Frank," somebody was saying from a thousand miles away. "Can't we cover him up?"

The policeman was getting back onto his feet. "Somebody get us the accident blanket out of the back of the Rover," he said.

Me, Jim thought, *he means me*, and without even being fully aware of what he was doing he turned around and began to trot doggedly toward the promenade wall. Someone passed him without even seeming to try; it was the youngest of the reserves, the one who didn't look much older than nineteen although he almost certainly was.

The boy was on his way back with the accident blanket before Jim had even started to climb the ramp to the upper level. It finally came through to him then that he was no longer fit to stay in the game, and that the best course would simply be to keep on walking away.

It was the ramp that almost wiped him out. When he reached the top he found himself facing a small crowd that had gathered at the rail, mostly old ladies and a few over-loud children on bicycles. Nobody looked at him or spoke to him; they were too interested in what was happening out on the sands.

Jim took a last look back. The red splash of the accident blanket was being drawn over the decaying halloween monster that lay with its swollen arms outstretched like a scarecrow's.

"That'll spoil the wool, for sure," he heard one of the old ladies saying.

Linda and Terry were at the table nearest the electric bar heater in Spencer's. They hadn't been there for long; mugs of tea stood in front of them, untouched. Linda didn't look up as Jim pulled out a chair, but she said, "Was it him?"

"I think so," Jim said, lowering himself wearily. His clothes, half-dried in the wind, were itchy with salt and full of hidden cold spots. "It's hard to tell. I thought you were with him, Terry."

Terry Sacks shook his head, slow and miserable. "We had an argument, and he threw me out of the car. He must have driven on and gone through one of the barriers while I went down the path."

Linda said, "Who's going to tell his parents?"

"They'll have procedures," Jim said. "Don't worry about it."

"That's not so easy."

"If you're feeling guilty, don't."

She shook her head. "I shouldn't have left him the way I did."

There was more to say, but Jim knew that he wasn't the one who should be saying it. The three of them sat in silence, and the blue-rinsed manageress came to see if there was anything that he wanted. He asked for a mug of tea, and left it standing with the others.

After a while, the men from the beach started to arrive. A couple of them nodded to Jim, and it was from them that he got the rest of the story. They'd been unable to remove Fedak's body, and at first they'd thought that it had been entangled in the Volkswagen's seatbelts. Somebody with nerve had reached down into the water and sliced through the webbing, but it had made no difference. Then they decided that he was jammed under the steering column and was too stiff to be maneuvered; by this time the light was fading and the tide was really starting to roll in, and since they still couldn't get the heavy cutting gear out onto the sand they tried to break out the column, with no success.

In the end, the sea had driven them back. True high-tide would be in another four hours, but already the car had been reclaimed. Their last sight of it had been as the waves had lifted the accident blanket away, leaving Fedak's outstretched hands to disappear under the water.

The constable came in a short time later, and he sat at their table and listened as Terry Sacks repeated his story of the night before with a few added details. By unspoken agreement, none of the three had mentioned their trip out to the Moynahan house. The constable was beginning to look grey and weary.

He said, "Let me know where you'll all be tomorrow, and I'll have formal statements from you." And then, to Jim; "Better get yourself changed before you get pneumonia." And then he walked out, his working day only half over.

Well, that was it. A one-day shot that had been good while it lasted, except that it hadn't. It was ungenerous and faintly shocking for him to realise it, but he couldn't help thinking that Fedak had managed to find a way to ruin the Jim-and-Linda idea for good.

The boyish-looking reserve, a self-employed glazier with the name of Tommy Herron, had offered to drive him back to the house. There Jim had changed his clothes, drained off the last inch of the Glenfarclas malt to suppress the shakes, and sat on his folding bed before the open door of the oven trying to warm himself through. He wanted to lie down and sleep it all away, but he couldn't. At midnight he put on his overcoat, locked up the house behind him, and began to descend the path again.

Tommy Herron's van was now just one of many vehicles lined along the promenade under lights that had been rigged on scaffold towers. The constable had been in touch with his main station, and a salvage firm had brought in caterpillar-tracked sandwagons on the backs of articulated flatbed trucks. If they couldn't pull the Volkswagen out, they'd simply scoop up a chunk of the beach with the car still embedded.

Jim stood at the promenade rail with the reserves, part-time policemen who would look odd in their uniforms and who would be more used to dealing with traffic foulups and lost children. He felt accepted, one of the group; somebody passed him a styrene cup full of chicken broth from a vacuum flask. They were all watching the sea, at a point where two angled spotlights from the shore converged.

There wasn't much conversation as they waited for the falling of the tide. An hour later, they were turning to go. The beach was uncovered, the pattern of the sandbars had been altered slightly, and the car wasn't there. It was as if Fedak had crawled back inside and turned the Beetle around to head for his new home.

But Jim knew where he really was.

His body might be feeding the fishes, but his spirit would join the others who now belonged to the jealous old town forever. He'd be out at the end of the pier, part of the all-night carnival of souls where the dancing never ended and the applause was for a five-piece band that the living would never hear.

Jim would catch the music, though. It would come drifting up to him late at night in the coldest parts of the approaching winter, beckoning him down to join in the warmth and the fun. And perhaps the bandmaster would turn from his music every now and again to see if Jim had arrived, and he'd scan the hall with blind-white eyes before giving a slight nod of his head to go on with the party.

The blind man was in no hurry, and he could wait.

Jim was certain of it.

NINE

A preliminary inquest was held a week later, in a room over the Friends' Meeting Hall by the library. Jim attended in a borrowed suit, and he gave his identification evidence standing only a few feet away from Stephen Fedak's father, who sat alone and said nothing. The entire hearing took no longer than fifteen minutes, which disappointed the three elderly ladies who had come along to sit at the back of the room and who were obviously hoping for more of a free show.

There was no legal requirement for Linda to attend and Jim didn't see her at the actual session, but when he finally stepped out into the plaster-and-wax scented corridor he saw her looking for him in the crowd.

"Jim," she said when she saw him, "you look terrible!"

"I know," he admitted as they stepped aside to let others pass. "I should have listened to advice. I've been laid up for most of the week."

"In that place? You'll kill yourself."

"I think it must be making me tougher. I'm nearly out of it, now."

The words sounded hollow, even in his own ears. The fact was that the last few nights had been some of the worst that he'd spent since his first weeks back in England . . . but at least at that time he hadn't been cold and alone, and he'd known that somebody would come when he called out.

Linda, who wasn't looking so hot herself, said, "I thought you'd been avoiding me."

"You've had enough to worry about," Jim said, but she shook her head as if he couldn't be more wrong.

"Look," she said, "I've got to talk to you. It's important."

"Whenever you like. What's it about?"

The skinny seventeen-year-old reporter from the local newspaper brushed by, knotting the belt on his trenchcoat. It was a good stab at image-making, but the woollen bobble-hat killed it. Linda touched Jim's arm to draw him aside a little further, and said, "I can't tell you here. Can we go somewhere?"

"Have to be later," Jim said. "I promised Terry I'd give him a hand to pick up some of the cleaning gear now that his van's been fixed."

"You don't look in any state for work, Jim," she said, and she was so genuinely concerned that he quickly tried to reassure her, although not too hard.

"I'm okay," he said, "honest. I always look a bit blitzed, even when I'm fit." She was still looking doubtful, so he added, "I don't think it's muscle that he needs, anyway. More like someone to listen."

Linda hesitated, as if she wasn't quite sure how to phrase what was coming next. She said, "There's something I've got to tell you about. I shouldn't, but . . ." She looked around, and shrugged helplessly. "This has changed everything."

"How about tonight?"

She managed a weak smile. "You may not like me very much afterwards."

"I don't think that's possible," Jim said.

Linda began to say something else, and found that she couldn't. She suddenly turned, and left him there.

The suit that Jim had been wearing had originally belonged to Terry Sacks' older brother. It had been passed along to Terry, and Terry had been intending to get it altered to fit because his interview suit was falling apart from the inside out. He'd walked up to the Cliff House and offered it to Jim on the Wednesday before the inquest, just at the point where Jim had been at his lowest. He'd had the feeling then that Terry was wanting to tell him something; fixing up help with the cleaning gear was just a way of putting it off.

All the same, it had been a decent gesture and Jim only hoped that he'd shown enough appreciation of it at the time. If Linda thought that he looked rough now, she ought to have seen him then.

That was the day on which he'd unearthed his bag of pills and tablets from the bottom of his suitcase, and started himself back on the prescription routine that Franks had originally devised for him. Maybe he'd brought this on himself, maybe if he'd stuck with the dosages instead of trying to be smart and self-sufficient then he might never have slid back so far and so fast. He'd noticed a slight improvement already, but nothing that he could call a cure.

And, by *Christ*, his back could really ache sometimes.

Terry arrived at the house in his van shortly after two o'clock, his hands and his fingernails blackened by some last-minute tinkering. He lived in a small bedsit extension over his parents' garage, and they'd let him store the van and the steam-cleaning equipment down below. The gear was presently at the site of their last contract, and it would be a two-man job to bring it back.

Terry kept the engine running as Jim folded the borrowed suit, now back in its polythene, and laid it on the seat between them. Then they moved out.

There wasn't much conversation at first, not until they were some way past the broken barrier and the strings of plastic danger flags that marked the spot where Stephen Fedak had left the old lighthouse road. They were almost down to shore level when Jim said, "Will you carry on with the business?"

Terry didn't seem keen. "Technically there's a half-share reverted to Steve's people, but I haven't had the nerve to ask them about it. The whole thing's a bit of a dead loss, anyway."

"You mean it doesn't pay?"

"Not the way we went about it. There was a slight lack of enthusiasm and commitment, it just wasn't our line. And with Steve having been the business brains and the salesman, I can't see me making a go of it alone."

"So, what's it going to be, then?"

But to this, Terry could only shrug despondently.

They were heading for one of the Edwardian seafront hotels that Jim had passed on his first day, six floors of rooms with three-year-old décor and eighty-year-old plumbing. Terry drove around the back and reversed the van under a glass awning that definitely wasn't a part of the public face of the hotel; the rear wall of the bay was a stack of furniture throwouts and dead fluorescent tubes, and as Jim stepped down to the ground he scared off a stray cat that had been weaving sinuously in and out of the wheels of a bicycle.

A monkey-faced old man in a blue jacket was carrying out rubbish, and he recognised Terry and let them in. As far as Jim could see, there was nobody else in the building.

It was quite a trek through passageways and unpainted fire doors to get to the kitchens. These were newly cleaned and had the look of a large operating theatre in fawn tile and dull stainless steel. Terry's gear stood in the middle of the room, a wheeled trolley that was about the size and weight of a small generator with several coils of hose and five large plastic jerrycans of solvent. They took the trolley out first, a twenty-minute job because of all the doors and some steps for which planks had to be laid. After that they took out some overalls and empty containers, and after that they took a break. The signal for the break was when something in Terry Sacks seemed to give, and he said "Aw, *fuck* it," and flung a bundle of spraying rods into the back of the van without even looking to see how or where they'd land. Then he stamped off back into the hotel, and was in the kitchens again by the time that Jim caught up with him.

Terry was slamming a kettle onto one of the gas ranges, where it looked like an undersized toy. One of the boxes that they hadn't yet taken out included some teabags, some powdered milk, and two chipped mugs.

"Here," Terry said. "You're the guest, you can have the one with the handle."

He stamped and growled around like a pint-sized bear for a while, running water and rinsing and doing everything with more force and more noise than was called for. Jim waited, saying nothing. Finally, when all the stuff was set out and there was nothing else left to do, Terry paced up and down the kitchen and stole a quick glance at Jim as he turned. His anger was too uncharacteristic and too hesitant to last; his look was almost furtive, like that of a dog caught sneaking a quick drink out of the toilet bowl.

And he knew it. All of the fury went out of him in a rush.

"I wasn't made for this," he said miserably, sitting on one of his own crates. "If someone had told Mrs Sacks' little boy that his life's big achievement was going to be scraping the grease and the dead flies and the crap out of other people's kitchens, I think he'd've hung himself on the climbing frame right there and then. We never even covered our costs. We were so cheap, we were as good as paying these people to use us so we could call it work and still hold our heads up. Where's the fucking human dignity in that?"

Pulling over another box and sitting next to him, Jim said, "You don't have to tell me, I know all about it."

"I mean, I don't *have* to be like this. I could do a bank, if I wanted to. I could do a bank and nobody would ever even know."

"You serious?" Jim said.

"Sure I'm serious," Terry said bitterly. "I've got it all worked out. I'm a bona fide keyboard genius, didn't Steve tell you? The genius with more rejection letters than you can fit into a toy boy's arse. Companies have been known to go bust rather than give me an interview. I know exactly what I'd do and I know exactly how I'd do it. I could pick up all the basic data I'd need just by sticking a CB aerial and a wide-band TV receiver into the van and then reading off their terminal screens through an outside wall. Next time I get through the door somewhere, if I ever do, I'm tempted to do it first just so that I can leave them with something to think about. Just kind of mention that if I don't get the job then they shouldn't be too surprised if their entire system crashes the next morning."

"Sounds great," Jim said. "Why don't you try it?"

"Because I haven't even got a bloody computer of my own," Terry said sheepishly, "which makes it kind of difficult to get started," and it was then that the water in the kettle began to boil.

They sat and they talked about Trojan Horses and Password Grabbers and worms and viruses; *Maggie*, the virus that Terry had written, was apparently designed to keep on eating up memory space as it dedicated all the resources of a target system to calculating the millionth digit of Pi. Any system that was network-linked to the target system stood a pretty good chance of picking up the infection as well. Terry also said that the commonest password was *Password*. Jim said that he thought it might have been *Swordfish* but Terry, being no Marx Brothers fan, didn't get it.

Jim said, "You know, when you stormed away from the van like that, I thought perhaps you were pissed off at *me*."

Terry looked genuinely blank. "Why?" he said.

"Because of what happened the night that Steve died."

"But that was nothing to do with you."

"I know that. I just wasn't sure how you thought about it, that's all."

But Terry was shaking his head. "I'd known him just about forever, I think I've a rough idea how he probably felt. It doesn't matter how old you are, when it comes to things like that you're always fifteen on the inside and nothing makes sense or looks straight. I just wish you'd known him before, as well. I just wish you could've seen something of what he was really like."

"Tell me about him," Jim said.

So Terry told him; about their school, the time they went to Greece on holiday together, the car which they pooled their savings to buy and which, like the van, had spent most of its time off the road. The trip to York where they missed their train home and had to spend the night on the station. The way that life had looked when McAndrew was on the rise and nothing seemed impossible; and the way that it had been after his fall, when the only options had been government schemes that had the look of real work but which tasted of nothing but air.

He hardly had to look at Jim as he spoke. Jim's presence had been the necessary trigger, but this was mostly for himself.

Linda McKay had entered the picture only a few weeks

before. She'd taken a room in Kim Pryor's house, she knew nobody in town, and so Kim had brought her along to Spencer's and introduced her around. The rest was history.

"A few weeks seems an awfully short time to go so far overboard," Jim said. "That's really all he'd known her for?"

"A few weeks is like forever in a place like this. I mean, you've been here for a while, now . . . what do you think of when you remember the time before?"

"It all seems pretty remote," Jim admitted, but probably not for the kinds of reasons that Terry had in mind.

"There you are, then. Linda was the most interesting thing to arrive around here in ages, it's only natural the old antennae should start to quiver a little. Steve wasn't the only one who felt it. But he was the only one who went lumbering in and made a dickhead out of himself, the poor old sod, and that's the real tragedy of the whole sorry mess . . . nothing you did, and nothing you could have prevented. Make you feel any better?"

"A little," Jim said as they got to their feet.

"He was cut up about you," Terry added, "but he'd have got over it. Especially when he came to see the way that it was going with the two of you."

"Meaning what?" Jim said.

"Oh, come *on*," Terry said with a pained, wry kind of a smile, and he took Jim's mug from him to throw what was left down the sink.

When everything had been cleared out and stowed in the van, Terry offered to drive Jim back to the house. Jim said thanks, but he felt that he needed a slow walk. "I could do with some cold air and exercise," he said, looking out at the darkening sky from under the awning at the back of the hotel.

"No shortage of either in this town," Terry said. And then he added, after an awkward moment, "Keep well, Jim. I'll see you around."

"You too, Terry."

"I didn't really mean it about the bank, you know."

"I know."

"I'm not saying I haven't got the ability. Maybe I've even

78

got the nerve. What I don't have is the front. I see it the same everywhere. The times may be lean, but the sharks are all getting fed while the decent people just go for groundbait."

And with that thought in the air between them, Terry set off in the van for home and Jim set out on foot for the place where he lived.

TEN

Sometime early in the morning, while Micheline Bauer had still been lying in the damp half-coma that passed for sleep around these parts, the cobbler had come back and set up his stall again. Now he was hammering on the pavement three floors below her window, his woodpecker-tapping adding a counterpoint to the chorus of streetcars and bicycle bells and singsong human voices in the dusty public square. Yesterday one of the Cubans in the room below had complained to the hotel manager, and a couple of boys had gone out and made a big show of yelling at the cobbler and slapping his rows of shoes down from the hotel shutters. The cobbler hadn't played his own part too well; he'd sat nodding and smiling and showing teeth that were the colours of different kinds of wood. Micheline had guessed that he and the boys were probably family, or else he paid them some kind of unofficial rent on his patch of ground. However it worked, he was back.

Patches of her cotton night-dress were sticking to her as she sat upright and tried to shake herself awake. She was in an Asian's idea of a European hotel room, conceived by an Asian who had never been to Europe. Three plaster ducks in graded sizes were pinned to the wall over her washstand, and a switch by the bed would give her a muzak channel where the same half-hour Johnny Mathis tape played over and over. Micheline had expected her grip on reality to take a knock after a journey of more than thirty hours, but she'd also expected to be adjusting after a couple of days. This was her fourth morning, and she didn't feel any better. She levered herself off the bed and went to the open window, looking out through the insect screen and hoping that she'd at last be hit by some sense of familiarity.

Zero.

The south side of the square was a rolling sea of coolie hats amongst market-stall awnings, while the once-formal gardens before the Colonial Administration buildings to the north had become a bare-earth football pitch for barefoot children. It was still an alien landscape to her. Micheline felt as if she were having her first peek at what it would be like to get old; the world had moved on, and she no longer seemed to have the ability to move with it. So what had happened to the confident kid who'd been prepared to go wherever the company sent her?

The answer to that one was easy. *Bruno*, she thought as she looked down.

Even though the passing of time had started to dull the edge of her bitterness, Micheline could still imagine herself giving Bruno Weingartner some painful surgery with a hot knife. It was because of Bruno that the Englishman had died in the dog pens, and as a result she'd seen the shutdown of the research centre and the dispersal of its staff throughout the extensive Risinger-Genoud business empire. Her own posting had been to one of the chemical plants in north-eastern France, acquired some years before when Werner Risinger had married Rochelle's widowed mother, gained control of the Genoud group of companies, and then effectively disenfranchised the rest of the family; Micheline had spent a year on the plant, batch-testing bulk vitamins and popping tranquillisers to fight off her own depression. Sometimes, she'd wonder what the company had done with Bruno. She never doubted that he would still be on board somewhere, kept silent and in line with pressure and unspoken threats and maybe just a little hope in the far distance to keep his attention in focus; all that she hoped was that wherever he might be, he wouldn't be enjoying it at *all*.

For herself, she was determined to come out ahead. This new posting might not look any more promising than the last, but at least it was movement. She'd had no briefing yet, and had no idea even why she'd been sent; but now that she was here, she was going to be looking to earn a few gold stars and get herself back into the high-flyers' league.

The rickshaw boys outside the hotel were leaning back in the shafts of their carts, watching without interest as mule wagons laden with sacks rolled by. They, too, had known better times. The tourist trade had never really returned, and few of the Russian advisors ever seemed to go out of doors; but still the rickshaw boys hung around, and when a likely mark appeared they'd shout for the business in accented French and American-English. They wore caps with earflaps, and wraparound green jackets. For them it was still the cold season, even though for Micheline it was as sticky as a low-heat sauna.

Something had their attention; they were craning. Micheline looked across the square and saw an old Moskvitch taxi, nosing through the crowds and puttering smoke. It was a rare enough sight. She began to wonder if things were going to start moving at last.

The taxi pulled in by the hotel's main entrance, which meant that she wouldn't be able to see whoever was getting out. In spite of this, she was washed and more or less dressed by the time one of the manager's nephews came tapping at her door with a visiting card on his worn brass tray.

The Risinger-Genoud logo was all that she needed to see.

He was sitting on one of the cane chairs in the hotel's lobby, leafing through a four-day-old copy of *Le Monde*, but he stood up when he saw her. He wasn't what she'd expected; she'd imagined that her contact would be some worn-out and warmed-over outpost man in a straw trilby and a stained white suit. He was actually around her own age, tall and lightly tanned and with fair hair bleached by the last summer's sun. His shirt, slacks and desert boots were all the same dusty khaki; he had the open and energetic look of an Agency volunteer.

"You're Micheline Bauer?" he said, putting out his hand. He was English, but his French was more than passable.

"That's me."

"My name's Peter Viveros," he said. "Shall we go and get a drink while we run through what's going to be happening here?"

There was nobody else in the bar so early, but the pint-sized barman was already there and waiting in his maroon jacket and black tie. He hopped off his stool and switched on the air-conditioning as they walked in. Viveros went to the bar and ordered two Tiger beers as Micheline seated herself at a table under a plastic chandelier. She smoothed her dress across her knees, and hoped that her handshake hadn't been a damp one.

"The Tiger's always warm and pretty awful," he said as he sat down opposite, "but the water can't be trusted and you've got to drink *something*. Here's to the Oktober project."

"The what?" Micheline said politely.

First Viveros smiled as if she was making a joke. Then he saw that she wasn't. He lowered his glass. "You don't know what the Oktober project is?"

"I never heard of it before."

"But what happened to the expert they said they were sending me? The one who was supposed to have been in on it right from the beginning?"

"Search me," Micheline said.

Viveros looked around for a moment, like an actor who'd belatedly realised that he'd learned the wrong script and was casting around for the inspiration to improvise. "Damn," he said at last, when nothing came. "I'd better telex Basle and find out what they're playing at before we get into a briefing, then."

"Oh, great," Micheline said. "Does that mean another four days of sitting around the hotel, doing and knowing nothing?"

"If you've never worked with Laevo EPL and you've never had any contact with Harper, I don't see what else I can do."

"Harper?" Micheline said, seeing light at last. "You mean, the Englishman who died?"

"I mean the first test subject to survive an EPL overdose as something other than a vegetable," he said. "Are we talking about the same person, or what?"

It turned out that they were, although their two sets of information didn't exactly interlock. As far as Micheline had been concerned, Harper had been dead and that had been the end of it. Viveros had been told that Harper was a consenting volunteer in a UK study being run by a small-town doctor on a company grant, and he listened as Micheline went over her version.

"Seems like nobody's working with the full picture here," he said with a weak smile when she'd finished. "Perhaps that's why we've been making so little progress."

"So, now we've established that I was in on the start of the Oktober project without actually knowing it, do I get to find out what I'm supposed to be doing?"

It was now more than half an hour later and they were still alone in the bar, but Micheline could see two Cubans standing just outside the doorway and making a poor job of showing no interest in them. They were both short, heavy men, dressed in neatly cut safari suits and carrying Samsonite briefcases; they were probably waiting for the government saloon that came to collect them every day at eleven and brought them back at six.

Viveros had seen them, too. "We'll be taking a drive out this afternoon," he said, "and I'll explain when we get there." And, with a glance in the direction of the Cubans, he added "The situation's kind of delicate. In fact, after what you've told me it sounds even more delicate than I'd thought. Better if we play it with caution."

The two men were walking out to their limo as Viveros and Micheline were stepping into the lobby. Back in the room they'd just left, the barman was switching off the air-conditioning. As the Cubans opened the door to the outside, a bus crashed its gears in the square and a faint odour of smoke as harsh as the scent of burning chestnuts wafted through the lobby from street traders' fires.

Viveros said, "You'd best get yourself changed into some rough-country gear. I'll pick you up in an hour."

And with a farewell nod, he turned and walked across the lobby and out of the hotel.

This had changed everything.

Now when she looked out of her window, Micheline saw just another square. Peter Viveros was already out of sight; because of his height and his colouring, there was no way that he could have hidden himself in the noisy mass down below.

She hadn't been out much alone. If a white face had become a rarity, a white woman was something that you called your friends over to see. Wherever she'd gone, she'd been followed by a mob of polite half-caste children who carried bamboo begging-bowls and wanted to ask her about life in the West. Most of them had American fathers that they'd never seen, although one or two of them did have old photographs which they showed her. None of them had asked for money, but by the end of the first half-hour she'd blown all of her currency.

She was waiting in the lobby when Viveros returned, on the hour as he'd promised. Their transport was an old US Army jeep with its insignia painted over in a green that didn't match, their driver a mahogany-skinned local in a faded Hawaiian beach shirt. Viveros told her that the man spoke some French, but not much. He'd been partly deafened in an air raid when he'd been fourteen.

They set out through the broad avenues of the centre that had been laid out by the French, Micheline sitting in the jeep's open back and hanging onto the rollbar. She knew from her ride in the battered airport bus that they'd soon be into the winding medieval pattern of streets that was the true city, each area named for the crafts that could be found there.

Viveros half-turned in the passenger seat, and said, "According to your papers, you'll be a detail worker representing the firm."

They hit a bump, and Micheline tightened her grip on the bar. "Does that mean I have to do any selling?"

"No, it's strictly a cover. Our local people have been warned about it, and they'll back you up if there are any queries. We'll be making a stop, soon. There's someone I want you to meet."

Ten minutes later, they pulled in to the side of the road by a city park. Viveros climbed out and Micheline looked around. They'd stopped before a pink villa that had old-style colonnades and balconies; the low stone wall that had marked its original perimeter was now topped with six feet of new-looking cyclone fencing. Viveros was walking through the open gate, and he beckoned for her to follow.

A man came down the steps to meet them, grinning like a split melon. He grabbed Viveros' hand in both of his own and pumped it like the hand of a long-lost friend, and then after an introduction in pidgin French he did the same with Micheline. He called over to the house, and five children came spilling out and formed themselves into a graded line to be introduced. The oldest was a girl of around fourteen, the youngest about five. It was a quarter of an hour before Viveros could politely disengage himself and get them outside the gate again. Everybody came to the fence to wave as they drove away.

When they were back on the main route to the city outskirts, Micheline said, "What was all that about?"

"That was Hoang," Viveros told her. "He more or less controls the black market for drug supplies in this area."

"He treats you as if you were family."

"I don't deal with him directly, but it's as well to keep up good relations. And I wanted him to get a look at you." Noting her expression, he added, "There's a lot goes on around here that you won't read about in the annual company reports, Micheline."

The jeep gave them an uncomfortable ride, but nothing else could have kept going on the red clay roads that got worse and worse as they left the river plain and the rice fields behind. They were climbing, and the jungle palms and mangroves crowded close on either side and darkened the trail ahead.

During the slower stretches, Viveros explained about the cross-border bicycle convoys which took goods in one direction and brought back a variety of currencies in the other. It was a six-day journey each way, but the turnover and profits were high – as he was explaining when three armed soldiers stopped them at the ravine bridge that marked the border.

"It's okay," Viveros reassured her. "Everybody knows the jeep's got safe passage." But as he stood up to talk to them over the windshield, Micheline could sense his tension.

The three soldiers seemed no more than boys, but already Micheline had learned not to be fooled. They could be anything from nineteen to thirty-five, at which time they would instantly become old men. They held their rifles at the ready, but they kept them pointed away as their leader spoke to Viveros.

A soldier was hurt, his leg broken in a fall, and he needed transport to the area hospital. That's where Viveros was headed anyway, so it wasn't worth an argument. They carried their splinted casualty out of the jungle and lifted him into the jeep beside Micheline. He lay there for the rest of the journey, not speaking and barely breathing.

They'd been on the trail for more than five hours when they began their final descent into the valley where the area community hospital had been set up. Viveros touched the driver's arm and made a sign, and the jeep slowed as they approached a clearing in the bush.

This was for Micheline's benefit. The clearing was man-made and paved with stone, an overlook that had so far managed to resist being reclaimed by the jungle. The jeep came to a stop in the middle of the terrace, and Viveros climbed out stiffly.

"Come and take a look at this," he said. Micheline followed him over towards the edge of the clearing where they could look down on the rolling green panorama of the valley. Flanking the built-out platform on which they stood were two immense flat-nosed heads, carved in stone and now crumbling. Viveros was looking down towards their destination.

"It's a hospital now, but it used to be a temple," he explained as she joined him. Behind them, there was a clang of metal on metal as their driver refilled the jeep's tanks from jerrycans. "People heading along this trail used to stop here and say a prayer of thanks."

It was now late afternoon, and the sun was low and golden. Micheline looked down across two or three miles of solid greenery to where the bomb-damaged temple stood. It was a long, low building, with an ornate pagoda roof and a tiled dome with towers which topped the structure at one end.

By some trick of the afternoon light, the deep shadows where the dome had burned and fallen inward seemed to give it the look of – what would you call it? A stoved-in skull?

"Programme, sir?" a voice behind Jim Harper said. "If you'll take a seat, the show's about to

"Now I've got to find the medical officer," Viveros told her when the tour was more or less over. "I'm going to leave you here for a while, okay?"

"Does it have to be *here*?" Micheline said, uneasily.

Apparently, it did.

The hospital had begun as an emergency field centre more than fifteen years before, and much of the layout still had a makeshift feel about it. There was only one doctor and a small team of nurses, and they divided their time between patient care and the training of village para-medics. Everything else – feeding, bathing, turning the infirm to forestall bedsores – was done by the relatives of the patients. They camped outside under the pagoda's eaves or in the inner courtyard of the temple, entire families in some cases sitting on straw mats and bedrolls around cooking fires that gleamed like rubies in the evening twilight.

It gave the 'wards', such as they were, an open, informal atmosphere. But this one was different.

The windows were screened with muslin, and there was a lock on the outer door. The twelve patients, all of them young-looking men, lay unmoving and unvisited. Most were on drip-feeds, and one or two were beginning to hunch up into the fetal curl of the long-term comatose. If their charts were to be believed, none of them even had names.

Viveros left the door unlocked when he went out and left her; she was alone with twelve near-corpses and an elderly ward-orderly who was down at the far end of the room. The light came from a single hurricane lamp overhead, and Micheline had wondered how the orderly was managing to find his way around in the deep shadows. Then she'd glimpsed his eyes as he'd turned toward her. They were cataract-white, glazed with blindness as if each pupil had been lightly touched with a hot poker.

Alone with twelve specimens of the living dead and their blind curator. She thought that Viveros had better have a damn good reason for leaving her here like this.

And perhaps he had, at that; perhaps it was up to her to guess what the reason might be.

Over in the darkness, the orderly was coming her way. He was round and white-haired with a mandarin string of moustache and beard, and he wore loose black pyjama-like robes and wooden sandals. He clacked toward her, one hand briefly touching the end of each bed to check his orientation, the handle of a twig broom clutched in the other. As his face came fully into the light, he stopped.

Micheline held her breath. His empty eyes were staring straight at her, but his head was tilted slightly to one side and he was listening. She didn't make a sound, didn't move. Then he smiled, and Micheline knew that he believed himself alone.

He leaned the broom against the iron frame of the bed, and shuffled around the side of it with one hand outstretched. He found the single sheet and drew it back, uncovering a wasted body that was as bent as a puppet's. The boy was naked under the cotton.

The orderly leaned on the mattress. He slid his free hand between the boy's knees. It was playtime.

After a few moments, the young man in the bed nearest to Micheline was beginning to stir. There were rustlings from the darkness. Every body in every bed was reacting, as if they were on a shared line to the same bad dream. There was a low moan from somewhere, and it didn't even sound halfway human.

The moan became a low-register whine of anguish.

Micheline saw that the orderly had now moved his hand lower to take a pinch of the meagre flesh on the boy's leg, and he was twisting it so hard that he seemed to be trying to rip a piece away.

Micheline coughed, loudly and deliberately.

The blind man stiffened, as if he'd been unexpectedly whipped. He released his grip and then drew the cotton sheet back over the boy. Then he picked up his broom and slowly walked past Micheline and out of the ward. He didn't turn toward her, or acknowledge in any way that he knew that she was there. His eyes were like drilled holes peeping down into hell.

When Viveros returned, he was with a nurse who pushed a trolley loaded with newly made-up drips. Micheline told him that she had to talk to him, and alone.

He took her out into a citronella-scented herb garden in the shadow of the temple dome, and as they walked between the eucalyptus rows she told him what she'd observed.

"He hurts one of them," she concluded, "and they all squirm." Viveros was watching her carefully in the weak light that spilled from the unshuttered temple. Out over the darkness of the jungle, a razor-edged moon was rising in the night sky.

He said, "We've noted the phenomenon before, but never in so extreme a form."

"What's in the drips?" Micheline said.

"Low-concentrate EPL in a new formulation. Without it they'd just decline and die. The boys were all soldiers, they were given the stuff to keep them sharp. We haven't conceded that the drug caused their present condition, and we're not going to. It hasn't happened anywhere else. We think that a single batch of the stuff is responsible, but we don't know why."

"And that's the batch that we were given at the centre?"

"Presumably so. But you couldn't know that when you gave a shot to the Englishman. It must be the fact that he survived it and recovered that makes him so interesting to the company."

Micheline thought back to her time in the dog station.

EPL, short for Ephetelin; a patented Risinger-Genoud drug, a central nervous system stimulant that had been on the market for about seven years now. Its only real medical use was in the treatment of narcolepsy, the 'sleeping sickness'; otherwise it was just an upper with amphetamine-like properties, including the production of temporary psychoses with a prolonged overdose. It had been a fashionable slimming drug in America for a year, until the FDA took note of a lot of fat ladies who were suddenly hearing voices out of nowhere. At the time Micheline had been puzzled to receive an assignment to look for potential side-effects in a drug that had already been tested and marketed, but a rogue batch made a lot more sense.

Even the use of the sled dogs made sense, now that she'd seen that weird communal reaction on the ward; their natural pack empathy would have made them ideal subjects for displaying whatever mechanism was at work here. All the bad feelings she'd had for Bruno were now redoubled, because of the way that he'd cut short the programme and stopped her from getting to this first.

Viveros said, "I'll warn the chief about his orderly and then I'll show you where you'll be staying."

"Don't tell the chief anything," Micheline said quickly, and from the way that Viveros looked at her it was obvious that he didn't understand.

"But I thought you told me that the blind man's a sadist."

"That's right, and in two minutes he showed me more than I learned in a month with the dogs. I'll need him."

Without waiting to see what Viveros thought of this, she turned and moved back towards the temple lights. Whatever her status here might be, she was going to find a way of coming out of this with results that would get her a first-class ticket back to Basle.

Peter Viveros followed, but slowly.

ELEVEN

When Jim wasn't looking, someone had flipped over the showcard on the easel at the end of the stage. Now, instead of *Gargantua and Perpetua: Feats of Strength and Decorous Beauty*, he read *MR GRUNDY's highly amusing and astonishing exhibition of SCIENTIFIC ILLUSIONS!!!!!* One line below that, the sign went on in smaller-case lettering, ***Ably assisted by MR TOM SAYERS, GENTLEMAN BOXER***. Jim checked the running order against the handbill on the table before him, but half of the paper was water-stained and had rotted away.

He sneaked another look at the crowd around him. Most of them had turned aside, and in the moving diamanté light of the overhead mirror-globes it was impossible to see far into the shadows. None of them seemed to have faces.

This was his confirmation; it was the carnival of souls. Jim couldn't remember when he'd been given his ticket, or how he'd come to be here. He only knew that he wanted the show to keep on going, to run and run for ever. Because when the show was over, then the band would strike up and the dancing would begin.

The stage was small, a magic-box of darkness and red velvet fronted by a row of limelights. Tom Sayers, gentleman boxer, stood at its centre. He was handsome in a brutal and brilliantined kind of way, and he wore a loud check suit in a style that Jim hadn't seen outside of silent movies. The backs of his hands were so heavily tattooed that they almost appeared to be burn-scarred. He was holding out a folded scarf. He shook it, and the scarf seemed to double in size. He shook it again, and the scarf was a sheet.

He laid the sheet on the boards of the stage, held it by the centre for a moment, and then whipped it away. Mr

Grundy crouched beneath. He slowly unfolded and stood, unsmiling.

There was a murmur of appreciation from the crowd, and some applause. Jim glanced across to the next table. Nobody was moving, or even appeared to be watching.

Grundy was as pale as death, dressed in a bowler hat and a shabby suit to which he'd added a muffler and gloves with split fingers. He wore small, round, wire-rimmed glasses. Their lenses were black, but Jim already knew the colour of the eyes behind.

The unlikely magician moved toward the side of the stage. His walk was slow, and spidery. Tom Sayers was there before him, turning over another showcard to reveal *ILLUSION OR ESCAPE?? ** The Chinese Water Torture Cell*. Grundy turned, and indicated the empty stage with a sweep of his arm.

Except that the stage was no longer empty; a double-trap the size of a freight lift was opening up at its centre, and something was being chain-hoisted out of the water tank beneath. It came up in jerks, splashing waves out onto the boards and pouring water from every seam. It hung unevenly in its harness. It was a green Volkswagen.

The big doors rocked back on their hinges, brass pull-rings rattling, and the car began to turn under the stage lights. It was much as Jim remembered it before the windshield had been sprung and Fedak had come surging up out of nightmare country. Grundy crossed the stage before it, facing the audience all the way but pointing toward the car behind him. He was indicating Stephen Fedak, still alive and struggling to get out.

Jim gripped the edge of the table. The linen was ripped, and the wood underneath it felt mildewed and gritty. Fedak was fighting to open one of the doors from the inside, his cheeks blown with bad air and his eyes screwed shut against the sting of the seawater. It was still pouring out of the car, but its level wasn't getting any lower.

Some of these bugs are nearly airtight, Jim thought. They drift before they sink.

Fedak's strugglings were getting weaker. One or two shouts were coming over the heads of the motionless audience, like a tape playback across a graveyard. Fedak made a fist and tried to take a swing at one of the Volkswagen's side-windows, but the water took all of his energy away. He didn't even make contact. Silver bubbles were beginning to stream from his mouth and nose, the life forcing its way out of him even though he fought to keep it in.

He tried the door again. The car rocked a little with his efforts. He clawed at the windows. The scratches made no sound.

Jim knew that he ought to do something, but he didn't move. He couldn't even shout.

Fedak's head went down, his hair waving like drowned weed. Jim could no longer see his face, but he saw Fedak's life come boiling out as his hands dropped from the glass. More shouts came from behind.

Tom Sayers, Gentleman Boxer, stepped forward. He'd removed his jacket and rolled up baggy sleeves to reveal oak-beam forearms that were crisscrossed with the tails of Chinese dragons. The rest of his suit protected by a stained apron, he walked to the edge of the tank and inserted the blade of a shovel into the crack of the Volkswagen's door.

He banged it home twice with the heel of his hand. On the second blow, the door sprang open.

From out of the car came a flood of water and a cascade of live fish, hitting the stage so hard that the boards trembled under their force. Tom Sayers stood back as the mound grew and slithered and spread, some of the bigger fish flopping so hard that their death-throes came over like drumbeats. A few made it back into the tank, but not many. The stage writhed with more than a ton of dying silver.

Someone moved close to Jim; he looked up quickly. Grundy had descended, and was standing by his table. Both hands were held up before him, and between his spread fingers was a plain wooden birdcage. A canary was fluttering around inside, trying to find a way out. Grundy's black lenses were looking straight at Jim.

We have to remember why we're doing this, he said, in a whisper that was like fingernails across a damp shroud.

And we have to remember that such things can't always be humanely carried off. And then, without any warning, he made as if to fling the birdcage into the air; except that the birdcage suddenly wasn't there.

Grundy began to smile, slowly. It was like watching old paint starting to peel. Even through the dark lenses, Jim could see the featureless whites of his eyes gleaming. Grundy held out one of his hands, uncurling his fingers to show the dead canary. There was a single cherry-bead of blood at its beak.

Now, he whispered, *Let's strike up the band*, and he moved aside.

Tom Sayers was standing behind him. The stains on his apron seemed to be of dried-on blood and pus, layer upon darkening layer like the working coat of an old-time surgeon. In his tattooed hand was a surgical scalpel with a three-inch blade. It sparked in the limelight as Sayers moved forward.

Jim lifted the table. It seemed to weigh nothing at all. It sailed through the air toward Tom Sayers, Gentleman Boxer, tilting like a shield and meeting him head-on. There was a dull *thwack*, and two full inches of blade appeared through the underside. Jim almost fell over his chair in his haste to turn and run.

They were coming after him; he didn't have to look to know it. He heard the furniture smash as Tom Sayers kicked it apart to retrieve his knife. He brushed by somebody, feeling them move as if they were made of nothing more than rags and straw; two more tipped as he pushed his way through, and he heard their skulls bounce upon the table. A dead hand was thrown out against his leg, and he knocked it aside. A couple of yards further on it happened again, but this one grabbed him and wouldn't let go.

Jim spun around, trying to pull himself free. Sayers was scrambling over bones and dusty rags to get to him, silhouetted against the bright stage where the fish were still jerking around like hanged men. Something snapped, and Jim was running again.

A door fell open under his weight, hardly slowing him at all. He was out of the music hall and into the long arcade.

The arcade was burning.

Everything was red, red, red. Carousel music was playing and he stumbled toward it, one arm raised to protect his face. He was running down an aisle of penny machines and shies and fortune-telling booths, and he almost tripped and fell a couple of times as loose boards gave under him. He *did* fall as he came out into the main area where the big rides were run, but he was on his feet again in a moment.

The carousel was in motion, its black horses rising and falling in the long seesaw gallop to nowhere. Most of them had riders, but the riders were speared on the carousel's twisted poles. They slumped forward, arms hanging down by the horses' necks. In the flicker of firelight Jim saw a baby going by, its arms and legs waving as it was carried up and down, up and down, pinned six inches above the saddle.

Tom Sayers was calling his name.

He had to be headed in the right direction; there *had* to be a way out. He ran around by the side of the carousel. Weakened fingers plucked at his shoulder in passing, as if reaching for a brass ring. He faced more rides, more booths, and deep shadows that danced in the firelight. Whichever way he turned, he could be wrong. He looked back.

Jim could see the boxer across the platform of the carousel, but Sayers hadn't yet seen Jim. He was standing, knife in hand, watching the dark horses as they went by. If Jim could melt back into the shadows without being seen, he might even get away.

Some of the impaled figures began to stir. They were raising their arms to point toward him. He did an about-face and a fast takeoff.

Way ahead, he saw his last chance.

She sat cross-legged in a glass booth, her delicate wax head tilted slightly forward. Dust hadn't reached the Eastern robes that she wore, but their colours were fading. *THE ALL-KNOWING AUTOMATON*, the hand-lettered sign above her read; and below, *any question answered*. Jim's breath fogged the glass as he fell against it and made his request.

Seen from this close, her pale wax skin was a maze of tiny cracks. *This is the carnival of souls*, she said in his mind. *There isn't any way home* And a single crystal tear ran like glass down her cheek. Her eyes were blue, shading into violet.

Two hands gripped his shoulders.

"Jim," Linda said, shaking him hard. "Jim, what are you *doing* here?"

There was no carnival, and no carousel. There wasn't even any fire; just the on-off red glow of the pier-end's sea navigation light that shone down through the holes in the arcade roof. It helped to fill in the shadows around the beam of Linda's flashlight as they made their way back toward the boardwalk and the promenade gates.

Jim said nothing for a while, and Linda didn't push him. He was embarrassed, he was uncertain . . . and more than anything, he was scared. The gates were wide open, the temporary wire that had secured them untwisted and hanging in pigtail spikes. He could feel the cuts on his hands from where he must have pulled it free.

They walked under the promenade lights, with Linda keeping a tight and reassuring hold on his arm. A sea breeze made spindrifts in the blown-over sand, and carried them away into the darkness. Jim realised that he didn't even know what time it was.

"I waited for nearly two hours," Linda said. "I couldn't think where you might have gone."

"How did you find me?"

"When I got to the house, all the doors were open. I knew there had to be something wrong. I read your diary, Jim." She must have felt him go tense, because she quickly added, "I'm sorry. I wasn't snooping, it was the only way I could think of to find out where you might be. I suppose you're mad at me."

"No," he said. "I just feel like a fool."

He realised after a while that they were heading away from the Cliff House path, away, in fact, from the town itself; a few hundred yards ahead, the promenade petered out and gave way to sand dunes and couch-grass. He said, "Where are we going?"

"Wait and see," Linda told him.

She snapped on the flashlight again as they stepped down from the rough end of the tarmac. Jim was about to take a last look back at the pier, but he stopped himself. He knew with utter certainty what he would see. Grundy would be there, a tiny figure in the distance, his coat-tails flapping in slow-motion. He'd be flanked on either side by two dogs of indeterminate breed, dark as leopards and with jewelled eyes as white as his own.

Jim looked back. There was nobody on the pier.

Linda seemed to know where she was going, so Jim went along and asked no more questions. There was silence here among the dunes, where even the sea was no more than a faint wash in the distance. Last season's bottles and cans were half-buried in the sand around them like Sargasso wrecks; every now and then, a piece of driftwood cast a long sawtooth shadow.

They came to a duckboard path, a raised level of slatted wood that ran from the beach across to a dark stand of trees about a quarter of a mile inland. Sand gave way to marsh as they followed the track, and reeds were growing up through the gaps between the planking. They passed a large wooden sign, but it was too dark for Jim to read.

The trees sheltered a woodland caravan site, closed for the winter and apparently unsupervised. The trailers were large and modern-looking, each with a piece of private land around it and a couple of small outhouses. Two or three that passed under Linda's beam as she counted down the row had picket fences and rockery gardens. Jim looked around nervously, expecting at any moment a light to show, or somebody to shout a challenge, or a dog to bark. But the silence was complete.

"This way," Linda said, and she unlatched one of the gates. As Jim stepped through after her, she was tilting the zinc dustbin by the van's door and taking something from underneath. She came up with a key, and the key got them inside.

Linda already seemed to know her way around. As Jim was closing the door behind them, she was into a cupboard and turning on the gas supply. She came out with matches, and moments later there was a sunburst of warm light as the first of the backup gas mantles caught.

Jim blinked a little. This mobile home was one of the big luxury models, too big to be a trailer in anything but name and panelled and fitted like an expensive apartment.

"It belongs to the Pryors," Linda explained as she straightened from the gas heater. "They let it in the season."

"Do they know we're here?"

"Kim said we could use it, if we wanted."

"But why?"

At this, Linda seemed to hesitate. In the way she looked at Jim there was no lead-on, and no discouragement; perhaps she was trying to read him, but that was all.

Read him, hell. She'd already read his thoughts about her in his diary, hadn't she?

She found him in the pre-dawn mist and twilight. He'd discovered a gallon container of Elsan fluid in one of the outhouses, and he was splashing it around outside the van. A few more yards, and the ring would be closed.

She said, "Jim? What are you doing?"

"It's for the dogs," he explained in a whisper. "They'll never find us if I can kill the scent."

"There aren't any dogs, Jim. You were dreaming again."

He stopped. There was less than a pint of the disinfectant left. Linda was standing in the doorway of the caravan, a blanket hastily pulled around her shoulders against the morning's chill. Jim was wearing only his overcoat. He hadn't even noticed the cold until this moment.

No, there were no dogs. Not here, not now. He said, "I'm losing it, aren't I?"

"It's been a bad time for both of us," she said. "Come back inside."

Linda relocked the door, but she didn't try to hide the key. They dropped the blanket and the overcoat in a heap on the floor, and climbed back under the bedcovers to get warm. The gas heater was still burning, set as low as it would go.

Linda settled quickly, her head on Jim's chest and one arm thrown across as if to protect him. They lay quietly for a while.

And then Jim said, "What were you going to tell me?"

Linda was caught almost on the edge of sleep. "What?"

"This morning. You said you had something to tell me."

"Not right now, Jim. Please."

He let it go. She was breathing deeply within minutes. Grey light was already starting to show around the edges of the curtains.

TWELVE

Morning.

They left the caravan as they'd found it, and Linda replaced the key under the dustbin. The site's gates were locked, but they were able to get to the lane outside by walking a couple of hundred yards through the trees and climbing over a low wall.

"It's going to rain again," Jim said, looking at the sky after he'd helped Linda to jump down. The trees on either side were bare, and the roadside was a mush of dead leaves.

"Tell me something new about this town," she said, dusting off her hands. "I'll lend you an umbrella."

They walked for half an hour, taking it slowly. The lane joined a country road, and the country road led them back into town. This was already as alive as it was going to get for the rest of the day.

In the hallway to the Pryor house, Linda sorted through a heap of coats on a Victorian stand to find her folding umbrella. A radio was playing somewhere in the back.

"Here," she said, pulling out the umbrella and offering it to him. It was blue and with a pattern of flowers, but as long as he kept it collapsed-down it would disappear into one of the pockets of his overcoat. "It may be a bit gaudy for you, but it'll be better than nothing."

"Thanks," Jim said, thinking that he'd take the first polite opportunity that he could find to hand it back.

"Well," Linda said with a glance down the hall that betrayed a slight nervousness, "I'd better turn you around and boot you out before Mrs P knows that you're here."

"House rules?"

She smiled, apologetically. "You've got it."

Walking down along the seafront, Jim noted with relief that the sky was already beginning to clear. The threat of yet another rain had been no more than that, a threat. As he reached the Cliff House path and started to climb, he took a small rubber ball out of his pocket and began squeezing it methodically in his left hand.

The old place was even starting to look something like home. A couple of days after moving in he'd taken a cautious trip upstairs and found not only that the bathroom was usable, but that the water heater was on a working circuit. Now, two hours after getting back, he was bathed, dressed in clean clothes, and feeling brighter than he had in a long time. From his backlogged stock he took a couple of the yellow pills and one of the white ones, as prescribed, and as he washed them down with tapwater he wondered how long it was going to take him to become stable again. He felt guilty for playing around with his own treatment the way that he had. Franks knew what he was doing, after all.

He decided that he could probably afford to take Linda to lunch at Spencer's. It was hardly the Ritz, but then they were hardly the Rothschilds. With this plan in mind, he made his way over to the Pryor house again after he'd made his regular call at the bank. None of the doorbells was marked, so he picked one at random. Moments later, he was facing Kim Pryor.

"Day off?" Jim said.

"Half a day, but it's better than nothing. You looking for Linda?"

"Yes. Is she around?"

Kim Pryor stepped back to let him in. She was wearing

100

jeans and an old pullover, not exactly bankers' business-wear. She said, "She had to go out, but she shouldn't be long. You can wait upstairs, if you like."

"Isn't it against house rules?"

Kim Pryor smiled briefly. "No rules in this house. Come on, I'll open up for you."

She took a key from a ring in a kitchen cupboard, and then together they climbed two flights of carpeted stairs. Jim said, "Won't she mind?"

"I shouldn't think so, not if it's you. You should have seen her face when I first told her you'd arrived."

"When was this?" Jim said. He was beginning to wonder whether he wasn't losing the thread of the conversation.

Her voice echoing back down the stairway, Kim said, "Oh, I suppose I shouldn't be telling you. Linda asked me to watch out for you at the bank and to let her know when you turned up, but I hadn't to let on. I can't see it mattering now, though. I suppose you know each other from way back."

"Something like that," Jim said.

They came to a narrow half-glassed door on the upper landing. All of the carpets in the house seemed new, and all of the woodwork was old under new white paint. She opened the door and stepped back.

"I've got to run," she said. "I'll see you later."

The door let onto a narrow attic stairway. Jim climbed slowly, nervous even though he knew there was nobody home. There was a windowless square landing at the top with a choice of two doors. The first was for a bedroom, most of the space taken up by a double-divan with a pink spread and a wooden chest of drawers that had been squeezed in under the sloping ceiling. A one-eyed teddy bear of indeterminate age glowered back at him from the pillow. He didn't go inside, but pulled the door closed and turned to the other room.

It was clean and it was pleasant enough, an odd mix of styles like the layout of any furnished flat. His eye was immediately caught by the laptop computer by the phone on the writing-desk.

He went around the old sprung sofa for a closer look.

She'd said that she worked for a computer firm, once, so this probably dated back to those days. It was a classy-looking machine, made by some French outfit that he'd never heard of.

As he was studying it, the phone started to ring.

It rang out four times before he overcame his hesitation and picked it up. Not knowing the number he said, "Hello?" but the line sounded strangely dead and all that he heard for a moment was an echo of his own voice over a background of what sounded like tape hiss.

"*Please engage the modem*," a synthesised voice said out of nowhere. And then the request was repeated, first in French and then in German.

He switched on the power to the laptop, and as its six-inch screen began to glow green he pushed the phone receiver into the rubber sleeves of the modem at its side. Then he stood back and watched the machine come alive.

It barely took a minute to load up whatever information was being transmitted, the screen flashing out beeps and patterns as it went. Finally it cleared, and Jim settled onto the desk's bentwood chair to read:

RISINGER GENOUD AG CP-V AT YOUR
SERVICE — R/G*OEOO
11.24 SEP 20 USER # 41A LINE # 103
ON AT 11.24 SEP 20
LINDA MCKAY 1274 9AP
CLEAR WS
*   ]LOAD OKTOBER 14170001*
OKTOBER 1410001 — DATAFILE HARPER, JAMES
PASSWORD?

He tried to think of a password that Linda might use. People always went for something obvious; their own names, their phone numbers, the name of their dog. But he didn't know Linda well enough even to make an educated guess.

It seemed that he didn't know Linda at all.

He typed in her name. The screen cleared immediately, making him think that he'd hit lucky on his first try.

But after a few seconds, he realised that he'd only succeeded in triggering some security sub-routine that had dumped the datafile out of the computer's memory. The screen was going to stay blank, no matter what else he did.

So then he switched off the power, and replaced the telephone's receiver in its cradle.

With any luck, she wouldn't even know that he'd been here.

Thirteen

Audrey Ellis had been behind the reception desk at the Lady DeLisle clinic for just over a month now, and she felt that at last she was getting the hang of the job. It was mostly a matter of running things in a way that the doctors were least likely to mess up, which meant that she'd had to watch them pretty closely for a while to get some idea of how each of them worked. Doctor Sims, the clinic's head and the most highly paid psychiatrist in the section, expected her affairs to be run with oiled precision even though she always came in late and never noted down her appointments; but at least she was easier than Doctor Franks, who would disappear for entire afternoons leaving Audrey to make excuses for him.

She had a little office with a sliding reception window, but mostly she preferred to stay at her desk out in the open area with the lounge seating and the rubber plants. The clinic was a ten year-old single-storey building, a mini-complex of prefabricated units with a roof that had begun to leak at the end of year one. It was always in the shadow of the main hospital block – itself built over a hundred and fifty years before as the city poorhouse – and it was on a service road that was used almost continuously by laundry vans. Now, after four weeks, Audrey was beginning to look on it as her second home; give it another four, she kept telling herself, and you might even start to feel comfortable.

There had been nothing to make her nervous. If anything, most of the patients that she met every day were so normal that they were completely unmemorable. This was pretty much as Adele, the girl who'd held the job before her and who'd left to have a baby, had said it would be; but in spite of this Audrey was still working with a nine-to-five feeling of apprehension. Twice she'd put her old Vauxhall in for the inexpensive carwash service that was run by a co-operative of some of the long-stay patients, and both times she'd had to check the boot before she could drive away. She couldn't rid herself of the image of one of them crouched in there, grinning and waiting until she got home and switched off the lights in the drive. After all, where did the movies get these ideas, if it wasn't from life?

"I need to see Doctor Franks," the man said, and Audrey looked up, startled. She hadn't even heard him come in.

He was wearing an overcoat that was a couple of sizes too big, and there was a cheap suitcase under his arm. His eyes showed intelligence, but also an unmistakable desperation. They burned in his pale face as if with a hunger that he hadn't yet found a name for.

Audrey said, "Doctor Franks isn't here today." Even if Franks had turned in as he'd been expected to, he'd probably have gone by now; he never stayed around beyond the mid-afternoon.

"Can you call him?" the man said.

"Appointments start at ten o'clock tomorrow. If you want me to fit you in . . ."

He leaned forward, putting his free hand on her desk. "It's an emergency," he said. "I can't explain."

Audrey stared at his spread fingers on the teak-effect desktop. It was as if he'd taken a first step into the safe space between them.

She said, "Are you a patient?"

"Harper, James Harper. He knows me."

104

"Just take a seat," Audrey said, grateful for the excuse to be able to slide her chair back and out of reach, "and I'll see."

Jim walked over and lowered himself onto one of the black vinyl lounge chairs in the waiting area. They'd been throwouts from the gynae unit and they farted like whoopee cushions if they weren't approached with care. He sat with his case across his knees; it was actually an effort after a few moments to set it down on the floor and look away, as if he was beginning to get abnormally attached to it.

Well, that was hardly wrong. The suitcase represented just about everything that he had. Everything he had that could be relied upon, anyway.

He hadn't been away for long, but the place was already beginning to look different. Even a new receptionist to replace friendly Adele, who'd called him Jimmy-boy and always offered him coffee. This one seemed as nervous as a bird; he could see her now, peeking out through the Enquiries window of the inner office as she tried to get Franks on the phone.

Franks wouldn't mind, when he heard Jim's story. Jim closed his eyes for a moment, and held it all down for a while longer.

From along the corridor in the large playroom, he could hear the live-in children of Doctor Gupta's Disturbed unit. He was glad of the chance to sit for a while. Long busrides always made him feel a little queasy. After a few minutes, the receptionist finally emerged.

She said, "Doctor Franks is on his way over. I told him you said it was an emergency. He's coming in from home."

"Thanks."

"He said you could wait in his office."

Even this has changed, he thought as he stood in Franks' office and looked around. The yachting pictures and the trophy case and the soft tweed Torture Chair were all as he remembered them, but Franks had added a desktop micro terminal to his range of executive toys. Almost everything in the room seemed to be evidence of the psychiatrist's desire to be out doing something else. Where other doctors might hang their diplomas, Franks had a colour shot of his yacht *Rosebud* in the Fastnet race of nine years before.

Jim started to smile as he read the name. *Rosebud*. Oh, come *on*!

The receptionist was back; she hesitated on seeing that Jim was on the 'wrong' side of the desk, but then she seemed to think again. At least this way the furniture was between them.

She'd brought him some magazines. "I'm sorry," she said, "this is all we have," and she laid down two copies of *She*, a *House and Garden*, and a *Beano*. They were all months out of date.

Jim indicated the micro. He said, "This is new."

She smiled nervously, already inching back toward the door. "It's just on a tryout," she said. "Nobody's quite used to it yet."

This time, she closed the door behind her. Jim realised too late that he'd left his case outside.

He went to follow her. The door was locked.

He'd raised his fist to start banging, but then he stopped himself. She was probably already fantasising him as a multiple rapist or an axe-murderer, and he didn't want to encourage her in the idea. It was an annoyance, but the prefabricated walls were hardly those of a prison; and if he needed to get out in a hurry, he could simply drag a chair over to where two filing cabinets blocked off an unused doorway. The transom overhead was already open an inch.

But after the day that he'd had, he could have done without this. Sometime soon, Kim Pryor would be getting home from her half-day at the bank. It couldn't be long before Linda would know that he'd been in her room and perhaps that he'd taken her phonecall as well. She'd know that her cover was now useless. It had been a scramble to get packed and to make it down to the bus terminal in time, but at least Jim had now reached the one place where he knew that he could feel secure.

He was prowling. It was starting to get to him, and he mustn't let it. He stopped by the desk again and picked up two golfballs, Franks' oversized worry beads. Jim sat on the edge of the desk and rolled them between his hands, around and around. Behind him, the telephone *pinged* once as someone elsewhere in the clinic dialled for an outside line.

After a minute he went around the desk and sat in Franks' chair, a deep leather recliner. He wondered how long it would be before Franks could get in from home. Jim had never felt such a strong need to talk, and keep on talking.

There was a printed logo on the side of each of the golfballs, and he switched on the desklight and held them under it so that he could read. The print had faded, but it was clear enough for Jim to be able to make out the words *Epheteline – the* safe *anorectic*. Below this in a circle was a company name that had been mostly rubbed away. It was a salesman's freebie; they'd turned up everywhere during Jim's stay, overprinted pens and block-edged memo pads and any kind of desk junk that could possibly carry a brand name.

Franks would be annoyed at Jim's self-directed experiment in survival without medication, but he couldn't really do anything other than come clean about it. He set down the golfballs, and looked around for something else to play with.

There was an oversized noteclip in yellow plastic — *Iversin Inhaler*. A pen tray – *Probotine Supplement*. *Metastatin. Zonalin Antibacterial.*

Jim turned the light across the desk. Under each product, the same company name.

The room seemed a few degrees colder.

Slowly, Jim pulled the chair across to the micro at the end of the desk. There was a small oblong patch under the screen where something, a piece of tape or a sticker, had been peeled away. The computer didn't look cheap. He switched it on.

THIS IS MEDIC, the screen glowed. *WHAT'S YOUR PASSWORD?*

Jim thought it over. Then, with one finger, he typed *ROSEBUD*.

GOOD AFTERNOON, DOCTOR FRANKS,
WHO'S OUR FIRST CASE?
JAMES HARPER
TRY AGAIN
HARPER, JAMES

HARPER, JAMES, IS A SPECIAL FILE, ACCESS
IS RESTRICTED TO KEYHOLDERS ONLY.
WHAT'S THE PASSWORD?

Jim sat there, putting it off for more than a minute.
If he left it for much longer, the machine might switch itself
off.

OKTOBER, he typed.

The screen was immediately filled with dates and data.

He touched the power button, and the screen went
blank. It was time to go.

The filing cabinets rocked dangerously as Jim climbed
aboard. The transom opened with a giveaway squeal, but it
opened into an empty surgical store. He clambered
through and briefly tested his weight on a shelf that wasn't
meant to take it, and from there he jumped down to the
carpet tiles. Half of the mass behind the noise of his landing
belonged to the overcoat.

He listened at the door, but nobody came running. The
stores were locked, too, but they could be opened from the
inside. Jim stepped through into a corridor that was lit by
skylight panels in the flat roof overhead, the glow of a day's
end on a grey vinyl floor. If he could quietly get his case and
go, he'd be away before anyone knew it.

The receptionist had retreated from the open area to her
inner office. She was talking on the telephone, her back to
the sliding window. Jim picked up his case and started
toward the door.

Two male nurses in hospital whites were climbing the
steps outside. One was small and red-haired and wiry, the
other had the build and the doleful expression of a polar
bear. Jim wasn't aware of ever having met either of them;
but as they came in through the glass doors, he could see
from their faces that they knew him in an instant.

With his case under his arm, he turned around and took off.

He was down at the end of the corridor before the nurses had even made it across the Reception floor. He burst through into the playroom, jumped over a fingerpainted moonscape-in-progress while six multicoloured children watched his passing with their mouths hanging open, and hit the fire doors on the opposite side without slowing. The crush bar gave way, the doors exploded outwards, and Jim was out onto the waste ground beside the clinic as the fire sirens started to howl.

He ran across the service road. The nurses were emerging after him, one of them limping badly and spattered with paint. The hospital towered overhead like a redbrick cathedral bound with the iron galleries of its fire escapes. He hurdled a planted border and ran on across grass; somewhere behind, the blare of a van's horn was added to the sirens as the two nurses tried to dodge the laundry service.

Jim had increased his lead, but he could easily lose it. He wasn't even sure where he was going, he only knew that there was a ten-foot perimeter wall that would face him squarely if he should make a wrong turn. He had to make it through the grounds to one of the main-road exits.

Rose bushes tried to catch at him. His case felt as if he was toting an anvil. He passed under the counterweighted ladder of one of the escapes, knowing that he had no chance of reaching to pull it down. Staying close to the high gothic wall of the hospital, he dived for the nearest corner and around.

He was on the wrong side of the building.

All of the main doors, and therefore the main road, were around on the other side. He'd run into a U-shaped garden between two of the hospital's main wings. Five floors of windows looked down from three sides, and not a single door.

Behind Jim, one of the nurses had enough breath to call out to him. He didn't have enough breath to make it intelligible.

They'd be in sight at any moment. Jim looked for the

nearest window, *any* window on the ground floor that might be open; saw one, made for it. He posted his case through, heard it hit the floor, and hoisted himself up and dragged himself after.

He came headfirst into the steam heat of an autoclave and incinerator room. There was so much noise from the heavy equipment around him that he could have entered with a fanfare and it wouldn't have drawn attention. He was alone.

Before anything else, he peeked back over the sill. Both of the male nurses were in the garden, and they were looking around for him; from their point of view, it must have seemed like a vanishing act. Moving back from the window, he picked up his case and went to the door to listen for a moment.

Somebody was coming.

The room wasn't large, and Jim could see only one place that he might be able to hide; there was just enough space for him behind the autoclave drum, as long as he crouched and didn't move. If somebody caught him there, he was going to have an interesting time trying to explain exactly what he was doing.

There wasn't enough room for his luggage.

Outside, something bumped the door and stopped with a clatter of stainless steel. The only off-the-floor space that Jim could see was on a shelf alongside stacks of new bedpans packed in tissue paper; his case slotted in perfectly, and he went to ground just as a Jamaican nurse came backing into the room pulling a ward trolley behind her.

Jim was breathing heavily, but he tried to keep it quiet. Bent double as he was, his side was beginning to cramp into a stitch. He closed his eyes and tried to wish it away.

"You know what Sister does to peeping Toms," the Jamaican nurse said, and Jim's bowels turned to icewater.

He began to straighten. He almost had, when he realised that the nurse wasn't talking to him.

"Leave it out," another voice said, "I'm knackered." It was coming from outside the window, and it sounded like the Polar Bear. Jim ducked down again, hoping that no-one had been looking his way. The voice went on, "Has anybody been through here?"

"No," the Jamaican girl said. "Why?"

"There's a paranoid from the psychiatric unit running around."

"*Another?*" the nurse said. She sounded weary and incredulous, both at the same time.

"Yeah. Close the window, will you?"

The case, Jim was thinking. *Don't look at the case*.

"It's already like a bloody sauna in here."

"It's only until we get him," the Polar Bear said, and already his voice was fading. A few seconds later, Jim heard the window being slid down a token few inches.

Don't look at the case, he kept thinking over the next couple of minutes as the nurse unloaded bags of soiled dressings from her trolley, *and for Christ's sake don't look over here, either*. She sang as she worked, and she was still singing as she finally wheeled her trolley out of the room.

Jim was sweating like old dynamite.

He only had to make it through the hospital. There were too many ways in and out for them all to be watched, and it would take too long to organise. Take it slowly, he told himself as he slipped out of the incinerator room, and try to look as if you belong here.

He'd covered fifteen yards. "And where do you think you're going?"

Jim knew that she was talking to him and nobody else; it was the kind of voice that could be targeted like a whip. Jim turned around, and saw a girl in the uniform of a nursing Sister. She was barely more than five feet tall and she looked like a teenager, but her tone of authority was a thousand years old.

Jim said, "Did I take a wrong turn?" and the Sister sighed and glanced up once as if to count the tiles on the ceiling.

"This way," she said. "There's only five minutes left."

He followed her to the corridor's end and through a double set of swinging doors, too dazed to wonder where he was going or why. They came through into a fifty-bed women's ward. It was visiting time.

"Thank you," Jim said, and he carried his suitcase on past the nurses' station with its charts and flowers. He walked down the centre aisle as slowly as he dared. He passed beds on either side, most of them in hospital linen but some of them with hand-crocheted spreads brought from home. About half of the women had visitors; some of the beds with empty chairs beside them looked empty themselves, their occupants so frail and old and shrunken that they barely made a bump in the covers.

By the time that Jim reached the end of the row, they'd have spotted him for a fraud. There wasn't another way out, and when he risked a glance back he saw that the Sister was still looking in his direction.

He stopped by the end of an unattended bed. The old woman in it was as yellow and parched as a mummy, her off-white hair neatly brushed even though it was dull and beginning to fall out. Eyes like dry beads stared into the middle distance, not even registering that Jim was there.

Feeling guilty and mean as he did it, he set down his case by the bed and drew up a chair.

She seemed as fragile as a tissue-paper kite. Jim said in a low voice, "I hope you don't mind. It's only for a couple of minutes, and then I'll go."

But go where? His last home had been the clinic and beyond that, he had nowhere. The Sister was talking to one of the nurses at her desk at the end of the ward, and again she seemed to look at Jim. The old woman's hands were loosely folded over her Angora bedjacket, and Jim reached over and took one of them in his own. It felt like a handful of twigs. She didn't resist, but for the first time Jim sensed a stirring in her awareness.

Her hand trembled like a bird's. Like the canary so casually crushed and thrown aside by Grundy in Jim's walking dream of the evening before. Perhaps he should have taken more notice; there was more truth in it than he'd cared to see.

"I know who you are," the Sister said from the end of the bed, and Jim was brought back to the moment as if by a

112

dousing in cold water. The old woman's hand still quivered in his own.

"Mrs Allenby's always talked about her George," the Sister said, moving around toward him and looking down at the bleached head on the pillows with professionally tempered pity. "Never used to talk about anything else."

"Really?" Jim said, glancing down and almost expecting to be given away.

"She said you wouldn't break a promise."

Grace Allenby stared on into the middle distance, all of her spent energies being consumed by the simple act of keeping her life-signs going. Feeling about as low as he'd ever been, Jim said, "I couldn't get away before. And I can't stay."

The Sister leaned forward, and seemed to detect some change in rhythm that Jim couldn't see. "She wants to say something."

She wanted to call him a liar. Her shrunken lips twitched; Jim moved closer to listen, knowing that he deserved it.

George, she whispered, *George*, and her skinny hand put the slightest pressure on his.

Oh, Linda.

FOURTEEN

Evening.

Piccadilly Circus, London; the Underground.

Jim hovered in the striplight shadow, just out of range of the video camera that was angled down onto the street exit behind him. Every now and again he'd glance up to see if the camera had moved, but its position seemed to be fixed. The single red eye of a power indicator shone through the grime on the camera's mount, the fifty-cycle heartbeat of a monochrome witness to all of the deadbeats and down-beats and sightseeing tourists that passed under its lens.

He'd been waiting and watching for almost an hour. He was feeling lonely and hungry and his head ached with dull ferocity; they'd threatened to throw him off the National Express coach that had brought him into London because of the noises that he'd made after falling asleep in his seat. There seemed to be only one dependable certainty in his world at this moment, which was that the people supposedly treating his condition were the ones who were actually responsible for it; how or why he didn't know, but he *did* know that he had no allies when it came to finding out.

Well, if he had to, he'd manage alone. He'd started to say as much aloud once, but it had sounded too hollow and unconvincing.

The station concourse beneath the Circus had become a winter home for the streetlife that found the streets too cold. It was low-ceilinged and dark, cream paint gone yellow with a floor of off-white stone tiles. The main crowds were around the telephone booths and the lit ticket machines where turnstiles led to descending elevators; but whereas most people kept on going through, some only moved around enough to avoid being noticed.

There were two in particular that had taken Jim's interest. They never seemed to go far from the chipped yellow zoo-bar enclosure that was the control point for arrivals – at least, not until two uniformed policemen made their regular half-hourly circuit, and then they seemed to vanish like geckoes from a garden wall. Otherwise they received contacts, held deep conversations that never lasted more than a minute, and generally seemed to be carrying on some kind of covert trade.

Jim finally decided to take a chance. He went over and said, "Can we talk business?"

The darker of the two looked at him with instant suspicion. Both seemed to be in their early twenties, and both had bad skin and night-people eyes. The dark one had a sparse pencil-moustache that had been helped along with real pencil. He checked Jim over, took in the suitcase and the Oxfam-shop clothes and the general look of him, and decided that he was probably on safe ground.

He said, "What kind of business?"

So Jim explained what he needed to know, and the dark one glanced around quickly, and then he indicated his companion and said, "Go with Benny. He'll sort you out. He's got no record, so he does all the handling."

Benny the Banker set off and Jim followed, not without some feeling of nervousness. Under the lights and in a crowd he'd felt reasonably safe, but the empty number one subway was something else.

They passed the dark basement windows of the store that had once been Swan and Edgar's, and started to walk up a fifty-yard tiled incline past poster-ads for cinemas, museums, jeans, jobs, and pregnancy advice. Before they reached the steps at the end, Benny indicated a dark side-spur with a pinned-back iron gate.

"Step into the office," he said, as any sales clerk might, and he waited for Jim before he followed him in. They stood in a corner piled with trash and echoing with the whine of hot-air dryers in the toilets further down the tunnel, the air scented with old urine from those too drunk or too lazy to walk a few more yards.

None of this seemed to bother Benny. He said, "Okay, what have we got?"

Jim showed him the bag, and he was starting to explain when Benny stopped him.

"That's okay," he said, and he sorted around in the carrier. He came out with four of the tablets, all different kinds; he sniffed, broke, tasted, swallowed. He crunched them up like sweets, and when they'd gone down he stood for a few moments with his eyes tightly shut. Then he shook his head, as if to clear it.

Jim watched the whole performance with some disbelief. He said, "Do you have to try everything?"

"Yeah," Benny said. "It's a perk. Better than paying Jacko's prices."

"Doesn't the mixture screw you up?"

"No, it usually cancels out. Although some nights you can feel as if you're going home with your head on backwards. Just give me a minute."

He spent most of it leaning one-handed against the wall, head down as he monitored his own reactions.

Finally he straightened, took a deep breath, and shook his head again. He said, "Milk sugar."

"What does that mean?" Jim said.

"Means they're all placebos, every one of them. You might just as well have been taking Smarties for all the good they'd do you. I can give you a fiver for the whole bag. Most of the kids Jacko trades with won't know the difference."

Milk sugar. Franks had explained them to him one at a time; this one's a tranquilliser, this one's an antipsychotic, this one's to protect you from the side-effects of *that* one . . . the lie hadn't even been casual.

Jim said, "I'm not arguing about the money, but . . . are you sure?"

Benny put a hand on his shoulder. "Trust me," he said. "I'm a professional."

Jim took what was offered and, when Benny had gone, he added the money to the rest of his funds. The total wasn't much.

But whether he liked it or not, it now seemed that he was going to have a long way to go.

FIFTEEN

At around the time that a lorry was dropping Jim Harper off at the harbour gates in Folkestone, a minicab braked to a halt on the service road before the Lady DeLisle clinic. The cab's meter was almost into three figures, but Linda told the driver to wait.

It was now nearly midnight, and only a dim security light burned over the reception area. The place seemed deserted, but when Linda tried the main door she found that it opened easily.

She'd never visited the clinic before. She stood in the near-darkness and tried to listen, but the only sound was the slow hiss of the door as it closed itself behind her. Franks was supposed to be here. He'd said as much in the panic phone message that Atalanta Pryor had taken while Linda had been up at the Cliff House, trying the locked doors and wondering where Jim might be.

Now, after speaking to Kim and learning that he'd been in her room, she knew that she'd have to assume the worst.

Her arm outstretched and her fingertips brushing the wall for guidance, Linda stepped toward the offshoot corridor behind the reception desk. Almost immediately, she saw light on the far wall where the passageway turned. There was somebody in one of the offices around the corner, and the glass panel over his door was the giveaway.

She walked to the door, and opened it. Franks was inside. He looked up guiltily, as if he had no right to be in his own office.

"It took you long enough," he said. He was behind his desk in a tilted-back leather executive chair, one hand frozen in the act of massaging his temple.

She said, "I didn't get your message until late. Where is he?"

"I was hoping you'd be able to tell me," Franks said, and he leaned across and placed something on the desk; a golfball. It rolled along the edge of his blotter and came to rest against the base of the desk light.

"But he knows about the monitoring?"

Franks could only shrug.

He said, "Audrey thinks that he took a look at his own file while he was in here. God knows how he's supposed to have managed that. But you can tell your people I've finished with him, I never heard of James Harper and I never heard of Oktober." He indicated the micro terminal at the end of his desk with a brief, rejecting gesture. "They can come and strip all of this out, and I'll look for another grant. I'm sorry I ever got into it."

"We can't just dump him," Linda protested, but Franks was already taking a creased-looking trenchcoat from a hook behind the door. "He needs help."

"We're the ones who are going to be needing help," Franks said, "if any of this ever gets out."

"Wait a minute," Linda said. "That evening at the house, when your people were in the kitchen and I wasn't watching. What exactly did they do to him?"

But Franks was already on his way out of the door.

"Ask the people who sent you," he said. "I was never even here tonight."

PART TWO

On the Road

SIXTEEN

Jim is on an escalator, and descending.

It was a thousand-mile tunnel angled down into the earth, the machinery was old and the ride was uneven; he kept a tight hold on the handrail and swayed every time that his step jerked or the drive chains ran slack for a moment. There was nobody ahead, and Jim couldn't look back. He tried, but he couldn't.

Most of the advertising posters had been ripped from their frames in the tunnel wall, but every now and again one had been left. It seemed to Jim that the glossy studio shots were getting more and more daring as the stairway went deeper; these were nearly all underwear ads, and some of the underwear was more see-through than cover. Every model was staring at the camera with a look that was something between an offer and a challenge.

He tried to make out where he was heading, but some of the lights were out and this was difficult. He'd lost all sense of when he'd started the journey, and why. The escalator clanked and rumbled, and when Jim looked down he could see that a kind of glow was escaping through the gaps where the steps didn't quite fit against the sides. It was green, and it seemed to pulse slowly. Jim knew that it was probably a string of working lights in the machinery down below, but it had the persuasive rhythm of something breathing.

Jim glanced at the next poster. The two girls in the shot had been messily killed, and their bodies hung up to be photographed.

There were even sounds under the running of gears and drivewheels that might have been breathing or perhaps a low, regular growl; it was the sound of something that laboured in chains and knew that its tormentors were only just out of reach. There was another jerk, one so hard that it nearly threw him off-balance, and as Jim clutched at the handrail and did his best to stay upright, he thought he heard a break in the rhythm that was like a deep, slow chuckle.

The posters were getting worse, their variations infinite. Over one of the black-and-whites that showed a carcase turned almost inside-out, someone had slapped a sticker with a feminist protest. Below the sticker was a single fingerprint in blood.

The stairway trembled. Something was happening ahead, he couldn't tell what; but a green light was starting to shine.

The next poster almost made his heart stop.

It was nothing like the others; they'd had the fascination of a car accident, but this was something else. She stood naked and apparently unconcerned, her body long and lean and posed as if for a Tarot card. Her hand was resting lightly on the neck of a swan. She looked out at Jim, and he saw that there was something slightly odd about the colour of her eyes.

If he could, he'd have reached out toward her. But she'd already gone.

Ahead, the green light was getting brighter. At first Jim thought that he was coming to the end of the ride and that the access plates in the floor had been taken up; but now he could see that the floor itself had been stretched out into an O, with the steel teeth of the litter-rake poised like fangs. The escalator steps were carrying on down into a deep pit that was ribbed like a throat. Jim was wrong; the escalator isn't powered by a beast. The escalator is the beast.

The speed suddenly increases, and Jim is thrown forward. He falls as fast as the steps, hurtling through the opening and then down towards the creature's belly.

Down among the garbage and the intestinal worms. Grundy is waiting.

Jim sees him look up, and sees his blind eyes shining green. Grundy is dressed for Oriental magic, in a long *robe that is covered with half-moons and weird symbols. His head is shaved, and he's wearing Chinese makeup. Jim is falling towards him, and there's nothing he can do to stop himself.*

Grundy reaches up. Playtime, *he croons, and as the sound echoes around it becomes the howl of a half-maddened dog.*

Jim tries to twist as he falls, but it's no good.

Grundy's hands are on him.

Jim sat up in the darkness. The pain punched him suddenly in the back, as if it had been waiting to be sure that he was awake. He froze, waiting for it to fade. He supposed that he must have been lying badly on the freightcar floor.

It had never been as severe as this before, but even his folding bed in the Cliff House had been more comfortable than unvarnished boards with a suitcase for a pillow. The poker-tip feeling slowly subsided to become a pounding ache between his shoulders, and after a while he realised that this was the best that he was going to get. It was time to take a look outside and see where he'd landed.

The channel crossing had taken a bite out of his cash reserve, but when he'd arrived in Ostend at around four a.m. and emerged from the terminal into the railway station he'd seen an opportunity to start making savings. The station had been open and, at that time, not very heavily manned; a single guard had been there to direct travellers to their platforms, and he hadn't been checking tickets. Jim had walked down by the Paris train as far as he could go, and then he'd climbed aboard and quickly opened the door on the far side of the carriage to let himself down to the trackbed. Then he'd carried on walking for a few yards, counting off the dusty maroon freightcars that were hitched to the end of the train and looking for one that might be empty and unsecured. When he'd found one, he'd slid back the heavy metal gate and clambered inside. Ten minutes later, they'd started to roll.

He had no heat and no windows, but the ride was free. He'd been so exhausted that the steel-mill racket of the car had actually helped to send him to sleep. He had no idea how long he'd been out, but the fact that the car was no longer moving suggested that they might finally have reached the Gare du Nord. Jim pulled himself over to open the door a crack and peek outside. And then he groaned.

Something had soaked into his jeans.

The floor was filthy and scattered with old straw, but he'd checked first and he'd thought that it was dry. It was only when he felt around that he realised that the mess was all on the inside.

Oh, no. This was *embarrassing*. It hadn't happened to him since the age of sixteen. He tried to remember what he'd been dreaming about, but it had already slipped away. Whatever it had been, it wasn't worth this.

Jim stood up. A part of his shirt-tail was sticking to his belly, and it peeled free as he straightened. He felt angry, as if he'd been interfered with as he slept. Even though he couldn't recall the dream, he knew that it had to be something to do with the blind man. He always left Jim with a sense of having been put on and used like a rubber glove.

He rolled the door open a couple of inches; the slides needed oil, and it took most of his strength. He was feeling soiled and depressed. Whatever else happens, he told himself, you go straight to the tourist bureau and get a one-star hotel with running water. There's a baseline to anybody's dignity, and you've just found yours.

Jim looked out. He wasn't in Paris.

In fact he couldn't have been on the move for more than a couple of hours, because he was looking out across fields and a distant mass of woodland that were greyed by a pre-dawn twilight. Everything stood in silence. Jim went to get his suitcase, and then opened the door wide enough to climb down.

His wagon was one of four, unhitched and abandoned in a remote siding. The rails were rusted, and the trackbed was wet cinders with weeds growing through. Jim looked around, his breath feathering in the cold air. There seemed to be no point in waiting.

There were some buildings and perhaps a road in the far distance – something to make for, at least, even though it meant a long tramp across farming land and fences to climb. Jim put his suitcase under his arm and set out, pushing his way through a sparse hedge to emerge into a field where straw had been newly ploughed-back into the soil and puddles had formed in low spots over the furrows. He switched his case around as he walked, but he couldn't get comfortable. The dull pain in his back wouldn't let him.

It was slow going, and much of the ground was water-logged. His boots and his jeans were quickly soaked, but Jim tried to close down his mind and keep on. As he got nearer to the buildings he was able to make out details; a farmhouse with a mansard roof, backed by a long redbrick barn with its windows shuttered with corrugated iron.

Two dogs started to bark. Jim changed his direction.

Eventually he came out by the side of some woodland into a field of cabbages. He could hear the far-off drone of an autoroute somewhere ahead, and this had become his target. Birds were starting to wake up and sing as he left the trees behind and walked down between planted rows; as far as he could see there was only one more hedge to go through, and then he'd be able to get out into a lane or a side-road and cover the rest of the distance without so much difficulty.

But when he got to the end of the field, he could see that there was no way through the hedge. He had no choice but to follow the boundary along, looking for a gateway. When he reached one, he looked through and found that he'd been walking around the outside of a campsite, closed for the off-season and with the grass re-establishing where too many tents had slowed down the growth. It wasn't a large site, just a field or a former orchard that had been put into use to bring in extra income for a family hotel. Jim was looking at the hotel now, as he stood at a padlocked gate; it was a converted farmhouse, white-painted and with a steep red-tiled roof. He was around the back, where ornamental tables with Cinzano umbrellas had been stacked under the eaves to wait for better weather.

Across the cobbled yard to his right, Jim could see what had once been the barn; now it was a block of six motel-style units with an iron gallery and stairway giving access to the upper storey. Three cars were parked out in front. Jim heard a door opening, and he moved back out of sight.

A woman stepped out onto the upper gallery. She carried a small red vanity case, and she was followed by a middle-aged man with two large soft valises. He closed the door behind them, and then they descended as quietly as they could and stowed the bags in the back of a small Peugeot that was freckled with rust around its headlamp mountings. Jim could see that they'd left their key in the unit's door for the cleaning staff to pick up; he could make out the plastic tag, still swinging as they started the Peugeot and reversed out across the yard. The car had Belgian plates.

The engine noise receded, and silence returned. Just two guests making an early start.

But now an idea had got itself into Jim's mind, and it wouldn't go away.

White metal shutters covered every window in the former farmhouse. There were no lights, and nothing moved. The sky was lightening perceptibly, and he wouldn't have much time; the question was, did he have the nerve?

Jim shifted position slightly. His shirt-tail had dried out, and it scraped him like cardboard. That decided it. He hauled himself and his case over the gate, and walked quickly toward the motel block. A glance around to be sure that nobody was watching, and then after a quick dash up the stairs he let himself into the vacated unit and closed and locked the door behind him.

The twin-bedded room was large and had a superficial kind of luxury; the departing guests had straightened it as they'd gone but everything seemed slightly askew, waiting for a maid's professional touch. There was a dressing table with a three-sided mirror on the wall opposite the window, and a colour TV on a raised wall bracket alongside this. Jim walked straight past the furniture, shedding his case, his overcoat, and his freedom fighter's jacket along the way. He was halfway out of his shirt as he stepped into the bathroom, and he was unzipping his jeans as with his other hand he turned on the bathtaps. Within moments, the bathroom mirrors were misted and the bathroom was filling with steam.

Some of the thick pink towels on the heated rail hadn't been used, and there was a bar of Lux guest soap by the washbasin that was still wrapped. Jim ran the bath as hot as he could take, then stripped out of his underwear and climbed in.

It felt so good, it almost hurt.

He sank back, feeling himself go loose. The pain between his shoulders started to unwind immediately. It was an effort after a while to sit up and start soaping down.

Ten minutes later, he was out. He'd found a coffee-maker with a left-over sachet on one of the bedside tables, and he'd washed out one of the cups and set it to fill. Now, wrapped in one large towel and rubbing himself down with another, he sat on the stool before the dressing table and watched himself in the three-way mirror.

Three Jim Harpers looked out in different directions. Two of them were strangers. Pieces of Jim Harper were trapped where the angled mirrors picked up reflections from each other. He didn't look too bad, considering; this meant that he looked pretty rough, but also that there was a lot to consider.

He went over for his coffee, and brought it to the dressing table. It was black, and hopefully would keep him going for a while longer. He sat side-saddle on the stool, and began to towel his shoulders.

After a few moments, he snapped on the makeup light and turned one of the side-mirrors a little.

Whatever he'd thought he'd seen, it had gone; he studied the skin of his back in the double-reflection and saw nothing. He threw the towel over, and drew it across again.

The scar showed white as his skin reddened, and quickly faded as it returned to normal.

It was small, and it was centred exactly over the area that had begun to trouble him whenever he stood for too long, or exercised too hard, or tried to relax on an uncomfortable surface. He tried to touch it, but the scar was positioned so that he could barely reach it with the fingertips of either hand. It hurt him to try, and when he was finally able to make slight contact it felt as if there might be some small, hard growth under the skin.

There was a noise from outside. Jim stepped over to the

window, and opened the floor-length curtains just enough to look through.

A family from one of the lower units was loading up to go, a man and a woman and two young fair-haired boys. Jim decided that he'd now pushed his luck far enough. He took the last of the clean clothes from his case, and started to get dressed. It didn't take him long.

When he looked again, they were still there; the two boys were bringing out carrier bags and standing them by the open back of the family's estate car, and their father was stacking them inside to make the most of the space. Jim's first impulse was to let them finish and get out of the way before he set foot outside, but a look at the sky told him no. Being seen by some guests would be no great disaster. Leaving it late enough to be seen by the management would be sheer bad planning. He opened the door, and stepped out onto the gallery.

He seemed to give the housekeeper quite a surprise.

She was only a few feet away. She wore a huge white apron over a grey dress, with a linen headscarf. She had the figure of a cottage loaf and the complexion of a trawler-man, and she carried a wire supermarket basket loaded with bottles and dusters and spare toilet rolls over one meaty forearm. She turned to face the main hotel, and yelled so loudly that birds were scared up out of the trees. And then, before Jim could back off out of reach, her hand shot out and caught his ear in a ferocious grip. There was nothing that he could do as she started to drag him toward the stairs.

By the time that they'd reached the end of the gallery, the owner had crossed from the hotel and was on his way up. He was dark and unshaven, wearing a sweater with no shirt. He didn't even slow as he reached the top, but slammed into Jim and threw him back against the wall, hard.

Jim took all of the impact across his shoulders. For a moment he was deaf and blind, all of his senses blow-torched by the sudden pain that exploded from a white-hot centre. He clawed his way back just in time to see his suitcase being kicked all of the way down the stairs; it was bouncing and bursting open as his collar was grabbed and he was thrown after.

He made it to the bottom without falling, but he was kicked and driven down every step. He staggered and grabbed at the handrail; both of them were yelling as they followed him, but Jim had no attention to spare to listen. There were tears in his eyes, and a skewer through his back.

His suitcase was open and empty, leaning on the bottom step. Jim tripped over it and fell onto the yard cobbles. His radio was a few feet away, and was smashed; his clothes and other things had been scattered. Jim tried to get up, but the hotelier hooked his feet from under him and brought him down again.

Now he had a nosebleed. He sat with his head in his hands and tried to make it stop as the hotelier sorted through his gear, presumably looking for money. Jim was vaguely aware of another voice that had joined the storm beating around him, speaking English with what sounded like an American accent . . . the guest who'd been loading up his car was trying to talk to the hotelier. *What's the matter*, he was saying, *Did he damage a room, or what?* But the hotelier only shook him off, and then gave Jim another rough push to tip him off-balance before continuing with his search.

That's it, Jim thought, *Enough*. Real life could be okay in small doses, but sometimes even the darkness was preferable.

And with a sense of release, he slowly sank until his forehead touched the cool stone of the cobbles. And then out.

SEVENTEEN

Jim's first lift was in an orange-and-white Citroen van which looked like a small bus knocked up out of corrugated iron and which also rattled like one. His second was in a red

Toyota driven by a shoe salesman. It was early evening when they came through Saint-Denis on the outskirts of Paris; fifteen minutes later they were in crawling traffic on the Rue de la Chapelle.

There was a chorus of horns sounding up ahead, and after a while they found out why. A *Police-Secours* Peugeot van had been parked at an angle in the middle of the road, and temporary barriers had been thrown up behind it. Cars and people on foot were being diverted away through a side-street. The people on foot were making it through, but the cars weren't.

Jim looked back at three rifle-carrying gendarmes who were waiting by the side of the van with a hand-radio turned up loud. There were more blue lights flashing a hundred yards beyond the barrier.

The shoe salesman sighed heavily. "Either a bomb scare or another shooting," he said. "This happened to me last month, and I was four hours getting home."

Jim, whose French was already beginning to lose the rustiness of a year of disuse, turned to face forward in his seat. The cars were packed as tightly as they'd go, and now nobody was moving. He said, "Who's behind it?" and the shoe salesman lifted his hands from the wheel and let them drop.

"The Arabs, the Jews," he said, "who knows any more?"

When Jim had finally come round after his blackout in the motel yard it had been to find himself on exactly the same spot, but alone. The Americans' car had gone, the hotelier and his housekeeper had been nowhere in sight. His stuff had still been scattered around his open case and there had been silence, no birdsong or any other sound apart from the muffled screaming of a small child somewhere deep inside the main hotel. When he'd stirred himself to rise, something had fallen from him; he'd looked down and seen a simple crucifix made from dried grasses, probably a relic of some Palm Sunday long ago.

Weird. He'd looked at the main house, but most of its shutters had still been down. So then he'd put everything back into his suitcase, noting as he did that none of his money had been taken, and he'd walked out unchallenged onto the adjacent four-lane highway. The screaming of the child had quickly faded into the drone of early-morning traffic on the autoroute. Had he scared them, somehow? Had they looked at him lying there and thought they'd injured him, (the thought *Let's get him out of this bearpit and into one of the treatment rooms* flickered momentarily in the back of his mind, but its lights had died away even before awareness had begun to register) or even worse?

Now he was stuck in a backstreet of Paris amongst people who were getting out of their cars and standing by them, craning to see more or else just passing the time. The shoe salesman cranked down a window and waited for the grapevine to bring any information to him.

"Bomb scare," he said finally after a few words with the driver of an Audi alongside, and he switched off his engine and looked at Jim. "You can stay or walk, it's up to you. Looks like I'm not going anywhere."

The salesman was right; they weren't too far out of the centre, and Jim could now make better time on his own. "Thanks for the ride," he said.

"Watch out for the *flics*," the salesman warned him as he climbed out of the car. "They're really cracking down, ever since they found somebody trying to plant a fire-bomb in the Louvre. And stay clear of the barriers if you don't want to be searched."

Jim told him thanks, put his battered case under his arm, and was on his way.

The chaos was near-complete. Some cars had tried to turn in the narrow side-streets and were now jammed in mid-manoeuvre. A gendarme wandered through the auto maze, rapping on doors with a nightstick to discourage horn-sounding and leaving more than a few dents behind. Jim kept pushing along against the crowd, looking for a street that would take him down towards the Gare du Nord with its accommodation bureau; the railway terminus was only a few blocks away, but every access seemed to have been covered. Every now and again, he'd stop and listen to the talk; the most detailed and reliable rumour seemed to be that a German-registered Pontiac had been left double-parked outside a Jewish-owned café, and the police were rigging degutting charges on the bonnet, boot and doors to blow it open. Confirmation came when Jim heard a dull bang like an exploding tin drum, echoing over the rooftops from several streets away. Some time after this, the traffic started to move again and he was able to get through.

He found the *Hôtesses de Paris* in a walk-in office under a white neon sign in the station, three sympathetic and sharp women who were starting to look just a little worn at the end of a long day. They found him a cheap hotel on the second try, and sent him out with a voucher and a city map with his destination marked.

On his way over he found himself thinking of the hard, cyst-like spot on his back again; if it hadn't been for the small but definite scar on the skin covering it he might have been tempted to suspect that it was the frightening beginning of some kind of spinal tumour. But the scar itself was a limited comfort; it opened up many more questions than it answered.

His hotel was squeezed between a bank and a bar in a side-street off the Rue Lafayette. The reception area was small and dark, hardly more than a counter with space alongside for two seats and a coffee table. Most of this space was taken up by frame backpacks standing two-deep. Jim registered, and then he was given his key and shown through to the stairs. The passageway was narrow and windowless, with cream walls and a red carpet; Jim thought that this was how a middle-market brothel would probably look.

The room itself was better than he had any right to expect for the price. With his case lying on the bed and the door locked behind him, Jim opened the tall double-windows and looked down into a courtyard three storeys below. It was getting late in the day and he'd travelled too far to be at his best; the morning would be a better time for him to make a start on the real business of the journey. He could rest his back and he could hope for a dreamless night.

And tomorrow, he would find Rochelle Genoud.

Eighteen

The switchboard at the House of Akira took more than a minute to answer his call. Jim did his best to screen out the low-level noise from the café behind him, but it wasn't easy; the pay phone had no soundproofing and was in a rear corridor that linked the kitchens, the toilets, and a back entrance through which delivery men were stacking crates of mineral waters.

On the reply, he covered his ear and turned to the wall and said, "May I speak to Mademoiselle Genoud?" The usual reply so far had been *who?* or *No Mademoiselle Genoud here*, but now as he strained to hear he got a different answer from the switchboard operator.

"It isn't possible," she said.

"Well," Jim said, "could I leave a message and ask her to meet me . . ."

"No messages," the switchboard cut in, "there's nobody here. Everyone's down at the Tuileries getting ready for the show."

"So how can I get in touch with her?"

A moment's thought. "Genoud. Is she the Swiss?"

"That's her."

"Then you'd better forget it. Her father's seen to it that she meets nobody."

"I'm an old friend," Jim said.

"Especially old friends. Goodbye, m'sieu."

Jim was starting to feel faintly disturbed as he returned to his place at the counter. There had been something implicit in the switchboard operator's attitude when she referred to Rochelle, like someone at a boarding school talking about the least popular girl in her class.

Jim moved himself over so that someone else could get through to buy a *jeton* token for the phone. This café was almost directly opposite his hotel, and although it was neither particularly clean nor particularly cheerful, it was the only place in the street where he hadn't had to step over a large sleeping dog to get in.

So, something was happening down at the Tuileries gardens. He'd have to approach this carefully.

Who could tell? They might even be watching for him.

Twice a year, the inner courtyard of the Palais du Louvre and the adjacent gardens between the wings of the palace were handed over to the city's fashion houses. Three flimsy marquee-style buildings had been assembled out of scaffolding and fibreglass and aluminium; more than a dozen designers would be giving shows here to packed houses of buyers and journalists and photographers, and also to tourists with the right kinds of connections. Security was going to be tight tomorrow, Jim could see; but today, because it was just a time for lighting pre-sets and run-throughs, nobody seemed to be too worried. The movable barriers alongside the museum's Porte Denon entrance had been folded back, and as aluminium-sided panel trucks reversed in and turned on the cobbled forecourt Jim was able to wander past without being challenged.

The marquees were bright, but they also seemed to be tacky; they were functional boxes with an on-site life of no more than a couple of weeks. Power and heat were provided by generators and blowers in a small enclosed park, and facilities lines and huge ribbed airtubes had been run overhead using the park's ornate railings and castiron lamps as support.

Jim walked on through, and tried to look as if he belonged. He'd been worried that he'd stand out too much, but on the Avenue de l'Opéra he'd realised that large numbers of Parisian males of his own age or younger were wearing window-cleaners' jackets or baggy overcoats with knotted belts and turned-up sleeves that looked no different to his own. Apparently he had instant chic.

The first marquee, the one with the press tent alongside it, was empty; a construction team was working on the outside, stringing extra guywires to hold down a ten-foot pelmet of coloured canvas panels that were meant to give the place a circus feel but which strained like sails every time the wind blew. Jim skirted around the ladders and the cable drums, and went through a narrow stone arch behind the press tent to get to the palace's inner courtyard.

And there he found her.

The battered aluminium double-doors of the Pavillon Perrault – the marquee nearest to the arch – had been pinned back so that the roadies from *Regiscene* lighting supply could carry their equipment cases through. Akira and his team were going over the details of their staging under the fluorescent working lights at the far end of the showhall. He was small, even for a Japanese, and he looked like a neatly-tailored doll in a grey suit; as he stood at the far end of the Perrault's white catwalk and flipped through the running order on a clipboard, half a dozen young men and girls waited around as if his decision was the most important thing that they were going to hear all day.

About eight hundred grey plastic seats had been set in rows on three sides of the walkway, and there was even more standing room at the back and around the press grandstand. Jim paused by one of the chairs. For the moment, the activity of the roadies covered him. He'd looked at Rochelle twice before he'd recognised her.

She was wearing an immense loose-knit sweater over skintight jeans, and she was standing on the stage at the catwalk's end and holding a stopwatch. From the way that he'd heard her talking a year before about her plans to make a name for herself in the fashion world, Jim would have expected her to be standing at least at Akira's shoulder; but now as he watched, she hardly seemed to be a part of the group at all.

Somebody switched on a cassette recorder, and a few tall skinny girls in casual clothes started to walk through their routine. Rochelle timed each walk and turn, making notes. She appeared to be learning the business the hard way, and Jim got the impression that she wasn't liking it too much. She had the skin of a baby and the bone structure of a princess and when the models passed close by her they looked gaunt and ugly by comparison, but Jim seemed to be the only one in the hall who was aware of this.

He started down the rows just as a shadow moved along the seating by the edge of the stage. Two *Regiscene* men were passing and, on seeing the shadow-shape moving into the light, Jim switched direction and walked out with them. He didn't look back.

The cause of his sudden change of heart had been his recognition of Daniel, Rochelle's bodyguard. He'd been prowling around and scanning the auditorium with faint suspicion; but then, Jim knew that for Daniel Mindel suspicion was a natural state. He was a heavily-set man in his fifties with a look of rough-cast concrete, a thousand-yard stare, and a haircut so close that it was almost a shave.

Jim waited around in the gardens outside until the lunch break, which the fashion people took late. Rochelle didn't go with the others, and Jim followed at a distance as she and Daniel went to an overpriced bar-tabac on the Rue de Rivoli. He watched them through the window from the other side of the street. Daniel chose the table, sat with his chair turned outward slightly so that he could watch both the door and the rest of the clientele, and settled the bill and left a tip at the end of the meal. Rochelle didn't speak to him once, or even look at him directly.

It was pretty clear to Jim that, unless he could come up with a good idea fast, this was as far as he was going to get. Daniel had always been a figure in the background in parties of friends and on the family's property; here, he seemed to be in control.

A taxi came at five, and Rochelle and her bodyguard got in. Traffic was so heavy that Jim was able to follow them on foot for almost a mile, but then he lost them.

He turned to walk back toward his hotel, thinking hard.

Dinner that night was inexpensive *crêpes* from the street vendors in the Boulevard Montmartre. His money was running out fast and he was no longer too sure about how he was going to proceed. He'd thought about going to the police, but what did he have? Nothing more than a tiny scar and a head full of bad dreams and a deep sense of betrayal.

He felt that he'd been set up for something, but he couldn't imagine what. He'd been depending on Rochelle to fill in some of the gaps, but Rochelle was as far out of reach as she'd ever been.

Someone stepped out before him. "A moment, m'sieu."

Jim looked up, sharply. He'd been mooching along with his hands in his pockets, watching the ground ahead and paying little attention to anything else. He realised too late that the street before him was a no-access way, and he'd been walking straight towards the barriers. Four CRS men had immediately surrounded him.

The CRS were known as the *flics des flics*; they wore black-on-black under sleeveless bulletproof jerkins, and they carried their revolvers cowboy-style for a fast draw. They were all watching Jim with a lazy interest that he didn't mistake for indifference.

He said, "Did I do something wrong?", and he deliberately degraded his French and gave himself the worst British accent that he could manage.

"Your papers, please," the *flic* said patiently.

"I left them in my room. I'm a tourist."

"Which hotel?"

So Jim told him, and was led over to their car. He thought at first that they were going to put him inside and drive him away, but it was only so that he could lean off-balance with his hands on the roof as they frisked him.

The man that had first spoken now opened one of the rear doors of the car. There was a radio in a shoulder-valise on the back seat, and he unhooked the microphone and called his base. "An *Anglais*," Jim heard him say, and he realised that they were assuming he wouldn't be able to understand. "Dressed cheap and kind of haggard-looking. Says that his papers are at the Hotel d'Abbeville. Do we have the registration forms yet?" There was a pause; Jim tried to take his hands from the roof, but one of the men gestured him back. There was a reply that Jim couldn't make out, and the *flic* said, "Anything from Interpol? Come on, I've got him sweating. Give me *something*."

Jim didn't know which annoyed him more, being turned over as a casual amusement or the way that he'd been described. Dropping the accent, he said, "You could always invent something."

It was a mistake.

Four faces looked at him, stony and blank. Their leader slowly got out of the car and stood up, staring hard at Jim all of the way.

"*Zero on the* Anglais," the radio inside the car sounded out clearly. "*No warrants, and the records aren't through yet.*"

The staring in silence continued. *Oh, shit*, Jim was thinking, and something along the lines of *Beam me up, Scotty* . . . Why couldn't he have kept his mouth shut? The side-street was quiet and there were no witnesses on hand. From what he'd heard about the CRS, witnesses wouldn't be much of a deterrent to a beating anyway. He thought of his back and the strange, vulnerable little tumour that appeared to be lodged between his shoulders; he thought of the explosive pain of that afternoon and he felt his insides clench in terror at the notion of having to go through it again. All that he could do was to shut his eyes tight.

> (*And if he'd been paying more attention, he might even have heard Micheline Bauer saying, "I want permanent rectal thermometers and galvanometers on each of them . . . and if they ever start screaming like that again I don't care what time of day or night it is, I want to know" . . . And then, "Wait a minute . . . What are they doing* now?")

And then somewhere on the far side of the Elysée Palace, there was a deadened boom. There were screams and an alarm started to ring.

One of the men pushed him away from the car; the others were already jumping inside, and the engine was firing. Jim was still staggering back as the car drew away, over-revving and spraying grit. Sirens howling, it made a showy turn at the next intersection and ploughed through the crosswise traffic.

Well, he thought. How about that?

Back in his room, he went through the rubber-ball routine with his dead hand and tried out a few stretching exercises

138

for his spine. They helped, but this time they didn't drive the ache away completely; he was beginning to suspect that some new damage might have been done when he'd been thrown against the wall on the upper gallery of the motel, almost as if something might have shifted inside. He didn't like to think about it too much. The only idea that he liked to think about even less was that of lying face-down on the table with the anaesthetic taking hold, and some friendly surgeon saying to him *Don't worry about a thing, Mister Harper, I've called in some specialist advice to help with the investigation of your case*, and then as everything started to fuzz out seeing the smiling face of Alan Franks coming in through the OR doors to join the team.

On the plus side, he was learning to handle his nightmares. They were getting no better, but after the previous night he'd felt like less of a wreck when he'd opened his eyes in the morning. Roughly speaking when the pain was at its worst his sense of control would be at its lowest, and last night hadn't been too bad. That momentary threat of blackout as he'd leaned on the CRS vehicle had to be an anticipation of trouble rather than trouble in itself . . . or at least, he hoped that it was. The experience had been pretty strange all around, and he couldn't shake the feeling that it had some extra dimension to it; he put it down to his state of mind and the simple fear of being hurt.

The morning's improvement had seemed like a good omen. But now that the ache had increased a little, he began to wonder whether he might simply have swapped the hot irons for the rack.

NINETEEN

There had been twenty serious terrorist attacks in Paris during the last couple of months, most of them on Jewish businesses and the rest on government buildings or foreign embassies. Police were responding to every alert, at the rate of ten or more a day; nearly a hundred cars had been wired and blown up as an extreme way of making sure that they were safe. Last night's explosion by the Elysée Palace had been the unexpected detonation of a Saudi-registered Ferrari, and by all accounts it had been something to see. Jim would have learned more, but the man on the next stool in the café had folded his copy of *Le Figaro* and stuck it in his jacket pocket.

Security was tight everywhere. And yet here he was once more, this time standing shoulder-to-shoulder with the over-spill Press corps in the darkness of the Pavillon Perrault.

He was being hammered by waves of high-volume music and dazzled by the reflected glare of more than a hundred spotlights from the white-sheathed catwalk that ran down the middle of a packed house. People had been crammed in as far as the back wall. A photographer just a couple of yards away from Jim had brought along a set of aluminium steps, and he'd climbed up to shoot telephoto over the heads of the crowd.

The music was a kind of Oriental-rock with breaking glass, the clothes like slashed pyjamas and old bedlinen. There was a spattering of applause whenever a new group of four girls appeared, and those photographers who were closest to the dais would rise for a moment as cameras flashed like jewellery in the sea of faces all around them. A woman next to Jim was muttering in German into a pocket Dictaphone, her eyes glazed-over and fixed on the show as if she'd been hypnotised.

He'd had a good run of luck to get himself in. Where yesterday he'd had no problem in wandering through with the deliveries, today a uniformed guard had been turning away both the ticketless and the bribes that they'd offered. But for Jim it had been a simple matter to wander down the covered and colonnaded walkway fronting the museum wing before dropping just a few feet over the parapet to land behind the barriers. The House of Akira show had already been running as he'd emerged through the narrow arch into the Louvre's inner courtyard, but the press doors had been open and somebody ahead of him had been getting in late. With a confidence that he wasn't even aware that he had, Jim had walked up behind and announced himself as an English journalist. They'd let him straight in.

The photographer squeezed by with his stepladder, looking for another piece of floor and a new angle. He had a white sweater slung around his shoulders with the sleeves loosely knotted over his chest, and he left a vapour-trail of some effeminate cologne. Jim shuffled back to let him past, and leaned around in case he missed seeing Rochelle.

The pyjamas had now given way to a vandalised 1920s look in blacks and whites. The attention of those around Jim was total. The models, some of whom he recognised from the previous evening, were all tall, all flat-chested, all with their hair pinned up with just a few loose wisps; they walked out without even trying to catch the rhythm of the music, and at the end of the catwalk each seemed to give the audience a deliberate look of arrogance before turning and slouching back. But Jim already knew not to look for Rochelle on the stage; he concentrated his attention on the audience.

Rows of upturned faces, all rapt, all of them lit from the catwalk; in some places, spectacle lenses caught the lights and gave their owners a blank-eyed stare that was uncomfortably like Grundy's. Jim couldn't see Rochelle. He guessed that she was probably backstage somewhere, but he was still scanning for her as the show ended.

All of the mannequins came out onto the catwalk for one final circuit, fifty or sixty of them showing the range of Akira's new lines. They gathered on the shallow forestage at the head of the walk and started to applaud; this was the designer's cue, and as he stepped out into the lights the house applause swelled to a maximum. Akira's show clothes were a dark suit with a white fedora, and as he came forward he took off the hat and tossed it back over his shoulder. One of the models caught it in a rehearsed move, and she passed it back toward the stage entrance.

Jim only got the briefest glimpse of the girl who reached out to take the fedora, but he knew immediately that it was Rochelle.

Akira took a brief bow, and then he turned and

disappeared back behind the flats. The mannequins followed in order, and ten seconds later the music came to an end and the catwalk went dark. The applause died away, and there was already an immense tide of people starting to rise and move toward the exits as the houselights came on.

He couldn't leave now. He had to get closer to Rochelle somehow, and in a backstage crowd Daniel would be less of a risk.

The auditorium had already begun to clear, and the news crews on the press grandstand were breaking down their Arriflexes and ENG video cameras and packing away lenses and magazines of film. Jim moved against the flow, down through the rows toward the catwalk. The floor around it was now a litter of discarded tickets and Ektachrome boxes, but already half a dozen cleaners in red overall coats had appeared with brooms and large plastic rubbish sacks.

Some flash photography was still going on, over on the other side of the partition wall that screened the models' changing area. Any chance of climbing onto the forestage and walking through was blocked by two of Akira's young men; in a uniform of sharp blue blazers and red ties, they stood one to each doorway and simply shook their heads at any approach.

Jim looked along the rows as he descended, wondering if somebody might have discarded some press accreditation that he could use to get through. Seat allocations were marked with red ink on pink cards that had been taped to the backs of the chairs; Macy's California, *New York Times*, *Observer*, Galeries Lafayette, Bloomingdales, Nieman-Marcus . . . Saks Fifth Avenue must have offended in some way last year, because their buyer had been pushed back to row six. Jim saw nothing that he could use.

There didn't seem to be any way through on the inside. So he'd have to try going around the outside.

Even though it was still drizzling, Jim blinked as he emerged into daylight. Most people had now gone, but some were waiting under orange-and-yellow beach umbrellas for the next *pavillon* to open. There was a narrow cable-draped alley between the two structures, and nobody paid much attention to Jim as he ducked in and made his way down it.

He hadn't covered half the distance, when Rochelle appeared at the far end.

He saw her hesitate and glance back once, as if she was afraid that she was being followed. Then she started to run toward Jim. He stopped, and waited.

The heels on her boots were too high for running; she almost stumbled as she reached him, but she caught his arm and said breathlessly, "Have you got ten francs?"

"Why?" he said, knowing in an instant that she hadn't recognised him.

"I just need to borrow ten francs," she said, and again she gave an anxious glance back over her shoulder. Still holding his arm, she started to hustle him back down the alleyway. "Come on," she said, "I haven't got time to explain."

There was a crowd around the press tent as they emerged from the inner courtyard. The Louvre in the rain looked nothing like a palace, but more like the rambling municipal building that it had become. Some way ahead, a youngish security guard was still arguing with tourists at the barrier; he moved aside to let Rochelle and Jim go out, and as they dodged through a group of camera-toting Italians Rochelle took another fast look behind. By now, Jim had guessed why; she was dumping Daniel and she didn't expect him to like it.

Rochelle obviously had something specific in mind, because Jim found himself being dragged through parked cars toward the museum's entrance. He couldn't help it, he had to look back.

He saw Daniel immediately, still some distance away but made distinct by the pale yellow canvas of the press tent behind him. He was looking around, but he didn't seem to be hesitating; the image was more like that of some kind of robot device making a slow scan before processing the information and choosing its course. Jim must have slowed, because Rochelle let her grip slide down to his hand.

"Come *on*," she said, and pulled him along.

Well, she certainly seemed to have a way with a stranger.

Jim was working it out as they climbed steps toward the glass doors; another thirty seconds for Daniel to become certain that his charge was no longer within the secure area, and then perhaps another thirty beyond that for him to get to the barrier guard and ask him if he'd seen Rochelle. And unless the barrier guard had a sudden blackout, one minute was all the lead that they'd have.

Rochelle's obvious intention was to lose her bodyguard in the museum. But as they came through into the Louvre's vaulted stone entrance hall, Jim felt her grip suddenly go cold.

There were ticket booths at the centre of the hall, whilst behind a line of pillars on each side were glass-fronted stalls selling postcards, books, and museum replicas. Two of the ticket windows were open, and there was a slow-moving line at each.

Rochelle obviously hadn't planned for any kind of holdup at this stage. Still holding Jim's hand but with her timing screwed completely, she stared down at the lines looking blank and desperate.

A couple in their early twenties were going by on their way to the museum turnstiles. The man was bearded, the girl wore a headscarf; both were in orange cagoules and denims that had been washed almost white and carefully patched. Jim stepped in front of them and said, "Fifty francs for your tickets," and from what was left of his bankroll he pulled a note and held it out. The two of them stared for a moment, and then the note disappeared so fast that he might have sworn that it burned off his fingerprints.

The couple returned to the lines, and Jim and Rochelle made for the turnstiles. Daniel couldn't be far behind . . . but Jim could now see why he wasn't going to reach them.

The way into the main part of the museum was through a broad gallery with a floor of coloured marble, the walk flanked on either side by rows of inward-facing Roman figures. At the far end of this impressive introduction, a wide dark stairway swept up to the Winged Victory of Samothrace, looking like a headless hawk poised to strike from the prow of some massive stone ship. For quite some distance there would be nowhere for them to hide; but for Daniel, the turnstiles would hold the trap.

The shoe salesman who'd brought Jim to Paris had said that security had started to get tight after an attempt to set a bomb in the Louvre. They were taking no chances now; everyone who reached the control point halfway down the gallery was being given a once-over with a metal-detector paddle before they were being allowed through. And Daniel, because of his profession, was bound to be armed in some way.

A quick check, and they were past the point.

Rochelle seemed to want to break into a run, but she held herself back somehow. Releasing Jim's hand at last, she looked up once and clenched her fist at heaven as if she'd won a small but significant victory. Jim was now being left to fall behind, as if he was being discarded now that he was no longer required.

There was some kind of flare-up behind them in the gallery. A bell was ringing, and there were shouts. Jim glanced over his shoulder. He saw Daniel being held back by two security men as he tried to push through without a ticket. Red lights were flashing on the detector gear, and more guards were coming from the direction of the ticket hall. Daniel obviously knew that he couldn't win in the end even though he could probably have maimed all of the security men in seconds and walked on over them, and his struggles were no more than token.

He saw Jim.

Their eyes met as Daniel's knife was being taken from him, and Jim knew then that he'd been recognised. He also knew in that same moment that he wouldn't be forgotten. As he turned away he was still aware of the Frenchman's gaze, burning into the sore spot in his back like a needle of concentrated starlight and marking him for another time.

Rochelle had gone.

He finally caught up with her in the maroon-marbled corridor outside the Venus de Milo gallery. The gallery was almost empty, and Rochelle was sitting on a backless bench and stretching like a cat as if revelling in the freedom that she'd won. She became aware of Jim standing before her and she gave him a brief, empty smile.

"A little excitement buys a few hours of freedom," she said. "Whoever you are, thanks. Call round at the *pavillon* tomorrow afternoon and I'll see that you're paid back."

Jim said, "I don't think I can wait until tomorrow."

Her expression became tinged with weariness. "Don't be a bore, *chéri*," she began, but then she stopped as if she was really seeing him for the first time. Her casual manner seemed to freeze over.

"Oh my god," she said slowly. "It's you, isn't it?"

"I wondered when you'd notice."

"But . . . what's happened to you?"

"I was hoping that you'd be able to tell me."

He sat beside her as a party of ten-year-old schoolgirls went by, being marshalled by a nun on their way to the Venus. Rochelle's eyes followed him all the way, as if she couldn't believe what she was seeing. Had he changed so much? He supposed that he probably had. It wasn't something that he'd cared to reflect on more than was necessary.

It only took him a few minutes to tell her the story of his year. He saw her interest changing as she listened; it went from freak-show fascination at what he'd become to something much deeper.

"You think I look a mess, Rochelle," he said finally, his voice louder and less steady than he'd intended, "you should see it from the inside."

"I'm sorry," she said quietly, still watching him.

"Don't be sorry. Just tell me what happened."

"But I don't know. The last I saw of you was the day we all went out to the dog centre. I think you left somewhere in the middle, but I really don't remember."

"*Dog* centre?" Jim said.

They left the museum; Rochelle wanted to be somewhere else when Daniel got his liberty back. She said that she'd tried to give him the slip two or three times before, but this was the first time that she'd actually succeeded. Her stepfather's idea of protection was so tight that it was stifling, and Daniel would only answer to Werner Risinger himself. When she went to the bathroom, Daniel would wait outside the door and listen; once she'd run the taps to cover any sound, and he'd knocked to see if she was all right. Early this morning he'd taken a call from Basle, and in the hours since then it had been even worse. Jim wondered if this meant that he'd been expected, and guessed that it probably did.

They left the palace grounds and the tourist buses parked nose-to-tail along the *quai*, and they walked down by the Seine toward the Ile de la Cité. The rain had stopped, and the livestock shops of the Mégisserie had rolled out their crates and cages of fowls and songbirds and dogs onto the pavement.

Rochelle picked up on the word *Oktober*. She said that in the past three or four years the company had been using the names of the months as codewords for various major projects at least one of which, *April*, had been exposed in the international courts as an illegal scheme to give kickbacks to doctors favouring company brand names. Her family's company was big enough simply to have shrugged off the embarrassment and to have arranged a jail sentence for the employee responsible for the original leak.

Jim said, "If it's basically a family business, how come you're in Paris having a lousy time?"

Rochelle smiled, but there was more bitterness than amusement in it. "I was starting to take an interest in the company, but Werner didn't want to know."

"Why not?"

"Because I'm a Genoud," she said simply, as if that one fact explained everything else.

She wanted to know if they were anywhere near his hotel. They weren't, but Jim was prepared to spend a few more francs on Métro tickets in order to hold onto her for a while longer. It wasn't quite as simple as he'd hoped it might be, but affairs had definitely taken a step forward; his worst fear – that of getting this far and then finding that Rochelle had been coached to support the official version of events – hadn't been realised.

As they walked through a flower market towards the

Cité subway station, Jim told her about the scar that he'd discovered on his back. He already knew that he'd caught her interest, but now there was added something else. It was excitement, and she was doing her best not to let him see.

She looked at his room, called it a cupboard, said that this was the worst year of her life, and flopped onto the made-up bed. She groaned with the sheer pleasure of relaxation, and locked her fingers behind her head.

She said, "Would it offend you too much if I admitted that I've forgotten your name?"

"Not any more," Jim said, giving the hot water tap on the washbasin an extra half-turn in an attempt to stop it dripping. It had dripped since he'd arrived, and he hadn't had any success so far. He hadn't had any hot water, either.

Rochelle sat up, and said, "What are you going to do now?"

"I've really no idea."

"Lawyers won't do you any good, and you can be pretty sure that the company will have itself covered from every angle."

"I know."

"Have you got any money?"

Jim turned around one of his two chairs and sat, facing her. "No," he said. "And nowhere to go, and no-one to go to."

She gave him a little smile that was part wryness and part sympathy. "The worst year of your life?"

"I've had better."

She lay back again, and Jim waited. A year ago this would have been a scenario for one of his fantasies. Now it was just business. Rochelle hadn't changed so much, but any hook that she'd put into his heart was gone and its place had healed over.

After a silence, she said, "I could help you."

"How?"

"I don't know, yet. I'll have to call Roger – he's a cousin, another Genoud."

"What is this, some kind of family grudge?"

"It's too complicated to explain. But listen; if we help you, then you've got to let us handle everything."

"And what about Daniel?" Jim said. "He recognised me."

"He would. And he takes that kind of thing personally. Now they'll know we've been in contact, which means that I can't go back." Seeing the wariness in his expression, she added, "We're dancing with the big boys now. You're going to have to trust me."

"But what's your interest?"

"That's my concern. Just be grateful that I *am* interested."

Even so Jim found himself wondering, as she left with some of his change to find a telephone, whether she'd come back. Talk about trusting her was fine, but he barely had enough to settle that night's hotel bill and even that would depend on their keeping Rochelle's presence a secret from the concierge. She carried no cash at all. This had been one of her stepfather's ideas for keeping her more closely under Daniel's control.

Her plan for getting herself an afternoon away from her 'jailer', as she called him, had been a neat one in spite of the unforeseen hitch over the ticket lines. Unfortunately, Jim was going to be blamed for it. Looking at it from Daniel's side, Jim had snatched the woman he was supposed to be guarding and left him looking like a fool. Another meeting with Daniel was something that Jim would be able quite happily to live without.

Rochelle was back after ten minutes. She threw his room keys onto the bed and said, "Roger's coming. We'll meet him in the morning."

"Why do we need him?"

"Roger's an assistant director at a company plant in St Nazaire. The director's a Risinger man. We've been looking for a chance like this for some time, James."

As she stretched out again, Jim said, "What do we do about money?"

"Roger will handle that, too. Trust me."

Simple enough words, but for Jim they'd become a

danger signal. Rochelle had seen something of interest or use in his story, but the preoccupations that moved her would be entirely her own.

And it would be as well for Jim not to forget it.

TWENTY

"Are you sick?" Rochelle said as Jim eased onto the café stool beside her the next morning. The stool was high and the angle was awkward, and he'd winced without meaning to.

"It'll pass," he said, and he caught the owner's attention and ordered some coffee and plain rolls. Another bite out of the sixty or so francs that they had left. Jim said, "How long do you think we can go on like this?"

"That depends on how long it takes them to trace you. How did you register at the hotel?"

"As Bruno Weingartner."

"Odd choice of name."

"First one that I could think of."

Rochelle watched the steam rising from her coffee for a while. Unlike Jim, she seemed to have slept well; but then, also unlike Jim, she'd been on the bed and not on the floor. He'd succeeded in holding the door shut on his bad dreams for another night, but he hadn't been able to do anything about the trouble with his spine.

Getting off her stool, she said, "I'll call Roger's number. If he doesn't answer, I'll know he's on his way."

Jim turned around to look out of the window as she went down to the other end of the counter to buy a phonebooth token. It was only just after nine, but for once the narrow side-street wasn't blocked by cars waiting to get into the Rue Lafayette. His back wasn't easing off as he'd hoped that it might. At some time during the early morning, he'd awakened to the light of the room's low-wattage reading

150

lamp and he'd turned over to see Rochelle, stripped to her underwear and kneeling on the edge of the bed. She'd drawn down the candlewick spread that he was using as a cover, and she was looking for his scar. He'd sleepily pointed out the place, saying that there was normally nothing to see. She'd reached out to run her fingers over the skin between his shoulders, tracing the ridge of his spine. Her touch was cool and probing, and in that moment he'd experienced a stirring of the feelings that he'd once had for her. But it had passed.

A grey van came down the empty street, and stopped before his hotel. The rear doors opened, and men from the CRS jumped out. They went straight into the building, five of them with weapons drawn.

Jim didn't move, although his heart was hammering. A second, smaller van drew in at an angle behind the first, and two men brought out a German Shepherd dog. Daniel was with them. He strolled after, in no hurry.

Rochelle came by, showing him the token. "Give me five minutes," she said.

"I'll come with you," Jim said, and he dropped some change on the counter as he stood. Rochelle didn't understand.

She said, "That's not necessary," but Jim was already with her.

"Take a look across the street," he said in a low voice that was almost a whisper, "and tell me if it's necessary." He gave her a moment, and then he was guiding her away toward the back of the café before she could react.

The road had been blocked at both ends before the security police had been sent in; that was why he'd seen no traffic. As Jim led the way into the café's back corridor for the telephone, Rochelle said, "How did they find you so fast?"

"Probably by showing a photograph at the accommodation office." He ignored the telephone, but tried the door alongside it. Open. He held it back, and hustled Rochelle through before anybody noticed.

Jim had seen deliveries being brought in this way, so he knew that there had to be some route to the outside. They found themselves in a windowless stone-flagged corridor with daylight at its end. Rochelle didn't need to be pushed again.

It led them into a tiled courtyard, the tiles uneven and coloured with moss. The backs of three buildings came together with a fourth high wall completing the square. The walls were cream, washed-down with soot and starting to peel at the edges.

Across and to their right was an archway, running a building's depth to link the yard to the outside world. It was wide enough for one car, and blocked at the far end by gates of iron and frosted glass. There was a chain between them, but it wasn't secured. Jim unlatched one gate, and opened it far enough for them to slip through.

They came out into the noise of the Rue Lafayette, only a few yards from the spot where gendarmes were holding back the crowds to let an officer's car through. The mass of craning people was enough to let Jim and Rochelle get by without being seen.

As they walked away, Rochelle said, "What now?"

"Head for the Métro," Jim told her, "and don't run."

They avoided the nearest station, and the next was several blocks away. The streets were all cafés and banks and small businesses, but at this time of the day the pavements weren't nearly as crowded as Jim would have liked.

His back hurt. He tried to shut it out of his mind, but the pain wouldn't go. Slamming against the wall outside that Flemish hotel seemed to have begun a process that he couldn't stop; the rack was now getting to be as bad as the hot irons had ever been. Rochelle was ahead, and he struggled to keep up; in the distance he could see one of the familiar art-nouveau arches of creepers and vines supporting a lit sign that marked the steps to a subway entrance.

He descended too fast, and let out a badly-stifled cry of pain. It brought him several curious looks, and Rochelle's immediate attention.

"What's the matter?" she said, but for a few moments he couldn't answer. He could only lean against the wall just inside the station doors.

When he finally managed to speak, he said, "Something's moved. I can feel it."

"Okay," Rochelle said. "Just follow me, all right?"

He followed her. It was about all that he could manage to do. They rode a couple of stations, changed trains; Jim was aware of tiles, tunnels, the far-off echo of a busker, and for a while it was as if his senses of time and place had broken loose from each other. He was back under Piccadilly, with Jacko and Benny the Banker.

Finally, daylight again. Rochelle led him across a road, where he could barely see the traffic. Perhaps that last night on the hard floor had done it, or perhaps that was only a stage in some longer process, but it was as if his back was being slowly broken. He could feel himself running down.

"Not much further," Rochelle said. "Can you make it?"

"I don't think so," Jim admitted.

He was walking like a dead man. Awareness was being taken away from him piece by piece, and the spaces it left were being blocked-in with agony. It had never been as bad as this before, ever; it seemed to have come up and hit him faster than a tram, and just as he thought it would have to peak, it would double. He must *really* look like a wreck to her now, he thought. It embarrassed him, but he couldn't help it.

There was greenery, and the sounds of traffic receded. Rochelle was turning him, gently helping him to sit. Jim felt some kind of wooden bench behind him, and he allowed himself to be lowered. He didn't sit back, but stayed kind of hunched.

"Wait here," Rochelle said, her voice cutting through the haze. "We'll come and get you."

Jim managed to nod, and she faded away before him. He tried to breathe slowly. Sitting was better.

Over the next few minutes, he gradually got back a degree of control. He could see that he was in a small city boules park, on a spectators' bench that looked onto two long sandy enclosures. Undrained water lay on their surfaces, and at the far end of one of them a roller was going rusty. He was alone.

He wondered if she'd come back. From Rochelle's point of view, it might look as if the arrangement was going bad on her. Jim didn't fool himself that there was any sentiment or loyalty involved; they were together because they needed each other, Rochelle for her purposes and Jim for his, whatever his own plans might turn out to be. At the moment, he had none. He'd carried the ball alone for as far as he could go.

Someone was coming toward him, stepping through the motor bikes that had been parked on a narrow strip under the trees. At first he recognised Rochelle, but even as he saw her she seemed to melt and become someone else. The clothes were the same but she was darker, heavier, someone that he knew but couldn't name. She was pulling somebody else along by the hand, a man whose shape wasn't even fixed yet. Jim closed his eyes, and desperately willed himself to keep a grip on reality. It lasted for a few seconds, but then reality wouldn't co-operate any more.

The man was a pig, and then he was a goat, and then his form began to settle and became Grundy. It was Grundy as Jim had first known him, the shaven Oriental with the laser eyes, but when he spoke it was with a curiously inappropriate Breton accent.

"You didn't tell me he was half-dead," he said, and he seemed to hang back.

The dark woman tugged him onward. She was wearing a white hospital coat over Rochelle's sweater and jeans. She said, "Help me get him to the car."

But Grundy wouldn't come any nearer. "You don't want a car," he said. "You want an ambulance."

Micheline Bauer turned on him. "For fuck's sake, Roger," she spat (the voice was Rochelle's), "have I got to do *everything*?"

Grundy winced as if he'd been zapped with a prod, and he started toward Jim. Jim tried to say *No*, but nothing came out. He strained until he felt his throat would tear, but still nothing came out.

When Grundy's hands were on him, then Jim knew that he could manage it.

But then came the darkness.

TWENTY-ONE

This was the first time that it had ever been so bad that being unconscious was no escape. It followed him down through the darkness firing tracer-bullets of agony and scoring hit after hit, howling in triumph as each one went home, Jim twisted and writhed, but the long drop seemed to have no end.

But at least there was the doorway, down in a corner of his mind that he'd always avoided. He only had to think of it and there he was, standing before it. The door was firmly closed, but the handle would be easy enough to turn. He'd never opened it out of choice before but if ever there was a time, it was now. As long as he didn't go all of the way through and as long as he didn't let it close behind him, he could stand on the threshold – safely between the worst of two worlds.

The door swung open.

Jim eased himself off the sword's point, and then he opened his eyes again.

It took him a moment to adjust, but then the shock wasn't as great as he'd feared it might be. He was in territory that had started to become familiar to him.

He saw the turning of the black carousel, the one-way journey into dark country that had been bent around unnaturally on itself to bring its horrors screaming back into the light. He saw the shadow-shapes that moved across the landscape beyond, great slow beasts that stopped and swung their heads from side to side as they picked up the unaccustomed scents of life and clean air. He saw fire beyond the horizon, and heard the distant howling of wolves.

And close-to, walking across to stand between Jim and the place without a name, there was Stephen Fedak.

He was pale and he winced slightly when the brightness hit his eyes, but he looked more or less as he had in life. Jim asked him what was it like, to have stepped through without hope of return?

Damn cold for some of us, *Stephen Fedak said*. But I know now it was nothing personal. Go back.

Are you kidding me? *Jim said*. It hurts out there.

Fedak's expression didn't change. Doesn't hurt at all in here, *he said*. You don't feel much of anything while you're waiting out your time. Go back, Jim.

So Jim reached in for the handle, and it was like his arm going into ice water all the way up to the shoulder; and although he couldn't see them he could feel other hands touching his cold-deadened skin like fish nibbling at a corpse as he pulled the door closed. Stephen Fedak lowered his eyes as the edge of its shadow passed across him again, and then he was gone.

Jim took a step back from the door.

And on to other dreams.

For a moment after Micheline Bauer had snapped awake, she almost believed that it was because a lizard had rested its claw on her shoulder. But then she rolled over, and saw the outline of Do Minh through the mosquito netting. The young interpreter was crouched by her bedside, whilst behind him stood the small boy who accompanied him everywhere. The boy's job was to open doors when necessary or, as now, to carry a lantern; it must be late, Micheline thought, because the boy was pop-eyed and swaying slightly as if he'd been stunned.

"There's movement," Do Minh said. "You wished to be told."

Micheline pushed herself upright, holding the coarse sheet across her chest. She wore no nightdress. She said, "What kind of movement?"

"In bed number four. Some sounds also."

Number four. The youngest of the comatose group and occasionally the most responsive, although so far there hadn't seemed to be any pattern to it. She said, "Wait outside," and Do Minh turned and spoke to the boy. The boy set down the lantern for her, and the two of them withdrew to the corridor.

It was probably nothing, but she'd have to go and see for herself. When she'd dressed she took the lantern and went out into the corridor, where Do Minh and the boy had squatted down by the wall to wait for her. The boy had fallen asleep, but Do Minh elbowed him awake and the three of them headed in convoy through to the main part of the hospital. Micheline didn't look back; the interpreter always walked with his shoulders hunched and his arms crossed tightly across his chest to protect the vulnerable hooks that had once been his hands, and she still hadn't become used to the sight. He couldn't use chopsticks, and he could barely pick up a spoon; his fingers seemed to have been welded together, and the backs of his hands were so heavily burn-scarred that at first they appeared to have been tattooed. Without the boy, he'd have been lost.

There were still some fires burning low outside, and their drifting smoke scented the air. Micheline and the others picked their way through sleeping forms in the pagoda's inner courtyard, and then climbed the steps that would take them toward the hospital's locked inner wing.

On her arrival, she was disappointed. The ward was quiet. The blind orderly was waiting by bed number four. Being near him always made Micheline's flesh crawl a little, as if she'd put a hand into a pocket and found something slimy. Her research staff, all assembled. If she could trade in Do Minh's boy for a dwarf, she could start her own freak show.

She looked down at her number four subject. He was lying on his side with no pillow, and the mattress under his head was stained with spittle. Holding the lantern close to see if there was any reaction to the light, she said, "Ask him how long ago the noises stopped."

Do Minh translated the question, and the orderly replied. There was even something unpleasant about his voice, like rats running up above a ceiling.

"He says an hour," Do Minh reported. "Maybe longer."

"I was supposed to be told right away," she said,

straightening and looking around, and the interpreter hunched himself even more.

"Not so easy at night," he said apologetically. "He had to send someone to wake me, I had to dress and wake the mademoiselle . . ."

"All right," Micheline said, raising a hand to stop him. "Ask him, was it only this subject who got restless? Or did some of the others, or all of them?"

Another exchange, and then: "He says, this one only. He was moving around, like a bad dream, and he was talking."

"Talking? Does he mean actual words, or just the usual?"

"No real words. Only sounds."

Micheline looked again at the figure in the bed. He hadn't reacted to the lantern, and he barely even seemed to be breathing. Sometimes his catatonia could be so light that it *did* seem that he was only asleep and dreaming. Perhaps that was what this had been; without matched reactions from any of the others, there was no justification for supposing anything else.

She was no closer to finding an explanation for the strange empathy that they seemed to share than she had been on that first day. It came and it went, and it defied control. She'd tried separating her subjects and the effect had persisted even when one of them was out of sight or hearing of any of the others, but when it came to pinpointing the exact causes and conditions she was at a loss. It might be a spinoff of their EPL reaction, or it could be something that she simply hadn't thought of yet. She said, "Ask him again, is he sure that none of the others responded?"

"The mademoiselle must understand," Do Minh began, "that a blind man could not say for sure . . ."

"He'd know," she said. "If a flea farts in this place, he hears it."

"Fdak," the blind orderly offered eagerly. "Tee-vun Fdak. Dam co'." But Micheline could see that she was going to get nowhere. Do Minh's boy had curled up on the floor and gone to sleep, and Micheline suddenly felt like doing the same.

"Oh, forget it," she said wearily, and she turned and walked away. This was almost as bad as working with dogs. There was some rapid chatter back at the bed, and Do Minh called after her.

"He says that there appeared to be a pain in the subject's back," Do Minh said.

"So give him an aspirin," Micheline said more sharply than she'd intended. And then she headed on toward her mosquito shroud, and her dreams of home.

Bruno didn't like it when the dogs were quiet; he liked to hear them hurting.

They'd been hurting for some hours now, baying and howling and throwing themselves around – or at least, the stronger ones had. Bruno had gone through the building opening doors and pinning them back so that wherever he went he could hear his hated charges having a bad time. Bad times were what Bruno had promised them on Day One when he'd been left at the centre alone, and bad times were what they'd been getting. He didn't know what had brought on this latest bout, but he'd been making the most of it.

Now it was over, and Bruno wondered if it would be worth going down to the pens and stirring them to a little more action. He would have liked it if they'd fought more, but most of their spats were just quick scuffles to assert dominance. He'd tried starving them, but even then they only crowded up against the inspection windows and glared at him through the wire; it was almost as if he'd given them a common cause, and it was enough to make them forget rivalry.

Well, they couldn't hate him as much as he hated them. That Siberian, especially.

Everything at the centre had been put on hold after the almighty foulup with the schoolteacher. It had been the schoolteacher's fault for nosing around where he shouldn't, but it had been Bruno who had been busted down to janitor for an indefinite and probably lengthy period, and it had been Bruno who had been told that he'd better shut up and say thank you or else he'd never work for Risinger-Genoud or any other major company again.

He'd assumed until then that they were going to fire him, but now he could see that this wasn't how they worked. As long as he was still on the payroll, he was still on their leash; and as long as there was a possibility of reinstatement after his penance, they knew that he'd take whatever they handed out. They told him to clean up, dump the stock, and inventory all the equipment. And all for one little zap with a baton.

Bruno opened another beer and leaned back in his common-room chair. The stuff was beginning to make his head ache, but he couldn't think how else to pass the days. Any notion of a work schedule had gone straight down the crapper when he'd realised that he was to be left alone with no supervision and no checks on how he ran the place. Now the dogs got fed once a week, if they were lucky; he'd just open the service hatch in each pen and slide in an uncut block of the frozen offal that they'd always drooled over, and then it was up to them to lick it until it thawed and to make it last. He only worried about cleaning the pens when the smell was bad enough to reach him in the main part of the station; and then he would uncoil the hose from the wall and spray down the entire area, dogs and all. It made life a lot simpler.

He couldn't finish the can. He was feeling bloated and sick. A piece of his life was being wasted, and there was nothing that he could do about it. Of course, he could quit and walk out – that was, as long as he had no higher ambitions than that of selling contraceptives in some small-town pharmacy. The world was still turning and younger people were getting noticed in it; Bruno, meanwhile, had to switch on the radio to find out the day of the week. Back in the season he'd tried flagging down a train and riding up to the ski resort, but it had been a waste of time. He couldn't ski, he didn't have the money to spend in the overpriced bars, and he didn't have the looks or the poise to crash any of the chalet parties.

Bruno set the half-empty can down at his side, on a table that was honeycombed with sticky rings from other cans before it. He levered himself upright, belching as he went. If nothing else amuses, go and annoy the animals.

He called by the op room on his way. He'd left his electric baton there for a recharge, and it was about ready for use. He tapped the live part of the prod against the steel operating table; there was a whiplash crackle and a faint whiff of ammonia in the air. The steel was black where the baton had touched. Definitely ready.

They could hear him coming, he knew it. Every door from here to the pens was wedged open, and the dogs would be counting his steps and cringing as they waited for him to appear. Bruno took it slowly. Making them wait was part of the fun.

There was silence in the low-ceilinged corridor alongside the pens. Even the smell wasn't as bad as it might have been, because the dogs tended to try to keep themselves clean. Bruno went straight along to the Siberian's enclosure.

She was there and she was watching for him, her eyes like chips of ice as she stared at the wire. The others were staring his way, too, but the Siberian was all that Bruno could see. She was holding her head low, and the stiff hairs on her back were raised.

"*You don't like me?*" he whispered. "*You want to do something about it?*" And he raised his hand, and deliberately curled his fingers through the wire.

He'd done this once before, and it had worked like a dream. The Siberian would dive at the wire, and Bruno would quickly pull his hand away and jam the prod in its place. It would be too late for the dog to stop, and the wire would be live wherever it hit.

Except that the Siberian wasn't moving.

Bruno showed a little more skin, to make the bait more tempting. The Siberian tensed even more, but didn't make the jump. It couldn't be nerves; although she hadn't been the first dog to get EPL she'd been the first to survive it, and she was tougher than she looked. Bruno was watching her so closely that he didn't see the Greenlander until it was almost too late.

The big Eskimo dog had been crouched below the

look-through, pressed close to the wall so that Bruno wouldn't be able to see. He was aware of a dark blur and a growl like an approaching express, of teeth on the other side of the wire trying to close on his fingers; he pulled his hand back, fumbled the move, and slapped the live end of the prod against his own wrist.

It felt as if his arm would break. Bruno fell to the concrete floor and threshed around with a frightening lack of control, and the baton fell a yard away and lay there with its tip pointing toward him. The pain was intense, and it stayed with him as the trembling died away.

Hugging his arm like a dead thing, Bruno got to his knees. His wrist was burned, and badly. His face was streaked with tears, and his breath came in painful sobs.

When he looked up, the Siberian was at the wire and watching.

Bruno wanted to speak, but Bruno couldn't. Bruno was hurting. Half-blinded and beaten, he staggered toward the door. He couldn't think of anything other than a shot for his pain and some salve for his burns. He'd have time to be angry, but that would be later.

Bruno had all the time he could need.

PART THREE

In The Nightmare Country

TWENTY-TWO

Jim was on his side and there was a deep pillow under his head, and the pillow was scented with lavender. When he made a first tentative effort to move, he found that his chest and shoulders had been bound like a mummy's. He lay there for a while longer, wondering who'd undressed him.

The pitch of the roof told him that he was in an attic, the drawn curtains that it was night. His clothes were arranged neatly on wire hangers that had been hooked over the door of a solid oak wardrobe; this and a washstand and the chair beside it were the room's only other furniture. It was an old house, the ceiling beamed and the plasterwork white and new; Jim didn't know where he was, or who had brought him here, or why. He didn't even know the time, because his watch had been taken.

Someone else was around, because he could hear indistinct voices. He tried to push himself up a little, bracing himself for the stab of pain that he knew would come. It didn't happen. There was soreness, but the barb seemed to be gone.

He made it about halfway, and then he rested. Now he could see the washstand better. On its wooden surface were two steel dishes, some scissors, a dozen packets of some surgical blades, and a large half-used roll of cotton wool. There was also a bottle of some kind of antiseptic and, just behind this, a Kodak instant-picture camera. Under the washstand there stood a full-looking waste bag closed off with a wire tie. The survey took all of Jim's energy for a moment, and he let himself slide back.

The voices weren't clear, but one of them might have been Rochelle's. She seemed to be in the process of getting someone very upset, if the masculine voice that provided the counterpoint was anything to go by.

Levels changed as a door opened and closed somewhere in the house below, and there were footsteps on stairs. The one-sided argument ran on in the background as a kind of muffled buzz-track as Jim focused on whoever was climbing toward him.

The footsteps came to a stop outside. The door opened a few inches, and a man who was a couple of years younger than Jim looked in. He seemed surprised and suddenly nervous at finding him awake.

"Well," he said, "how are you feeling?"

"Doped-up," Jim said. His throat was dry, and his voice was scratchy. "How am I supposed to feel?"

"That sounds about right."

The young man picked up the chair from beside the stand and brought it over to the bed. This, Jim supposed, was Roger Genoud. He looked a lot like his cousin but it was immediately plain that he wasn't as tough, if you could apply such a brutal word to someone like Rochelle.

Jim said, "How long was I out?"

"About fifteen hours," Roger said as he sat. "You were in a bad way."

"And what happens when the dope wears off?"

"You should be okay. We've been fixing you up a little bit, that's all. Rochelle's going to explain it."

Jim eyed the instruments on the washstand, and wondered exactly what the 'fixing up' might have entailed. He said, "Can't I even ask where we are?"

"We're in the Grande Brière," Roger told him after a moment's hesitation. "It's in the marshes outside St Nazaire, about as quiet as you can get. Nobody will find you."

"Is this your place?"

Roger shook his head. "Rented."

There was more movement downstairs, and the voices seemed to have stopped. Jim heard a car door slam somewhere outside, and a moment later an engine turning over. He said, "I suppose Rochelle's been buying off the doctor."

"Not exactly," Roger said, and Jim could see that he was uncomfortable. Before Jim could ask what he meant, Roger went on, "A doctor would have been too risky. He'd

166

have to report what he found, and we didn't know what that might be."

"So who . . ."

"We brought in the head of research from the St Nazaire plant. Don't worry, he did a good job. He's done a lot of rabbits."

"You had me operated on by a *vet*?"

"He was very neat," Roger insisted.

"And what if he turns out to be another Risinger man?" Roger shrugged. "That's Rochelle's department."

Jim lay back. Fifteen hours, and a journey of nearly four hundred kilometres; he'd known nothing about any of it. There was a vague memory of unrest like a shadow across the back of his mind, but all of the details had gone. He had no wish to get any of them back. Instead, he felt a sudden sympathy for Roger; it must now be around three in the morning, and Roger would have been on the move without a break since before the previous dawn.

Rochelle came up a few minutes later. There was a gleam in her eyes that was a signal of an argument won.

She said, "He's either with us, or he's ruined. I gave him the choice."

"So why don't I feel safe?" Jim said, still unhappy at the idea of being carved up by a rabbit man.

"You're safe enough," Rochelle told him, and she went over to the washstand and began to sort through the operation debris. She explained that they'd lured the man out here by letting him think that he was being involved in a hot job for the company, digging out some scandal for use against a rival. Roger had photographed every stage of the procedure supposedly for use as evidence, and he'd been sure to include the man's face clearly in several of the shots.

"He isn't licensed to work on human subjects," Rochelle explained. "He's with us now, all right."

"With us in what?" Jim said, wondering if she was going to bring the pictures over to show him and rather hoping that she wasn't.

But Rochelle only picked up one of the steel dishes. "This is something important, James," she said. "We've been waiting for a break like it, haven't we, Roger?"

Roger shrugged, with something less than passionate enthusiasm. Rochelle came around and sat on the bed by Jim, and she held the dish out for him to see. She said, "This is what's been giving you all the trouble."

Jim looked. She was holding the tray at an angle, and a few ccs of blood and water were pooled at its lowest point. Lying in this was what looked like a small polythene bullet.

Jim said, "What is it?" and Rochelle looked to Roger for the technical details.

"It's a hollow plastic pellet," he said, "used for the slow release of certain kinds of drug over a long period of time. You dissolve the drug in a liquid silicone base, and it escapes through a diffusion hole. I've seen them used in rats and monkeys before, but I've never seen one like this."

It looked small and harmless. "Can you tell when it was put in?"

"Probably a few weeks ago. It would be very simple, just a quick shot with an air-pressure gun. It was sited so you wouldn't have much chance of feeling the pellet or finding the scar."

"Until it started to move," Rochelle added. "That's when you'd really know it was there."

A few weeks; he couldn't say how or when it had been done, but he *did* know that it seemed more or less to coincide with the return of his bad dreams from a year before. Roger told him that the pellet was empty, and whilst there might be a trace inside of the chemical used, he doubted it. But he couldn't rule out a link; the pellet technique had originally been devised as a way of drip-feeding amphetamines into animal bloodstreams, and the high levels and the long exposure had frequently created a kind of artificial psychosis.

"Could that be it?" Rochelle said, but Roger shook his head.

"Amphetamine psychosis is well documented," he said. "There wouldn't be any point. We're in the right area, but we need more information."

Hard information. Without it, all they had so far was a crank story for the Sunday papers. They needed to know what had been put into him, and where and when; and more than anything else, they needed to know why.

They talked it through but when it came to the most vital area, Jim's disappearance at the sled dog centre and his subsequent reappearance in the school a few hours later, he could only give them a blank. Roger had checked on the centre, but the company directory showed that it had been closed and the staff dispersed to posts elsewhere. After a while Jim began to get the feeling that Rochelle was growing angry with him, almost as if he was deliberately suppressing the information.

Perhaps there was even some truth in it. Didn't people often do that kind of thing, if the memories were bad enough?

Finally Rochelle stood up so quickly that the bed bounced and Jim felt a twinge from his new stitches. "I'm getting some coffee," she said sharply. "*You*'d better work on this."

Roger was caught in a bone-stretcher of a yawn as Rochelle stalked past him and out. The whole building seemed to shake as she pounded down the stairs, and moments later they heard the crash of a saucepan being slammed onto an iron stove.

"She doesn't mean it," Roger said.

"You could have fooled me. She seems even more desperate than I am."

Roger sat forward on the chair. He was weary, but it appeared that he was going to give Rochelle a cooling-off period before he followed her down. "It's a family thing," he said.

"Because you're both Genouds and not Risingers?"

"Our fathers were brothers. They formed Genoud chemicals just after the war and turned it into a fair-sized business. But then Rochelle's father died when she was two, and five years later her mother remarried."

"And her new husband was Werner Risinger?"

"Of Risinger Pharmaceuticals. He courted her on the ski slopes. The marriage gave him effective control of fifty per cent of the Genoud company, and then he set out terms for a merger which *my* father couldn't resist. Papa got a major

169

block of voting shares in the new company, and he moved to Basle as general manager with overall control of the running of the business. It looked like a good deal, but under Swiss law a general manager can't have any members of his own family on the board of directors. So when Risinger came up with a proposal for a new share issue that would only apply to his own family and would reduce Papa's holdings to a minority interest, there was no way he could fight the vote. Then when they had what they needed, they fired him."

"And what does Rochelle want?"

"Only what's hers by right. We both do, and we're the only Genouds that are left. The St Nazaire plant is one of the original Genoud factories, but I can never expect to get any higher than assistant director. Rochelle doesn't even have that, although she's been studying the way the company works ever since she was a girl. But then along you came, and . . ." Roger spread his hands, in a small gesture which implied that the rest was obvious.

Jim said, "What do you think of our chances?"

"It's like she says. We've found an interesting opening, nothing more. Allegations are no good, we'll need cast-iron proof. And unless you can remember who did what to you, we're not likely to find any."

Roger then leaned back in the chair, and tried not to yawn again. He almost managed it. Down below, there was a bang like somebody kicking a cupboard door. Jim moved a little to get his bandaged shoulders comfortable, and said, "You could be wrong about that."

"I could be, but I don't think so."

"Well," Jim said slowly, "when Rochelle's finished working her temper off on the furniture, get her back in here and I'll tell you how we're going to manage it."

Twenty-Three

The security guard behind the desk looked up and smiled neutrally. She remembered seeing him once or twice before, but she could tell that he hadn't recognised her.

"Linda McKay," she said, "special projects. My pass needs recoding."

He took the card that she placed before him and glanced at both sides of it. The photograph was about four years old and due for replacement; her hair had been longer then, although she'd recently decided to let it grow again. The guard said, "What's the problem?"

"I've been away on an assignment for the last couple of months, and now I can't get back into my old section. Have you been changing things around?"

"Could be," the guard said. He was around forty, greying slightly and gym-fit. Looking at his hands, Linda guessed that he'd had a manicure. She wondered if there was anything in the long-running rumour that most of the Risinger-Genoud security staff were gay, recruited as a matter of policy after a commissioned study in the mid-seventies. He said, "You know what this place can be like. Let me check."

He pulled his rolling chair along the desk to a built-in terminal, and inserted her pass into a slot at its side. The keys clicked as he typed, read, and typed again. As the display changed, he said without looking up, "Was everything all right at your home address?"

"Everything except the mail pickups. There was some stuff in the box more than a week old."

"Would you like me to pass on a complaint?"

"I'll send them a memo."

He read for a moment longer, green-skinned from the console reflection under the indirect lighting of the security complex, and then he removed the pass and handed it back. "You're right," he said. "It's a recode. They needed the office space while you were away, so they moved your stuff."

"To where?" Linda said.

"It's in storage. The record says no-one knew for sure how long you'd be away, so . . ." The guard shrugged.

"What do I do now?"

"Take your pass down to Gilbert Machoud in the computer room, and he'll handle it for you. Or you can leave it with me, but that means trusting the mailroom. You know Machoud?"

"I know him. I'll take it myself."

"You've got two boundaries to cross," he told her as she started to leave. "Ring 212 when you get to the doors, and I'll over-ride the lockout."

She was home. So why wasn't she feeling good about it?

Home wasn't the Rhine city, but the town-within-a-town that was the Risinger-Genoud complex. It covered more than a square mile within a twelve-foot-high boundary wall, an industrial theme park built up in decade layers with the latest and the brightest being dominated by the high-tech mirror-glass of the administration block. They'd still been clearing the site when Linda had first joined the company, dismantling old plant and tearing up railway lines; now it was three years since the block had been completed, and still they couldn't get the security programming right.

The building was zoned, with each zone requiring a different level of security clearance before access was allowed. Coding for clearances was held in the foil printed circuitry on the back of each employee's ID card. Doors between zones were referred to as 'control points'; low-power antennae in the fabric of the walls gave out a signal which was modulated by the card to produce a pass code. The code went back to the computer, and the computer opened the door.

Or, in Linda's case, it didn't.

This is a bore, she was thinking as she dialled 212 on a wall phone and waited for the security centre to respond.

The computer no longer recognised her pass code, which meant that it no longer recognised her. She couldn't even get down to the cafeteria, which like the computer room was in a multiple-access area; and if she tried to hop through the sliding doors after someone else, sirens would howl and the section would automatically seal.

The lockout was over-ridden. Linda had ten seconds to hang up and walk through. On her way down the corridor to the next zone boundary, she saw a dozen faces that were vaguely familiar and one or two that weren't. She'd spent most of her working life around here in one capacity or another after being talent-spotted in the UK subsidiary, but she'd never considered herself to be much more than a glorified clerk until this latest assignment.

And, considering how that had fallen apart, she was starting to wonder what her professional future might hold. Having her desk disappear might be only the beginning.

The computer room was reached by a passageway between two walls of tinted glass, almost like a Perspex walkway through a shark tank. The terminals were on one side, and the unattended processing power was on the other. Linda put her head through the door to the terminal room and said, "Hi, Gilbert. Remember me?"

Gilbert Machoud was the youngest section head within the company, but at twenty-nine he was the oldest member of his section. Most of the others didn't even look as if they'd have to shave too often. When he heard his name, he looked up from the timesheets he'd been checking.

"Linda!" he said with genuine pleasure, mangling the pronunciation of her name as always. "Back so soon?"

Linda went in. Of the other operators in the room, half a dozen were sitting with their backs to the terminals drinking coffee while a couple of others were reading magazines. It was usually the same scene, until something went wrong. She said, "The job kind of folded under me. I get back, and the doors won't open and they've given away my desk. Do you think they're trying to tell me something?"

"Nothing around here is that organised. Let me have your pass, and I'll run it through."

Linda handed it over. "Can I check the office allocations

while I'm waiting? I don't want to get pushed into some corner."

"Help yourself," Machoud said, and he grabbed the nearest castored chair for her. "There's nothing on terminal four."

Terminal four was right alongside the desktop laser printer that they used for listings to check on any queried sections of programming. Linda called up her own name in the office directory but no location followed it, not even her department's name. What she *did* notice was that she'd been flagged – a small coded symbol which wouldn't have shown on a screen but which came up now because terminal four had been set by the programmers in their main suite upstairs to include all hidden texts in its display. The effect of this was to tell Linda that somebody, somewhere in the building, had asked for notification of her arrival and whereabouts.

Machoud had just finished her recoding when she returned to him.

He said, "There's not much I can do until the people upstairs get their paperwork through to put you back into the machine, but I've given you a basic coding so that you can walk around the de-restricted areas without bumping your nose on the doors. Anywhere else, you'll have to call security and ask them to clear you through."

"What a pain."

"It's only for a couple of days," Machoud said. "And it's a good excuse for me to have you come back."

Linda moved toward the door. "See you later, Gilbert," she said, and Machoud put a hand to his heart and pretended to be doomstruck.

"Could I be so lucky?" he said.

Out in the glass corridor, someone was hurrying to meet her; someone who moved as if he'd been waiting to be told that she was around.

"Linda McKay?" he said. "My name's Peter Viveros. Can we go somewhere and talk?"

There was a small bar-café overlooking a city park that they'd all used back in the early days, before most of the others had moved on to other departments or even other companies. The décor hadn't changed, although the management had. They sat at a corner table. It was still early, and the place was almost empty.

Viveros had admitted on the way over that he was the one who'd requested the flag on her name. "I wanted to speak to you before anyone else did," he'd said. "It's about the Oktober project."

"Is this official, or what?"

"I think 'or what' probably covers it best."

Now, sitting across from him in the muted light of the bar, she could read some of the signs of his anxiety. He had the look of a man who'd glanced back over his shoulder and seen something coming up the road behind him faster than he could ever hope to run.

He said, "I wasn't briefed on the full story until I got back from Asia. It was bad enough then, but nothing I couldn't live with. This is something else, and I'm scared because I'm already in it up to my neck."

"If you're going to ask me to leak details, I don't think we ought to take it any further."

"Sit down. There's nothing you can tell me that I don't already know. Like, you got personally involved with the Oktober subject and you were on the point of telling him that he was under observation."

Linda was caught off-balance; having started to rise, she dropped back into her seat. "Where did you hear that?"

"I didn't. I was given the various reports to analyse and I worked it out. The first part was obvious, the rest is just a guess that I've been keeping to myself. But it looks like I wasn't far off the mark."

Linda said nothing.

Viveros went on, "You're assuming that because you've come back to no desk and no big welcome that you're going to lose promotion and professional credit over this. But this morning I saw copies of the memos that have been sent over to personnel, and *they* say that you're for an upgrading and a company apartment on the better side of the river."

"But why?" she said.

"Because you've hooked him, and they want to use that. The idea is to keep you sweet until they can get their hands on him again, at which point you'll become his keeper. That's the way the management thinking's going, but what's staring *me* in the face from the documentation is the possibility of you taking his side and turning whistleblower. And if that happens, then I want it on record that I didn't know the full extent of the project and that now I do, I'm getting out as soon as I can without arousing suspicion."

"So tell me what you think I don't know," she said.

He leaned forward. Linda didn't think she'd ever seen anybody who looked as serious as Peter Viveros in that moment.

"You know he was overdosed with EPL," he said.

"I knew that we were covering for some kind of medical accident with embarrassment potential for the company," Linda said.

"But you're familiar with the product line?"

"It's Epheteline," she said. "A central nervous system stimulant, still under patent."

"It's only been licensed for three years. We had a problem getting the manufacturing process straightened out, because there are two mirror-image versions of the EPL molecule. They're not symmetrical, and the right-handed molecule is about ninety per cent more efficient as a drug than the left-handed molecule. But then we found a way to separate them out, and the stuff called dextro Epheteline is the stuff that actually got licensed. Laevo EPL was just a waste product, fifty per cent of the factory's turnout but fit for nothing better than being pumped out into the Rhine at midnight. That was, until somebody in R and D came up with the idea of reprocessing it and putting it on the market as a low-strength EPL with much higher dosages."

"I don't see the point."

"The point lay in selling it under the existing EPL brand name in any country where the local regulations were loose enough to let it through. All of the packaging was to be stamped with a lapsed expiry date as a defence against any comeback, and then sales would be through black market outlets. We've often shipped substandard and short-dated batches to underdeveloped countries and there's nothing new in us manipulating the black market, either. But the Oktober project is the first example of a planned strategy from the design stages upwards."

"*Christ on a bicycle*," Linda said distantly. And then; "How does any of this relate to Jim Harper?

"Side effects," Viveros said.

He waited for a moment as three men, business types taking an early lunch break, seemed to be heading for their corner. But the men didn't sit close, and so Viveros went on in a slightly lowered voice, "Batch one went to a hospital on the edge of a war zone. The EPL was mainly used by the staff to keep them alert for long stretches as they handled bombing casualties; one of the big advantages of EPL over speed was supposed to be the absence of psychotic reaction with sustained large doses. But with overdosage of the untested left-handed molecule, what we got instead was irretrievable coma. But it wasn't coma in the classic definition, because there was almost continuous brain activity; and there were some weird features relating to the victims that we still haven't been able to explain. You give one an injection and they all flinch, even when they're in different parts of the hospital. You pack one in ice, and they all shiver. Now Harper got the same type of EPL, but unlike them Harper recovered; but then when you compare his dreams and certain changes in his physiology to what's happening with these other people, once you correct the data to take account of the time difference you realise that his subconscious mind is going through exactly the same hoops as theirs."

"How do you explain that?"

"I don't. It's one of the most exciting developments in pharmacology that I've ever seen, but when I think about how it happened I just want to get out before the whole thing turns into the Nuremberg trials. That's just one scenario, but it's nothing compared to what *could* happen if it carries on the way that it's going. You want my reading of the data, I'd say that Harper and the others have not only confirmed the existence of the Jungian collective unconscious, but in Harper's case he's beginning to be able to enter and control it at will. He doesn't even know it himself yet, but he's the king of fucking nightmare country and I don't plan to mess with him any more."

Viveros stood. "Tell him that for me, will you?" he said. And then he left.

Linda sat in silence until one of the three men from the next-but-one table ambled over and tried to pick her up. She didn't look at him, didn't even reply; and she couldn't have said what it was that he called after her as she walked out of the bar and into the daylight again.

TWENTY-FOUR

After a twenty-five-hour sleep with knockout shots and two days of moving carefully around the old farmhouse, Jim took his first steps outside. The rabbit man's work had been neat. There had been worry that Jim might react with some kind of post-operative shock, but so far he hadn't felt it. He felt as if he'd had the crap whacked out of him with a carpet beater, but nothing worse.

All credit to Roger, it was a good place to hide. The Brière was a vast inland *marais*, a reed marsh with only a few roads and a lot of water. The water was mostly what Jim had been able to see from his window, when they'd first let him get out of bed and into his newly-laundered clothes. He would sit on a turned-about chair and stare out across the wide silent marsh, listening inside to the quiet sounds of Jim Harper healing. Every now and again, the wind would blow and the reeds would whisper like thunder.

Rochelle didn't want him to go out at all, so he waited until she wasn't around in order to try it. She'd had to drive into Nantes, because she'd been unable to find anywhere in St Nazaire that could help with the shopping list that he'd given her. Roger, meanwhile, was putting in his usual hours at the plant; Jim's scheme might take anything up to a couple of weeks to bring off, and there was no point in giving the Risinger faction anything to be suspicious about at this stage.

Their farmhouse had originally been a one-roomed stone cottage which had been improved and extended when better times had come along; now the early part of the structure was left as a crumbling lean-to with a roof patched with corrugated iron. It stood on an island, surrounded on all sides by the *marais* canal network and linked to the mainland by a bridge. The bridge itself was a simple brick arch, wide enough for one car to pass over or for two flat-bottomed boats to get under. Jim had seen these boats going through occasionally, poled along by short weatherbeaten men in a Breton uniform of denim overalls with flat cap and wellingtons. Sometimes their craft were stacked with reeds or turves of peat, while a few carried flat-framed nets on hoists to fish for eels. A reed-boat that passed more than once was followed by a large black hound that danced along the bank and slipped in and out of the water like a seal.

Another dog. Jim had watched it through the window, knowing that he was locked-away and safe and trying hard to dig up whatever it was that had sent them into his nightmares and made him afraid.

But was he, any more? It was hard to disentangle the memory of fear from fear itself. Anything that didn't relate to immediate self-preservation was just phobia and, as Alan Franks had always told him, phobias could be beaten. Damn it, he'd always *liked* dogs, couldn't stand to see them being whipped or hurt. Something had changed him, but why couldn't he get hold of it?

His first excursion was a simple walk across to the bridge and back. Rochelle found out about it that evening and she wasn't happy, but the next day he went out again and this time he managed to walk all the way around the island, a distance of just a few hundred metres. At its far end he found ducks and geese feeding in chickenwire pens that extended out over the water alongside a makeshift jetty of compacted turf held up by stakes and planks. The inlet that it served had become choked with reeds, but by following this back he came to a thatched boathouse with two tarred wooden punts that had been laid up under cover. One had been holed and fixed with a sheet of tin and some nails, but the other still looked as if it would float.

On day five, Jim went boating.

By this time, Rochelle had given up on him. Every time she said no, he waited until she wasn't around and then sneaked out. He'd been an invalid for about as long as he could stand. The tricky part came when he got down to the boathouse and hauled out the smaller of the two punts; he took it in easy stages, monitoring for any sense of tearing or new damage, but his back seemed to hold up without a problem.

Rochelle stayed back in the farmhouse, her supply work done and the rented Avis car returned. Telegrams had been sent, and now it was just a matter of waiting for a reply. She was spending the time absorbed by ten years' worth of company reports that Roger had brought from the plant and which her step-father had never allowed her to see. For Jim it had been like this from the beginning; no sense of companionship, no conversations by the stove lasting late into the evening, no discussion of their common purpose. Rochelle had become impressively serious and Roger was a willing if nervous lieutenant, and neither of them was any damn fun at all. It was always a relief for Jim to get out and into the air.

He stayed on the canals for less than an hour, turning around when his stitches began to tug. The message from the rabbit man had been that they'd dissolve and pull out in their own time, but Jim didn't want to help them along any more than he needed. The church spire of far-off St Joachim village was his only reference point on an otherwise flat horizon, and he used this as a rough navigation aid. It got him to within sight of the poles carrying power and telephone lines alongside the road, and he followed these back toward the farmhouse.

It was slow work, and now it was getting harder by the minute. His back gave a definite, deep twinge as he steered out into the middle of a channel to avoid the submerged branches of a storm-fallen tree. Come on, he told himself, almost home, and at that moment the high reeds on either side began to shake as a breeze crossed the fen. Jim thrust the pole down into mud to anchor the boat until it had passed over, and felt as if he was being slowly torn apart. The sensation ebbed with the breeze, but it left him feeling wrung-out and tired.

Rochelle had been right, it was too early for this. But he wasn't going to let her know, and as the farmhouse eased into sight around a curve in the bank he sat up straight and took a breath and promised himself a long flop in his room if he could only make it to the house without wobbling.

Roger's brown Ford saloon was out in front of the house, and Roger was standing on the bank and watching for him. He walked along with the boat as Jim drew level.

"Did Rochelle make you watchdog?" Jim said, but Roger wouldn't be baited.

"No," he said, "today I'm the mailman." He reached into his jacket and brought out a telegram envelope, holding it out so that Jim could see. "We got a reply."

Jim let the boat drift. "And?"

"He arrives tomorrow."

That evening, as Jim lay on his bed with his replacement radio tuned to a far-off BBC transmitter, Linda stood at the window of her new Basle apartment and looked out across the Rhine. On the riverside walk five storeys below, somebody was leaving the building; a neighbour, probably, going down the brick path to where his car would be parked under the trees. Linda hadn't met any of the block's other tenants yet, and wasn't sure that she'd know what to say to them when she did. A place like this, it was in a different league altogether to anything that she knew.

She'd spread her stuff around as much as she could, but still it hardly looked as if anyone had moved in. Three bedrooms – what did a woman living alone want with three bedrooms, even if one of them *was* hardly bigger than a walk-in closet? She ought to be standing in front of the view and blessing her luck, but instead she couldn't help thinking how wrong, how disturbing and out of balance it all was.

So far, everything was happening the way that Peter Viveros had predicted for her; praise instead of a reprimand and even a few brief words from the top man himself. In all of her time with the company she'd never even *seen* Werner Risinger before, never been any closer than the sight of his black Mercedes limo going by, but suddenly there she was in his deep-carpeted office and he was coming around from behind his desk like somebody's uncle. She hadn't been able to believe Viveros at first, but she was pretty well along the way to believing him now. Despite all of the classy treatment she hadn't been told anything new about the Oktober project or her continuing role within it, but she had a definite sense of being softened-up as a prelude to something.

And if so much was turning out to be true, what about the rest of it? There, she had to hesitate. She had no problems with the concept of a collective unconscious, a dark and eternal territory of the mind where myths and archetypes and primitive fears were common to all; she'd read commentaries on Jung and even struggled all the way through *Seven Sermons to the Dead* as an undergraduate, but she realised now that she'd only been learning the academic routines. When it came to dealing with the notion on any realistic level, she couldn't prise herself out from the wrong end of the diving board. As a theory it was fine, but to have to consider it as anything more . . . well, even closed minds had been blown by less.

Tell him from me, Peter Viveros had asked her. But was Jim Harper ever likely to listen to her again, in spite of what the company thought of her usefulness? She'd already intended to tell him what had been happening. She'd decided on that morning of their discovery of Stephen Fedak drowned at the wheel of his car, the first spin-off casualty of what until then had been looking like a good strategy. She'd promised him on the day of the inquest, and then she'd avoided keeping her promise that night in the Pryors' caravan.

After that, it had been too late.

She turned back into the room. Well, Mister Bear, what do you think of that? Mister Bear sprawled at the end of the sofa, his one button-eye staring at her in disapproval. Linda couldn't argue with him. She was thinking of the way that Jim had looked, terrified and without defences as he sloshed Elsan fluid around the caravan to drive off howling dogs that weren't there. Whatever they'd told her at the time, she hadn't been any part of a plan for his welfare; instead, she'd been a functioning element in the mechanism that had made him as he was.

Life didn't seem quite so good any more, and the future was no longer the bright avenue that she'd always been able to imagine. Wherever he was, Jim Harper probably rated her as low as his scale could get.

Now, what do you think of *that*, Mister Bear?

TWENTY-FIVE

Late the next day, Jim stood in the shadows by the side of the tumbledown part of the farmhouse as he watched Roger's Ford come bumping over the bridge. Roger was driving, Rochelle was beside him, and there was someone else in the back. Roger turned the car as he came onto the forecourt, putting it into a tight circle so that he came to a stop facing the water. Handbrake on, engine off. Roger and Rochelle got out, and the young man in the back looked around him in bewilderment.

Rochelle beckoned, and he opened the rear door and climbed out. He stood in the fading light of the Brière, awkward and uncertain and completely out of place. He was wearing a city suit and carrying an attaché case. Roger and Rochelle had probably told him nothing, so Jim decided to end his confusion as quickly as he could.

He stepped out of the shadows. "Hello, Terry," he said.

Terry Sacks turned sharply at the sound of a voice that he could recognise, and he stared at Jim. He was wearing the same suit that Jim had borrowed for the inquest, and although it had been altered and taken in, the style betrayed it as a hand-me-down. Stockbroker lapels and buttoned cuffs didn't match the biker haircut and the beard. Jim suddenly felt mean for the deception that he'd used to get Terry over to France, but he told himself that Terry would benefit even if nobody else did.

"What's going on here?" Terry said. "I'm supposed to have been offered a job."

"That's right," Jim said. "Come inside, and I'll tell you all about it."

So they all went into the kitchen where they pulled out chairs around the plain wooden table. Rochelle gave Terry some coffee, Roger brought in Terry's overnight bag from the car, and Jim did most of the talking. Terry sat with a glazed look in his eyes that wouldn't have been out of place on a Dresden shepherdess. As far as he'd known, he'd been on his way to a final selection interview with a computer company that owned a development plant in La Baule; a long telemessage that had supposedly been from an international head-hunting agency had set out the details, and the airline ticket that had followed by express mail had seemed to be confirmation. He'd been met an hour before at the La Baule-Escoublac *aérodrome*, and nothing had gone as he'd expected since then.

When Jim had finished his pitch, Terry didn't waste time over his decision. He said, "Deus isn't for sale."

"Nobody's talking about buying it," Jim said. "We only want to arrange a rental."

Terry glanced from one to another, warily. "It's not that simple," he said.

Rochelle was looking decidedly hawkish. "You *did* bring it with you?"

"I brought all my notes, like the telegram said, but they're not in any form you could run. It's strictly development-level only, and we lost our machine access pretty early on."

"So here's your chance to try it out," Jim said. "Plus a cash payment and your ticket home."

"And no ticket home if I don't co-operate? You know damn well I haven't got any money." He wiped his nose, and Jim saw with a sudden stab of shame that Terry's hand was shaking. It was easy to forget how he must have seen his hopes taking a sharp rise and an even sharper fall over the last few hours.

Jim said, "Nobody's trying to blackmail you, Terry. But you've got to believe me when I say that I need this."

Roger hadn't spoken so far, but now he was rocking back on his chair and looking unconvinced. "I think we're wasting our time," he announced in English that wasn't half as good as Rochelle's. "The whole thing is just a fairytale."

"That's not true," Terry said, stung where it really hurt. "The concept's sound, but we never got the chance to work it through properly."

"So, here it is," Jim said.

"I couldn't even start without a machine."

This was the objection that Jim had been waiting to hear. He stood up, feeling a pull in his back from his boatman act of the afternoon before. He said, "Come with me."

If Terry was going to be with them, then this next moment was going to be the key to his winning-over. Jim led him out of the kitchen and through into the main room of the farmhouse.

The new terminal was running, its screen showing an ever-changing moiré pattern that had no purpose other than that of display. The computer itself was compact and free-standing, while beside it were a printer and an unconnected phone hookup. Terry moved in for a closer look. Jim could see that he was hovering.

Roger had been the one who'd argued against buying-in hardware that would have to be replaced if it wasn't suitable, but that was easy to understand because it was Roger's money that they were using. Over the past couple of weeks they'd managed to clean out almost all of his savings, with Jim and Rochelle outvoting him on every decision. Jim had been sure that in a case like this the sight and the touch of so much computing power would do more than any amount of pleading. Terry was like a Cortina playboy being offered the keys to a Ferrari.

"It's on approval," Jim said. "If it isn't suitable, you can go into town with Rochelle and pick something else."

185

Terry was playing it guardedly, but his hunger was showing through. "What's the CP?"

Jim shrugged. "That's your department. Anything that won't suit, you can change it."

Terry considered for a while. "There were a lot of questions asked when you and Linda disappeared," he said. "A lot of strangers."

"So why do you think we had to play it so cagily to get you out here?"

A long pause, as the pattern turned.

"Whatever you're tied up in, I don't want to know."

Rochelle's patience had been stretched about as far as it would go. From over by the door, she said, "Is this a yes?"

"I haven't decided yet."

Terry ran his fingers across the keyboard, so lightly that none of the keys was disturbed.

Jim said, "Something that I forgot to mention. When the job's over, you get to keep the machine."

It took a moment for Roger to understand, and then he started to object loudly and in his own language. Rochelle hustled him outside faster than a casino bouncer.

Resistance broke. With such a piece of hardware Terry could set up in business on his own, and he knew it. No more trailing around between interviews with a CV that showed nothing worthwhile for the last three years. Terry was hooked, and *Deus X* was theirs.

"The machine's okay," Terry said, "but there's some other stuff we'll need."

Jim glanced at the door through which Roger had disappeared, but Rochelle had arranged it so that Roger was no longer within earshot. "Make a list,' he suggested

TWENTY-SIX

It was almost a week after Terry Sacks' arrival in the Brière when Linda McKay finally got her recoded pass. She still had no office and she still had no specific assignment, but at least now she could get around the building.

Or at least, that was the idea.

She dialled 212 on the push-button phone beside the door where she'd been stalled. After she'd listened for a moment, a male voice said, "Security."

"I'm at three-fifteen and the door won't open," she said. "Over-ride, please."

"Your name?"

"Linda McKay, special projects."

"One moment."

Linda waited. She could hear the sound of the guard's breathing, and below that his one-handed tapping on the plastic terminal keys. There was a short pause, and then he said, "I'm sorry, Fraulein McKay, you're at the limit of your clearance."

"That can't be right. Can you check again, please?"

"It's here in front of me."

"Then it has to be a mistake." As Linda was saying this two young men in unstained lab coats were walking by, their passes clipped to their lapels. They looked like bottom-of-the-grade lab assistants. The door opened before them, and they walked on into the next zone without breaking pace.

The guard said, "We can only act on the orders we get. If you'll take it up with the administrative section, I'm sure they'll straighten it out."

Some chance, Linda thought as she hung up. It had to be the administrative section that had engineered this foulup in the first place; it had taken nearly two weeks for them to get around to issuing her with a recoded pass, and now it wouldn't get her any further than the temporary issue that Machoud had arranged. And she needed to get through; if Peter Viveros wouldn't return her calls, she was going to have to confront him directly and insist that he should come up with some evidence for what he'd told her. It had occurred to her that the entire scenario might be some carefully-planned loyalty test; she didn't quite believe this, but at least it was an alternative to the snake pit of possibilities that opened up if it were true.

She hesitated at the doorway to the computer operations room.

The scene before her was like a Sunday market.

There had to be more than twenty computer personnel working at once, operators that she recognised and others who were presumably programmers from upstairs, and together they were making more noise than the machines. The main area of attention was around terminal four, the one configured for the laser printer. Printout was being generated in lengths of ten metres and more, and rolls of it were being spread out and argued-over on every available surface. Linda was about to withdraw, but then Machoud saw her. He beckoned her over, and came out to meet her halfway.

"Sorry, Gilbert," she said. "I didn't realise it would be a bad time."

Machoud's expression told her that this was an understatement. He said, "You wouldn't believe it. What's the problem?"

"The same old stuff about my security rating. I'm supposed to take it back to admin, but I thought I might check for myself."

"Yeah, and save about six months. Is it really desperate?"

"Well, I'm supposed to be on the Oktober project, and I can't even get through to the offices."

Machoud's reaction was immediate. "Oktober?" he said. "That's the little bastard that's giving us all the trouble."

She looked behind him at the shirtsleeve chaos, and said, "How come?"

"We don't know. The programming's all screwed, and we can't find a reason for it. We're having to go through all the original notes and records to clean up the mess."

Someone looked up. "Give me two more minutes," he said, "and I can tell you why."

"What have you found?" Machoud said, but the programmer held up a hand for him to wait as he continued a long scan down one of the rolls.

Machoud lowered his voice so that he wouldn't be a distraction, and it almost sounded to Linda as if he were telling her secrets. He said, "We've got copies of the original program in the security dump, but we've made too many changes as we've gone along. And if what we're getting here is a result of a fault somewhere in the writing, then we're only going to repeat it."

"So what's happening?"

"Something's modifying the data as it's moved around by the operating system."

"Something called *Deus X*," the programmer reported triumphantly from behind Machoud. The section chief turned.

"Another program?" he said, incredulous.

"That's right," the programmer said, "and it's not one of ours." To Linda he didn't look more than nineteen years old, probably some *wunderkind* who'd been solving equations by his fifth birthday. He gestured toward the paper in his hand and said, "You're going to have to read all this, Gilbert, or you won't believe it."

"Who put it in?"

"Telephone link to the database. The line's locked open, so we can get a trace and find the senders. Whoever they are, they know the access code to the Oktober files. But that's not the interesting part."

"Try telling that to the people upstairs."

"I said you wouldn't believe it. We're talking about an AI program designed to seek and retrieve. It's so crude, they must have written it on a mini."

"Seek and retrieve?" Linda echoed, doing her best to seem no more than faintly interested. *Deus X* was as good as a signature for Terry Sacks, and as far as she knew Jim Harper was the only outsider who'd ever seen an Oktober access code – and that had been on her own machine.

"Like a gundog," the programmer said. "Feed it down the telephone line and then wait for it to come back with the information you want."

"Would it have worked?" Linda said, and it was Machoud who gave her the answer.

"Not a chance," he said. "But it rates as a nice try."

"Some of the ideas are worth a second look," the programmer insisted. "With the right access codes, you could scramble every file in a competitor's main storage.

Think what that could do, the day before a product launch."

"Or with the unprocessed data for a licence application," Machoud said, his imagination caught. "Stick with it, Jean-Paul."

"We'll take a copy and then clean it out," Jean-Paul said. "The access codes will have to be changed, of course."

"How long?"

Jean-Paul shrugged. "End of the shift. No longer."

He turned to rejoin the others, and Machoud gave Linda an apologetic smile. "Sorry," he said. "There's nothing I can do until this is cleared."

Linda made an *Oh, well* gesture, and started toward the door. Her thoughts were racing. She didn't want to leave; more than anything, she wanted to get her hands on the printout that all the computer people were studying and find out exactly what the hell was being carried off here. Which was the one thing that she couldn't do.

"Unless," Machoud said as she reached the doorway, "you want to get the night keys from Security and come in this evening. The place will be empty by then."

"Security wouldn't even give me the key to the toilet. That's why I'm here."

Machoud came over to her side. Again, he lowered his voice. "We'll be in the cafeteria from around seven," he said. "Drop by, and you can have mine."

"Are you allowed to do that?"

"Who's to know? The night guard's scheduled for his first check on the area at eight-fifty. Just be out of the way by then."

"But they change the schedule every day."

"*We* change the schedule every day," Machoud said, tapping himself on the chest and making the pens in his shirt pocket rattle. "Me and the great god Vaal. See you at seven."

At six-thirty, she dialled 212 again. "Security," a different voice said.

"This is Linda McKay, special projects. I've borrowed an office to catch up on my paperwork, and I'll be staying on for a couple of hours. Don't send the dogs out after me, will you?"

"Very well, Fraulein McKay, you're noted. No alarms."

The monitoring computer had a built-in loop of suspicion that called for a check if any employee failed to log out within an hour of the usual time, but her call would now have overcome that. As long as she stayed within the derestricted zone, she could go where she liked. She started by going to the cafeteria.

Most of the tables were roped-off and in darkness, but there were lights and a scattering of people in the all-night section. Machoud, Jean-Paul and a couple of the others were sitting around a white mica-topped table by one of the drinks machines. They all seemed to be on a high from the events of the day.

"The consultant's report said it all a year ago," Jean-Paul was saying. "If you want to run a computer on a network basis, the only way to guarantee security is with a block cypher system."

"And how many users have we got?" Machoud demanded. "You're talking about thousands of individual keys, more if you go for a multi-key system. And with the increased load, you only slow down the speed of handling even more."

"Is this the cafeteria," Linda said, pulling out a chair to sit alongside Jean-Paul, "or is it the new debating chamber?"

Jean-Paul hitched his chair along a couple of inches to make room. Machoud said, "Hi, Linda. You want a coffee?"

"Thanks, Gilbert, but I'm on a time limit, remember?"

"Sure." He took out an overloaded keyring, sorted out a single key, fiddled for a minute to detach it, and then passed it over. He said, "Maybe later?"

"If you're still around," she said. "What should I do with the key if you're not?"

"You'll find somebody here," Machoud said, and Jean-Paul nodded.

"Okay," Linda said, and left them to it.

She checked behind her along the way, but nobody was following. Even when she'd stepped into the glass-walled

191

corridor that ran between the two halves of the computer section, even then it would have been possible to pretend that she'd left something behind in the afternoon and had come along in the hope that there might still be someone around.

But once she'd produced the key that Machoud had given her, all other bets were off.

Linda had to take it on trust that she was safe until eight-fifty; Machoud ought to know, after all. Unless there was an alert, no guard would visit the section until the programmed time. She moved down toward the door. Her own dark outline moved with her on the glass.

As the door opened, Linda was met by a low-level sound that was ninety per cent air-conditioning and the temperature dropped a few degrees. She had only the emergency lights to see by, and it was hard to shake herself of the feeling that she was walking through a cave filled with nameless forms. Even though they were sleeping, their eyes glowed at her; pinpoint-green function lights, and the dull red burn of power warnings.

Can it, Linda, she told herself, and she switched on an anglepoise by terminal four.

Well, she'd known that it wasn't going to be easy. The afternoon's printout had filled three trash bags, and these had been wire-tied at the necks and left for janitors to take away in the morning. At least they hadn't gone to the shredder on the same day, but then everyone who worked in the main block knew that Office Services stopped work promptly at five and were all on their way to the underground car park at one minute past. Tomorrow the rolls would be nothing more than paper snow; but for tonight, they were dynamite.

Linda could program a little, and she was hoping that she'd know enough to be able to dig out what she wanted. She started by opening each of the bags and looking for line-codings on the crumpled printout inside. A long sequence of numbered lines, whether she could understand it or not, would be a sign that a piece of the program had been listed, printed in its original form of step-by-step instructions so that it could be checked by the people who had written it. The screens on the other terminals couldn't show more than about a couple of dozen lines at a time, which was why they'd gone over to the printer.

The second bag contained the low numbers that she was looking for, and so she pulled out a couple of lengths and spread them under the light. Scanning was made easier by the fact that there was so much she didn't understand; in fact, there was nothing on either of the two rolls that she understood at all, and so she bundled them up and put them to one side and spread out some more.

Linda lost track of how long it had taken her to find what she wanted, but when she checked her watch it had been, more than an hour.

The Oktober listing had begun with a security sub-routine that had detailed four different levels of access. She'd immediately known that she was onto something, because this independent existence under the overall security routine made it like a locked box within a shuttered room. Her own keyword, *Oktober*, let the user into the simplest and least controversial level of the file. Additional keys unlocked the more sensitive material, until *Valkyrie* – a listing with only a handful of authorised names and codings beneath it – unlocked the whole show.

She tore out the section, and put it on one side. This was the goldseam, but she wasn't finished yet. After she'd re-stuffed the trash bags and pushed them out of sight, she went around to the cartridge racks behind the terminal rows.

Even if Viveros hadn't convinced her, the listing had. Four levels of deep security with the most important information being available only to board members and division chiefs – she'd never come across anything like it before, and she was certain that a simple damage-limitation exercise after a medical accident wouldn't warrant it. If they caught her now, they wouldn't just fire her; they'd jail her. Industrial espionage would be the charge and, here in Switzerland, they could make it stick.

There were two sets of shelves loaded with cartridges, one set for use and the other for return to the condition-controlled library two doors further down the outside passageway. They held data and files and pieces of programming that were only called up for occasional reference. If Machoud had made a copy of *Deus X* as he'd said that he would, it ought to be here in the outgoing rack.

She had to put on another light to read the handwritten labels; the nearest was a bright overhead fluorescent that made her feel as conspicuous as a bug pinned to a bedsheet. She went through the fifty or sixty cartridges in the rack, reading sideways and coming upon the *Deus X* copy more than halfway down.

It was quite a relief to be able to return the room lighting to the single pool of the anglepoise by terminal four. Linda had been more used to handling the older Winchester disk drives where it had been a case of plugging the whole thing into a drive unit, giving it a half-twist to unlock the protective container, and then lifting the container away leaving the disks behind; but loading the cartridge reader was, if anything, simpler.

She pulled a chair over to the nearest screen terminal, and sat with the list of codes and keys to the Oktober files on the console beside her. She'd have to log on before she could get details of the source and the incoming line used for *Deus X*, but with the list she could use any one of the authorised names and codes from the highest-rated group. Breaking into one file was serious enough, but using the results to break into another would look suspiciously like the start of a career.

LOGON PLEASE, the machine glowed after the usual preliminaries, and so Linda checked the top line of the display where the logging-on time was always on show.

As she looked, it changed from *20.49* to *20.50*.

She was out of time, and the security check was overdue. Stay calm, she told herself, just close down and get out of the way and let the guard go through. Linda knew that she was close to what she needed; when the guard had reported in and moved on, she could return and complete the rest of it in just a few minutes.

But it wasn't going to be so easy.

She'd switched off the anglepoise and moved across the room to let herself out, but as she opened the glass door she heard footsteps. They were some way off but they were approaching, and she could expect the guard to appear around the corner in twenty seconds or less. She couldn't go toward him. She couldn't go the other way, either, because that was blocked by a zone boundary and she wouldn't be able to pass.

Linda had only one option, which was really no option at all. She stepped back into the computer room, and locked herself in.

She turned, looking for somewhere to hide. The layout designers had gone for an open, uncluttered approach, which considering her present problem was of no help. What she needed was somewhere to crouch out of sight until the guard had looked the room over and moved on. She couldn't think of any reason why he might need to enter. She hoped that the guard wouldn't be able to think of a reason, either, as she got herself behind a row of four-foot-high cabinets that had been moulded in grey plastic and smoked glass. She went down just as the spot of a flashlight zipped across the wall behind her.

Linda crouched, holding her breath and trying to listen. All that she could hear was the regular sound of the computer room's air fans, with a dull hammering beneath that might have been her own heart. Would she know when he'd passed on by? The glass that formed the corridor wall was probably a quarter of an inch thick, and she could hardly expect to hear him walking away. She'd have to wait a while, and then emerge slowly. And hope that he wasn't standing on the other side of the glass and watching for her.

A moment later, Linda knew that none of this would be necessary. The guard was coming in.

His passkey clicked in the lock, and Linda hunched down as if she'd been stabbed. There was nowhere to go, and no other way out. The guard came into the computer room, and his flashlight beam darted and spread across the floor as he walked toward her. She knew that she ought to stand and try to walk out of this with some dignity, but she couldn't.

The guard stopped, and switched off the terminal that Linda had forgotten. A moment later, he was back outside and relocking the door.

She gave herself time to recover; he'd be using the wall-phone at the corridor's end to report his progress to Security control, and if she emerged now he might still see her. Linda couldn't remember when she'd ever been so scared; the sensation wasn't as fierce as the utter horror that she'd felt at the sight of Stephen Fedak's Volkswagen being uncovered by the retreating tide, but it was enough to bring tears of relief as she slowly unwound. Squawking wouldn't help, she told herself as she wiped her eyes on her sleeve, and by the time she felt that it was safe to stand she knew that she was back under control.

There was nobody on the other side of the glass. Linda went around to her console and switched it on again.

When she got back to the cafeteria, Gilbert Machoud wasn't there. Jean-Paul and the other operators were still talking over cups of cold coffee; one whose name she didn't know was saying, "I did a year over at Berkeley and I worked with that system. You could cheat your way through to look at any file, and it was untraceable."

"From outside?" Jean-Paul said, disbelieving. "Down a telephone line?"

"The line didn't matter, just the terminal. The students were studying the operating system and breaking it."

"But that was a system that was never designed to be totally secure in the first place. Our setup's different."

Linda thought *not after today, it isn't*, and she said, "Sorry if I'm interrupting. Is Gilbert around?"

"He had to go," Jean-Paul said. "I can take the key for you."

"Thanks," Linda said, and she took it from her pocket and placed it on the table. As she was doing this she touched the folded paper that had the Oktober codes and her *Deus* notes on it. She'd been checking to be sure that it was still there all the way over from the computer room.

Jean-Paul said, "You got everything you wanted?"

"I had a useful time," Linda said, which was hardly a lie. "How are the terminal bookings for tomorrow?"

"About what time?"

"Say, ten o'clock."

"No problem," Jean-Paul said airily, in what was an obvious but unconscious imitation of Gilbert Machoud's relaxed manner. "There's always something free at that time, just turn up."

Linda would turn up, all right, but first she managed gracefully to turn down another offer of coffee. She'd quickly get lost in their technospeak, and she still wasn't sure that she could trust her hands not to shake.

Besides, she had work to do.

TWENTY-SEVEN

"Roger doesn't look happy," Jim said one day across the remains of a late breakfast in the Brière kitchen. Roger was leaning with his arms folded on the table, and he was frowning.

"Roger isn't," he said. "Roger's seen the last of his money being wasted on some crank of a kid. Roger is now broke."

Terry Sacks, the 'crank of a kid', had been sent in Roger's Ford to the market in St Joachim. There had been nothing more for him to do since *Deus X* had been finalised and transmitted the previous morning, and in the hours that had followed with no reply the last of the male Genouds had become noticeably upset.

Jim could guess how he felt. Roger wasn't weak, but he didn't have Rochelle's commitment; his situation would always shape him, rather than the other way around. Left alone, he'd probably have stayed as an assistant director with a few private complaints but no thought of any action. Add Jim Harper for opportunity and Rochelle for pressure, and he became an accomplice. Add Terry Sacks and a scheme which seemed to suggest that he'd flown over to France leaving most of his marbles at home, and Roger would see the whole thing beginning to degenerate into farce before his eyes.

He was uneasy now; but Jim wondered what he'd say when he saw the telephone bill.

The line had been in almost constant use, twenty-four hours a day for the past four days as Terry Sacks had run his basic code-cracker program to search for an avenue along which *Deus* could be slipped into the Risinger-Genoud mainframe. The mainframe had been defended against such approaches and would ring off after any three unsuccessful attempts, but Terry had found a way around this by routing his calls via the machine at the St Nazaire subsidiary using Roger's own logging-on code. Getting into the private company lines had been achieved by the use of a simple interface device that Terry called a 'cheesebox'; it had taken him half a day to make and no more than ten minutes to install when Roger had driven him into the works on a visitor's pass. Jim's vague memory of the access procedure that he'd seen on the display of Linda's machine had then served as Terry's starting-point; everything from here on, Terry had insisted, was just standard hacker routine.

Roger hadn't liked seeing his code put to use in this way, either. It was an extra strain that he would have preferred to live without. Every day he'd had to drive into the plant and betray nothing of his knowledge, reporting all of the company rumours back to the farmhouse every night. Rochelle's sudden disappearance hadn't been reported to the police yet, and so far had been treated as an internal security matter; the official version was that she'd run off with an Englishman who had a history of psychiatric disorder but who was generally reckoned to be harmless. It was the 'harmless' part that offended Jim more than anything else.

Roger ended breakfast that morning by throwing his chair back against the wall and stalking off into the next room. He wasn't made for anger, and it always turned into embarrassment.

But what could Jim say to him? Especially when he'd been able to sense it too, from the moment that Terry had set down to work; *Deus* was a dream, something that two friends had talked about and planned late into the night when anything had seemed possible and success was no more than a puzzle to be solved. Daylight was the time to see that everything came with a price, and that the puzzle was made out of sand. Daylight was now, and *Deus* wasn't holding up. Perhaps the worst thing that Jim could have done to Terry's dream was to force him to realise it; but these things, as Grundy had said, couldn't always be humanely carried off.

At the table next to him, Rochelle said, "You'd better be right about this, James. We've got a lot to lose over you."

"Whereas I'd already gone as low as I could get?"

"That's not what I meant."

But it was.

Rochelle's personal concern for Jim was probably so minimal that it couldn't be measured. He knew now that when he'd told her his story that morning in the galleries of the Louvre, she'd seen him not as a man in difficulty but as an opportunity for leverage. Her obsession and her frustration had been such that she'd grabbed the opportunity with both hands, dropping everything else, and Jim knew that he'd be dropped just as quickly the moment his value was seen to disappear.

With *Deus* a probable failure and with his memory for the details of his treatment an uncompromising blank, Jim knew that he was already there. It was just a matter of waiting for Rochelle to realise it. Somehow, he didn't think that it would take her long.

She'd been right. It *was* the worst year of his life.

There was a sound from Roger in the next room.

Within moments, they were standing at his side. The three of them watched the words and figures scrolling up the computer's screen so fast that they couldn't read any of it.

"What do we have to do?" Roger asked helplessly.

"Nothing," Jim said. "Terry left everything set up. Just don't touch anything until it's all finished." And, he thought, pray that it's what we were hoping for. He didn't dare to be elated, not yet.

The material took four minutes to run through and then the screen was suddenly clear, only a flashing cursor signalling the machine's readiness for new instructions. Jim sat down before the keyboard.

"Now let's see what we got," he said.

I'm setting this to transmit and then delete, they read. *Your line isn't secure, and can be traced. Oktober project information follows; wherever you are, take it and leave immediately. And next time, try sending MAGGIE instead.*

"Who's this from?" Rochelle said.

Jim was studying the screen. "I could make a rough guess."

The two of them moved aside so that Roger could get in to study the data that followed. "It's a product profile," he said almost immediately and then, after a minute or so, "It's EPL, but in an altered version."

None of it meant anything to Jim, but it obviously meant a lot to Roger. He watched for a while longer, and then he said excitedly, "It's all here. I'd need a few hours to sort it all out, but there's enough to hang them."

"We haven't got a few hours," Rochelle said. "James? We're moving out."

"Right away?"

"You saw what it said, they can trace the line back to us. We don't know how long they've had to get started."

"But they'd hardly go to the police over this."

"The police don't worry me. It's the idea of Daniel and a fast car from Paris."

The idea of Rochelle's bodyguard, with or without a fast car, was enough to send Jim sprinting up to his room for what was his current total of worldly goods; his new radio, two shirts, some underwear, and a pair of jeans that didn't quite fit. Rochelle's shopping for him had been well intentioned, but her mind hadn't really been on it. As he stuffed everything into two plastic carrier bags he thought of Daniel, his eyes two smouldering pits of hate as the Louvre security guards wrestled him back and his gaze burned its way onward across the gallery to Jim. His dreams might have become even more manageable in the nights since the removal of his implant, but still he'd had plenty of dark moments in which Daniel Mindel had featured as a leading player.

200

He went back downstairs. Rochelle wasn't ready, but she was close to it. As Roger was removing the all-important datadiscs from the machine's twin drives, Jim said, "What about Terry?"

"And what about my car?" Roger added.

"Forget your car," Rochelle said as she pushed a soapcase into a grip that was already well-stuffed. "We'll get out by the canals. You can leave a note telling Sacks to drive to the airport. Then you can report it stolen and let the *flics* find it for you."

Roger wasn't happy, but he couldn't think of any better way. Jim wasn't too happy either; he didn't like the idea of walking away and leaving Terry like this, but at least with a car he'd probably be out of it before trouble arrived . . . *and* he'd have transport for his new gear.

It still didn't feel right, but Jim let it go. He left Roger composing the note, and set out to get the punt from the boathouse.

Leaving by the network of marsh canals would be slow, but it would be safer than waiting around for one of the area's few taxis. They wouldn't have to go far, just enough to get away from the single-track road on which Daniel could bottle them up – assuming that he was close enough, and it wasn't really safe to assume anything else.

It was a cool day, and a breeze was stirring the grey surface of the *marais*. Roger caught up with Jim at the boathouse, and together they got the punt launched and scrambled aboard. Roots and reeds tugged at the craft, and Jim eased it out toward the deeper water in the middle of the channel. Algae rose and swirled under the water's surface in their wake. Roger took a hand with a second pole, and they were under the bridge and out in front of the farmhouse as Rochelle emerged with the bags.

"That was fast," she said as they helped her down from the bank.

"You can believe it," Jim told her, raising one of the poles and pushing them out into deep water again. "Suddenly this place doesn't feel so safe any more."

*

St Joachim was a small town and its market was a typically smalltown affair, with carpets and clothes selling alongside the foodstuffs. Terry's remembered school French was so awful that people were coming over from nearby stalls to listen, but he'd quickly learned that for anybody who wasn't afraid to make a fool of himself abroad there was no such thing as a language barrier. He got everything that they needed in two heavy bagloads, and as far as he could tell nobody had tried to cheat him.

He'd left the Ford in the town square, in the shadow of the church tower. The car was at least six years old, which probably said something about Roger Genoud's professional status. As Terry walked down the quiet main street away from the market and toward the square, he wondered what Jim Harper had got himself into. It certainly made no sense from the outside.

He'd have preferred to stay and see how *Deus* performed, but he could take a hint. Roger, especially, didn't seem to want him around once his work had been finished. Terry wondered if it was spying. Christ, they put you in *prison* for spying! But then the target for *Deus* had been company files, not government records, and the company wasn't even in the same country. It would be tough to trace, impossible to prosecute. He was probably safe.

All the same, it was better to be out of the way.

He could hear the voices of schoolchildren, playing on the other side of a high wall that was mossy and damp. They sounded about nine years old, the age that Terry had been when he'd first started going around with Stephen Fedak. But he'd promised himself that he wasn't going to think about it.

This wasn't a promise that he could easily keep. With Steve around to test his ideas and spot the flaws, Terry was sure that he could have made *Deus* work like a dream. As it was the program resembled a broken child, limping and half-blinded and barely breathing. They'd pressured him, and he'd done his best; but somehow he couldn't be confident that his best was good enough.

Although he tried to fight it, his thoughts kept slipping back. It wasn't something that he could control. As he opened up the boot of the car and raised the lid to put his groceries inside, he wondered if he was going to have to keep on reliving that night forever.

Probably so. He'd let down a friend, and he'd lied to the police. The second sin had ensured that he'd never be able to unburden himself of the first.

Fedak hadn't thrown him out of the car on the road down from the Cliff House. Terry just hadn't been able to take the way that he'd been talking about Linda, all tears and bitterness. Damn it, he'd barely *known* the girl a month! He'd never seen Fedak like this before, and it had embarrassed and disturbed him. Liking Linda hadn't helped, either, and so finally he'd demanded that Fedak should stop the car and let him out. Terry had walked away and left him there, sitting behind the wheel too sick and too drunk to drive himself home; Terry had known at the time that it was wrong, and he'd told himself so all the way down the cliff path, but still he hadn't turned around and gone back.

And now Fedak was dead, drowned in his car and then swept away with the tide. Terry wondered what it had been like. He couldn't imagine a worse way to go, with the car slowly filling and sinking and the outside pressure keeping the doors closed. The windows in the Beetle had always been tough to open anyway, and in a panic they'd have been impossible.

Or hadn't Steve cared? Say it was no accident. Say he'd run himself off the road deliberately, and then stayed in the car as the waves turned it around and around as he waited to die. However he read it Terry could have, *should* have prevented it. Now he'd be damned because he hadn't, and he'd deserve it.

At first he missed the turnoff for the narrow road to the farmhouse, and he had to swing around in a gateway to get back to it. Driving on the wrong side of the road wasn't a problem, but driving on the wrong side of the car would take some getting used to. The lane ran along the edge of the marsh for more than a kilometre; it didn't look quite the same from this angle as it had when he'd set out, but he knew that it was right. There was a well-worn *parc naturel* map on the seat beside him, but he didn't need to look at it; already he could see the farmhouse and the bridge that would take him back onto the island.

Visitors, he thought.

There was an expensive-looking yellow Saab parked in front of the house.

He pulled up alongside it. The Saab's arches and sides were dirt-splashed as if by some hard driving. He locked the Ford, and then went around for the groceries.

Something didn't seem to be right. He was thinking as much when he shouldered his way into the kitchen with the first of the bags. Nobody had cleared away after breakfast, and he had to make a space to set the groceries down on the table. The silence in the place was an empty-house kind of silence; and when he looked through into the next room he saw that the machine – *his* machine, the one that he'd been promised – had been switched off.

There was a note beside it, with Roger's signature at the bottom. This was almost all that Terry could make out, because Roger had written the whole thing in French and his handwriting was so small and crabby that it would probably take Terry a half-hour to decipher. Only two words in the top line stood out; there was *Deus*, and there was *succès* followed by a long string of exclamation points.

Deus had worked. How else was he supposed to understand it? The rest was probably to tell him where they'd gone and when they'd be back. He could get some lunch and then puzzle his way through the note later. His program had worked, and he hadn't even dared to expect it to. How about *that*, world?

He went back for the second of the bags, which had the wine and the baguettes. He broke an end off one of the bread sticks and ate it on the way back to the house. He had plans to make. Jim and his friends owed him some money and a ticket home, and he'd have to work out some way of shipping the computer and avoiding import charges. He might have to pay these out of his fee and then claim them back as business expenses at the end of the year; because that's what this was going to be, a decently-equipped and properly-run business. His days spent sitting at home watching Sesame Street repeats and cookery programmes were over.

As Terry was about to re-enter the kitchen, a man emerged from the reeds over towards the *marais*.

He seemed to have been looking for something, because he was dusting off his hands as he climbed up from the banking where he'd been out of sight. He saw Terry, and he smiled and gave a friendly wave. Terry couldn't wave back, but he waited as the man came over toward him.

The man was wearing a zippered quilted jacket and slacks, city clothes for the winter. When he was no more than five or six yards away, he reached into his jacket at an improbable angle and brought out a knife. He was still smiling.

Terry threw the groceries, and ran.

He could hear the heavy clunk of one of the wine bottles against bone followed by the man going down, but he didn't look back. Before he'd reached the car he knew that the man was on his feet again and coming after him. The doors were locked, the boot was still open; Terry didn't hesitate but hopped over into the narrow space, folded himself down, and pulled the lid down after.

Jesus, he hadn't expected it to be quite so cramped; the rim of the spare was right up against his shins, and his insides were feeling all doubled over and squashed. Inches away on the other side of the thin metal, the man was scrabbling at the lock and trying to get the boot open. But he couldn't do it without the keys, and the keys were safely in Terry's pocket; he could feel them now, gouging out a permanent place for themselves in his groin.

An inch at a time, he got onto his side. He was trying not to think of what might happen if the man decided to try spiking him through the lid. Bracing his back against the spare, Terry set his hands and knees against the sprung frame of the rear seat and pushed. The seat-back popped through into the car, and Terry squirmed out after it.

Fresh air.

As he came up into the back of the Ford, Terry could see that the man hadn't abandoned him completely; he'd opened up the Saab and was going through its toolkit, obviously thinking that Terry wouldn't be going anywhere. But he'd realise differently if he should see Terry scrambling over into the driver's seat.

The stranger ran to the Ford as Terry started the engine, the knife still in his hand. But Terry knew that he was almost home and dry. The Saab wouldn't be able to overtake him on the narrow road back to St Joachim, and the stranger wouldn't dare to do anything in the middle of a market crowd.

Or so Terry hoped.

The engine was running, and he crashed the gears. His right hand had never been used to the feel of a shift. The man dropped out of sight for a moment, and then Terry saw him jump back as the gears meshed and the car leapt forward.

He aimed for the bridge. It was when he found himself veering away from it that he realised one of his front tyres had been slashed.

Terry tried to fight the wheel, but it was too late; the car ran off the river embankment on the approach to the bridge, and thumped to a sudden halt on the soft ground. He had a start of more than a hundred yards. He couldn't waste it.

If he could get across the bridge and into the trees on the far side, he'd be away. He unlocked the door and jumped out of the car, leaving the engine stalled and its nose almost in the water. He scrambled up the embankment and onto the bridge, and he started to run.

He'd been a runner all his life; at school, at the tech, and for a couple of years in the harriers until he'd grown lazy. No middle-aged Frenchman was going to catch him now. Arms pumping and raising dust, he raced for the trees.

There was a light push in the middle of his back. It would have helped him on, but then one of his lungs filled with blood.

He ran on for a few more steps, all of his co-ordination going in a flailing tangle or arms and legs. He tripped himself, and fell forward in slow-motion. The jar as he landed on his hands and knees sent a languorous series of shockwaves through him. He coughed once, and blood spattered on the ground before his eyes. It was the most frightening thing that he'd ever seen, but he felt too dazed to be really frightened.

Terry couldn't hold himself up, and he sank onto the ground. There was no pain, but he suddenly felt too weak to stay up. He felt the knife being pulled out, and then he felt himself being turned over.

He didn't want this. On his back, he started to choke. He tried to tell the Frenchman, but he only managed to cough weakly and to spray more. The blood was bright red and dangerous-looking, full of bubbles, almost froth.

The Frenchman lifted him up and started to drag him, and that was better. Within a minute they were back at the Ford, and Terry was left propped against one of the wheels to look along the trail that he'd made as the Frenchman opened the doors. Then he lifted Terry again, and heaved him inside to lie on the rear seat.

Terry could see the damage that he'd done to the car as he'd kicked his way through, and now he was bleeding all over the seat. Roger was going to be really pissed at him. The Frenchman bundled his legs inside and slammed the door on them. Terry wanted to cough again, but he no longer had the strength for it. All of the colours were draining out of everything, and sounds were turning hollow.

The Frenchman started the car on his third try, and then he roughly reversed it off the embankment. Terry could feel that they were bumping along on one flattened rim, but he could no longer guess at direction or anything else. He didn't even know it when the Frenchman revved the engine hard and then left the car as it was moving.

He knew about the impact, though, and he realised what it had been when he saw the Brière water pouring in around the old rubber seal on the boot lid. Except that Terry didn't see Brière water; it was seawater, green and cold and salty, and he said, Is this what it's like, Steve? And Steve said Relax, Terry, it isn't going to hurt, and as the level surged up and over his face a hand came out of the depths and took a firm grip on his own. *Now*, Steve said, and together they stepped through the door and into darkness.

Daniel stood on the bridge and watched for a while as the car filled and settled into the centre of the channel. The roof went under with a final, gassy belch, and the water darkened with mud drawn up from below.

He kicked over the tyre traces at the edge of the embankment, and then he went over and did the same for the bloodstain where Sacks had knelt coughing. After that he ambled back to the Saab, whistling. He'd missed the *Anglais*, but the longhair had been a bonus that took some of the sting out of it.

As Daniel drove over the bridge, he slowed. There was nothing to see. Some boatman would probably find the car as he was passing over it, but by the time they'd dredged it out and found the boy Daniel would be far away.

Next time, *Anglais*.

Next time I'll be there ahead of you.

TWENTY-EIGHT

Jim and Rochelle had waited at Bellegarde as Roger had taken the train into Geneva, where he'd hired a car and returned to collect them. Showing Swiss plates, they'd been waved through without being stopped. Jim hadn't realised what they were doing until it was almost too late, and then he'd been forcefully argued-down by Rochelle. He'd have preferred to have been going in some other direction, *any* other direction than into the heart of the country where he felt he'd be least safe, but Rochelle had insisted that the only way ahead was to get him to the lawyers who were already in committed opposition to the company over claims relating to the April project. Once in their offices he could make a series of affidavits concerning his experiences and these, with the Oktober files as backup, would form a damning case against Risinger-Genoud. Werner Risinger might be able to keep himself out of prison, but Rochelle believed that international pressure would certainly get him off the board. The present management structure would start to fold, and the shareholders would panic. She and Roger could then take their case to Brussels, pointing to Werner Risinger's conduct and demanding the return of the Genoud assets.

Fine, said Jim, and he hoped that everything would work out for them, but his main concern was for his own immediate future.

They told him not to worry.

That evening, they booked into the Basle Hilton. The suite that they were given scored over the Brière farmhouse in a lot of ways; it had better carpets, fewer draughts, and room service. It also had Basle on the other side of its one-way mirrorglass windows, which meant that Jim was no longer inclined to go wandering out of doors alone. He stood nine floors up and looked down into the Aeschengraben, watching the city trams going by on their way into the main station square. People out there knew him, he couldn't say how many.

"I thought all the money had gone," he said to Rochelle a while later. A few of his stitches hadn't pulled out yet, and she was removing them for him with the aid of a pair of eyebrow tweezers and the blade of a ladies' razor. "How do we afford all this?"

"We don't," she said. She was being careful, not hurting him at all. "We charge everything, and then skip."

"I once tried that with some friends in a Chinese restaurant. I got chased by a chef with a cleaver."

"Then your attitude must have been all wrong."

That night he checked his back in the bedroom mirror, much as he'd done once before in a Flemish motel. The new scar was about three inches long, and neatly stitch-patterned like a zip. It was skin-sore, but that was all. Jim was in the smaller of the two bedrooms, while Rochelle and Roger shared the other; Jim thought this a little offbeat but, what the hell, they were family after all. Or maybe this was the same reason that made him feel uncomfortable. While Rochelle had been performing her minor surgery, Roger had been deep into a fan-file of printout that an office bureau had produced from the discs that afternoon. When breakfast time the next morning came around he was still engrossed, and Jim wondered if he'd taken any break at all during the night.

Breakfast arrived on a trolley, pushed by a small Egyptian bellhop in a shapeless blue-grey jacket. With him came a supervising assistant manager in his early twenties who was so charmed by Rochelle that he almost walked into a wall on his way out.

"Help yourself," she told Jim when the door had closed behind them. "We need you back in shape."

"I'm doing the best I can," Jim said. His stitches might be out, but he hardly felt ready to tackle pushups.

"It would help your credibility if you didn't look so much like a scarecrow. Why do you think we had to sneak you past the desk last night?"

"Sheer love of intrigue?"

"We've got all the intrigue we can handle," she said, lifting salver lids and looking underneath. "I'm going to ask the desk to call someone from a menswear shop to bring in a few samples. Try to show some taste, James. The way you're looking now, I wouldn't believe you if you told me the time."

He asked her, when were they going to make a move?

"Tomorrow," she told him. "Roger and I have a couple of things to get out of the way, first." And then, standing behind him, she touched his shoulder and said with a gentleness that he didn't fully understand, "Take a rest, James. You're going to earn it."

Later.

On his return to Basle, Peter Viveros had taken a lease on an apartment that was just outside the city in one of the upriver suburbs. If he'd been asked, he wouldn't have been able to say whether his new address was recorded in the Oktober file. It was his misfortune that it was.

Usually the drive home took no more than half an hour,

but on bad days this would double. Today had been one of the bad days, with the evening traffic backed-up and crawling slowly because of a spilled load of acid on an eastbound section of the ring road. His head was aching, partly because of the tension but mostly because of the fumes that had been drawn into the car as safety-suited policemen in breathing masks had waved him on past the cleanup zone. Cold air had helped, but half an hour on his back in a darkened room would help even more.

He pulled into his usual parking slot, and switched off the engine. He had a reserved place in the sheltered overhang of the apartment building, but he preferred to leave the car where he could see it from his second-floor window.

He sat for a moment, massaging his temples.

Linda McKay had stopped trying to contact him. He wasn't sure whether he was sorry or relieved. All that he knew for certain was that he wanted to get the lid back onto the pot of worms that the Oktober project had become and to cover his own tracks in getting away from it, preferably before the inevitable crap hit the waiting turbine. Doing this without arousing suspicion was no easy job, but so far he'd been managing it well enough.

He opened the door and got out.

"Excuse me," somebody called to him. "Do you know anything about cars?"

It was a woman's voice, too close for him to pretend that he hadn't heard. He turned to look for her, and she stepped out of the shadows of the overhang.

Half of his reluctance immediately disappeared. The other half still yearned for the darkened room. He said, "They either go, or they don't. That's about it."

"I can't get mine to start," she said helplessly, and Viveros realised that he was going to have to pretend to take a look. That was about as far as it would go, since the capsule summary of his mechanical knowledge that he'd already given her had been quite accurate. Cars either went, or they didn't. When they didn't, he called the garage.

Her car was in one of the residents' bays, nose-in to a

concrete wall. "How's the battery?" he said as they walked over toward it. She was close to him, and her perfume was in the air. He knew that it ought to make his heart race, but it only made his head worse.

"I didn't leave the lights on or anything," she said. "Do you live here? I haven't seen you before."

There was just enough interest in the way that she said it for Viveros to feel encouraged. "I only just moved in," he said. "I've been away for a while."

Her car was a compact red Fiesta, its bonnet already open. When he reached inside to try the ignition, he saw that there was a tag hanging from the rearview mirror. He said, "Isn't this a hire car?"

"I haven't had it more than a couple of days."

He tried the key. Nothing. "Well, if you call them, they should send you another."

"I can see sparks," she said suddenly, and so he had to go around and take a look.

"Where?"

"Down here," she said, pointing vaguely. "In with all these wires."

He leaned on the side of the car, wishing that they could have met when he was feeling fitter and in better conversational form, and also more able to follow up on any opportunities that may have developed as their contact went on. It didn't help to know that she'd probably remember him as a fumblenuts who had trouble concentrating on what was in front of him.

"Try it again," he suggested, hoping that he looked as if he knew what he was doing, and as she went around to get into the car he leaned forward so that he could watch for the sparks.

"I *have* seen you," she said, her voice muffled from the car's interior. "Aren't you with Risinger-Genoud?"

"How do you know that?" he said, but what was really puzzling him was the way that one of the terminal leads to the battery had been disconnected and laid to one side. He leaned in further for a closer look, which was how the sandbag that should have laid him out flat only stunned him and sent him sprawling against the side of the car.

212

His headache had vanished – in fact, he couldn't feel his head at all, just a split piece of rotten fruit that had taken its place on his shoulders. He tried to get up, and couldn't. Someone hauled him off the car and turned him around. He got a hazy image of a man and a woman – *the* woman – standing over him.

Get the pass, she said to the man, but her voice sounded as if she was calling from the far end of an empty swimming pool. *You barely grazed him.*

He moved, the man said defensively.

And you almost didn't. Check his jacket.

Everything was looking distorted and blown-out, as if it was being reflected in a hubcap. Viveros knew that it wasn't, because the Fiesta's wheel was against his back. The fault was all in this crummy surrogate head that he'd been given. The man leaned down toward him, filling his world from side to side. Viveros knew that he ought to struggle, so he tried. He wondered if he was having any success.

Apparently he wasn't, because the man was having no problem in going through his pockets. *He's bleeding*, the man said, and the girl said, *What did you expect?*

Bleeding. That meant he was hurt. He was lying there hurt, and they were robbing him. He couldn't fight, so he'd have to run.

Out in the parking lot, the porter would see him. All he had to manage was to get from the sheltered area into the open. Easy enough under normal circumstances, but not so easy when you were trying to think with a pumpkin full of maggots.

He tried to rise. The man pushed him back easily and carried on searching, but Viveros came bouncing up again with extra power and the man lost his balance and fell backwards. Viveros broke away, he was up and on his feet and the parking lot was straight ahead.

But there was some cruel trick, here. He was on slow time, and his best efforts wouldn't break him free. He saw the girl walk around in front of him. The air was thicker than honey, and he couldn't get through it. The sandbag was in her hand.

You're not flicking a towel, she explained to the man,

who was somewhere behind and out of sight. *It's got to be done hard, like this* . . . The sandbag became a blur.

Only a couple of minutes ago, Viveros had been looking forward to a darkened room.

Now Rochelle put him in one.

TWENTY-NINE

Jim listened to everything they told him. Roger didn't say much, but when his turn came he showed Jim the folded printout in its document case which he then zippered and handed over. Rochelle helped him on with his new jacket, and the three of them went down to the car.

This time, he didn't have to use the service elevator. With a haircut from the hotel barber and some decent clothes, Jim was probably looking more respectable than at any other time in his life. Nothing was paid for, but Rochelle could shoulder the guilt for that. Jim had to concentrate on the statement that he was going to be making to the lawyers.

And make it a good one, he told himself.

Rochelle had arranged everything. One of the partners would be expecting him, and him alone; there was to be no hint of duplicity, no reason to suspect this to be a company-sponsored ploy to discredit and undermine the April project opposition. Jim and the Oktober files were going to have to speak for themselves.

He and Rochelle waited in the air-conditioned hotel foyer, uneasy amongst the marble and chrome, as Roger went to get the car. All around them businessmen sat on low soft plastic lounge chairs and settees, reading newspapers and waiting for their contacts to show up. After a couple of minutes, Rochelle touched his arm. Their red Fiesta had drawn up outside, and they moved toward it. Rochelle seemed to be more tense than he was.

Jim kept his head down in the back of the car and Rochelle threw a rug over him, just in case. She sat turned halfway around in the passenger seat, keeping watch on the streets with her hand resting on him protectively. Jim lay gripping the leather folder as if it was going to save his life – which, in a sense, was exactly what it was going to do. He felt every turn they made, and after about ten minutes and a stop at some kind of automatic barrier he saw from under the rug that the inside of the car had suddenly gone dark. The car made another turn, and then started to descend.

When Jim was allowed to sit upright a minute later, he saw that they were in a long underground car park. Roger had stopped in a yellow zone before the elevators. He stayed behind the wheel as Rochelle and Jim got out.

"Fifth floor," Rochelle said, and then she kissed him quickly on the cheek. "Good luck."

She got back into the car, and Jim walked over to the elevator. The doors were open before he got there. He looked back, waved briefly, and stepped inside.

The doors closed. Jim touched the button for the fifth floor.

He couldn't help feeling that they'd gone over the top with their secrecy procedures; looking at his reflection in the dull steel of the elevator doors, he thought that he'd be pretty well unrecognisable from any description that Risinger-Genoud might have. Next time somebody wanted him to ride in the back of a car, he was going to ask for something bigger than a Fiesta. There were wool fibres on his blazer from the rug, and as he dusted them off he could feel that there was something in his top pocket that hadn't been there before.

He took it out.

It was a plastic card with some kind of metallic design printed on the back. He was still looking at it as he stepped out of the elevator onto the fifth floor.

A telephone rang in the Risinger-Genoud security complex. The duty guard picked up one of the receivers for the outside lines and said, "Security."

"I'm ringing about an employee of yours." The voice was a woman's, with no hesitation in it at all. "His name's Peter Viveros."

"I think you need to speak to the administrative section," the duty guard began patiently, but the woman cut across him.

"I need to speak to *you*," she said. "Somebody's stolen his pass, and they're using it right now. Check and see. And when Werner Risinger's had a chance to look at what's in the document case, tell him that his step daughter's ready to talk about a deal."

She hung up.

The duty guard sat back in his chair. They could always rely on two or three crank calls in a week when the moon was full, but this woman had known one of the direct-line numbers and also seemed to know what she was talking about. He swivelled his chair around to the nearest terminal, entered his personal code and requested a schedule on *Viveros, Peter*. The machine ran up two short columns of figures. The left-hand column showed times, and the right-hand column showed corresponding control points. Viveros, or whoever was carrying his card, had entered the car park under the administration block six minutes ago. Three minutes ago he'd taken the elevator up to the fifth, and he'd been scanned for clearance at each level along the way. By now he'd be in the fifth floor main corridor.

The duty guard sighed. They had a neat system, but a stolen pass was something that was hard to handle; and with such a large number of personnel, you were seeing strangers every day.

Two of his assistants were sitting on one of the desks at the back of the room, talking about a new club that one of them had found on the Freiestrasse. The duty guard stood up, and immediately had their attention.

"We've got a suspected intruder on level five of the main block," he said. "Seal the area, and we'll take the dogs in."

216

THIRTY

Jim was kept in the Lohnhof jail in the Leonhardskirch-platz for almost a week, and then he was moved in a windowless van to another prison that was a half-hour's drive out of the city. He spent a lot of the time lying on his bunk and staring at the ceiling. The cell was small and old, and it wasn't clean. The window was too high to reach and probably too grimy to see through, and the fluorescent light was kept on all through his first night. It was on the day after his move that someone from the British embassy in Berne came to see him.

The visitor introduced himself as Paul Phillips, junior attaché. He was around Jim's age, and he seemed to be suffering from a permanent cold. On the table of the interview room he laid out Jim's file, a notebook, and a box of Kleenex. He hadn't taken off his overcoat and scarf, as if he didn't expect to be staying long.

"Sorry it took so long to get around to you," he said, "but you got yourself picked up while we had three people on holiday. Have they given you a lawyer?"

"Public defender," Jim said. "I saw him for about ten minutes."

Phillips seemed gloomy. "They'll probably try to stick us for the bill. I hope you haven't got your hopes too high, because there's no way we can spring you from this."

"What's the charge?"

"Industrial espionage under article 162 of the Swiss penal code. I know it's not a criminal offence at home, but you picked the wrong country for it." He plucked a tissue out of the box, and honked into it like a seal. "Your only hope is that Risinger-Genoud will go lightly on you because of your – " here he paused, delicately – "because of your medical history. There's nothing official yet, but

217

we've heard that they may drop the charges if you'll agree to an open-ended hospital commitment." At this Phillips smiled and sat back, as if he'd just delivered the best present that Jim could have hoped for. "Who knows? You could be out in a year."

"I'd rather have a trial," Jim said.

Phillips left giving the impression that Jim was being decidedly unsporting, in his opinion, but he agreed to try to get hold of the magazines that Jim had asked for. When he'd gone Jim lay back on his bunk and stared at the ceiling again.

In most respects, the guards on his floor found him to be a model prisoner. Although uncommunicative he made no noise, he made no demands, and he didn't mess up his cell. He'd flinch when the door was closed on him in the evenings, but that was normal. He didn't seem to want anything to read other than the trade newspapers that the embassy sent over a couple of days after their attaché's visit, and even his interest in these waned after he'd found one particular item and torn it out. The wing supervisor went into his cell one morning during showers to read what Jim had pinned to the wall over his bunk; it was a short piece from the *Chemische Rundschau* announcing the appointments of M. Roger Genoud and Mlle. Rochelle Genoud as full members of the board of the Risinger-Genoud pharmaceutical company. It seemed innocent enough so the supervisor let it stay, but after a couple of days Jim took it down and threw it into his wastebin anyway.

His case didn't seem to be moving, with the reason being given as a delay in getting his medical records sent over from England. He had two more visits from the public defender's office, and during one of these the offer that had been outlined by Paul Phillips was formally put to him. He turned it down, and repeated his preference for a trial.

After a couple of weeks the wing supervisor lost interest in the odd Englishman, because he found that he had bigger problems on his hands.

They had to call in the medical officer because of a developing situation that seemed to be getting worse; it had started as a bad-dream epidemic on one floor but it had now spread to the block, and it seemed like something more than common prison hysteria. One or two of the inmates were beginning to scream as soon as the lights went out and more than a few were pacing their cells throughout the night in an effort to stay awake. They ruled out food poisoning, they ruled out toxins or bacteria in the water supply. Just one of those things, the medical officer shrugged and said, and that same night they had to transfer out a child molester who'd been so sick with night terrors that he'd thrown up and almost choked on it. As they lifted him out of his bunk onto a stretcher, one of the warders noted that his pyjama shirt was spotted red; he'd spontaneously begun to bleed from his left nipple like some stigmata-bearing statue in a Catholic shrine. For the rest of the night the block lights stayed on and there were regular checks on all of the cells. The Englishman, it was noted, showed no reaction to anything; he simply lay on his bunk with his hands locked behind his head and his eyes wide open, staring at the ceiling in the way that he always did.

On his twenty-third day in jail, word came through that the charges against him were being dropped. There would be no trial. He was to be deported.

His actual release wasn't processed until the next morning. He signed several sets of papers and was then taken to a dressing room, where his own clothes and his belongings – including his new radio and everything that he'd left behind at the Hilton – were returned to him. He dressed in a worn shirt, his old jeans and his freedom fighter's jacket.

"What about those?" the supervising warder said, indicating the expensive blazer and everything else that the salesman from *La Moda Volare* had picked out for Jim. He'd left it all heaped on a chair.

Jim looked at the officer. They were about the same size.

"Help yourself," he suggested.

From the dressing room he was taken down to an induction area, where a plainclothes detective was waiting for him. He was to be given a one-way ticket to Paris, courtesy of the state, and there he was to contact his embassy to find out about further arrangements for getting himself home. He wasn't to re-enter the country for a period of five years, and this ban could be extended without notice.

One more form to sign, and then they were walking down a parquet corridor that ended in a door to the outside. Jim had expected to feel something special when he stepped out into freedom, but he didn't. The light hurt his eyes for a minute, but that was all. The detective led him to a Subaru saloon with four-wheel drive, and the two of them got in. Five minutes later they were pulling into a parking lot below a small branchline railway station. The lot wasn't full, and young boys on bicycles were slaloming in and out between the standing cars. The detective checked once around his tyres for stones or broken glass, and then they set out across the lot toward the station ramp.

Jim said, "Do you have to come with me all the way to Paris?"

"No," the detective said, in a tone which suggested that he wouldn't have minded the trip. "But don't get any ideas. After here it's a straight run to the border without a stop."

The station buildings were at a level thirty feet above the road, and a part of the platform area ran out across a bridge where this same road passed underneath. When they reached the top of the ramp, the detective nodded to the man behind the ticket window and got a familiar wave in return. The platform was empty, as was the half-glassed waiting room that they went into.

The detective sat, and laid his attaché case on the seat beside him to open it. He glanced at the wall-clock and said, "Your train gets here in half an hour. Do you want a magazine?"

Jim looked down. The case was full of True Confessions magazines, along with a polythene sandwich-box and a small thermos.

"No thanks," he said, trying not to offend, and the detective shrugged and picked one out for himself. Jim moved to the window, and looked out across the platform and the tracks.

"Stay where I can see you," the detective warned, and then disappeared behind a cover splash of *ETs Ate My Baby*.

A local service pulled in. As Jim watched, about half a dozen people climbed down to the platform and immediately set out toward the exit. Nobody got on. Doors slammed, and the train started to move out again.

There was some kind of a disturbance; people were stepping aside as someone dodged between them. If she was hoping to catch the train, she was too late; the last carriage was passing and picking up speed as she reached the platform's edge.

She watched it go. Then, slowly, she turned to leave.

Their eyes met through the glass. Neither of them moved.

"Go on," the detective said from behind Jim. "You can talk. Just stay where I can see."

Jim let himself out of the waiting room. Linda, still breathless, was shivering slightly.

Jim said, "You want to go inside?" But she shook her head.

"I came to warn you," she said. "You scared them when you insisted on a trial. They've finally abandoned the project and erased all the files. I don't know what they're planning for sure, but I've heard rumours. If you get on that train, there's going to be some kind of accident before you get to Paris. You understand what I'm saying?"

"I understand," he said. "But why are you risking yourself again?"

"Oh, Jim," she said, and she shook her head slowly. And Jim looked away, embarrassed.

Linda said, "Is there just the one man? Can you lose him?"

"Looks like I'll have to." He thought it over for a moment. "Were those kids on bikes still messing around in the car park?"

"I saw somebody chase them off, but they came back."

Jim glanced down the platform. A bell was ringing somewhere, and the railwayman was on his way back to his

221

office. "There's a Japanese car, green with a vinyl roof. Give them some money to smash the windscreen, and make sure that somebody up here knows about it."

"They'll never do it."

"For you, they'll do it. While all that's going on, get in your own car – you're in a car?"

She nodded, nervously.

"Drive around to where the road goes under the track bridge, and wait. I'll be there as soon as I can. Now say goodbye, and make it look final."

They both hesitated and then they shook hands, awkwardly. A moment later the handshake had become a hard, loving hug that neither of them wanted to break. He rocked Linda, and told her that everything was going to be fine. She walked away without looking back, and Jim returned to the waiting room. The detective looked up as he stepped inside.

"Thanks," Jim said, and he sat on one of the contoured plastic seats and looked suitably despondent. The detective turned a page and started to read another True Confession.

It was a couple of minutes later when Jim heard a sound like a far-off shower of hail, with a distinct splat of breaking glass. The detective didn't even look up, but stayed with *My Brother, The Rapist*. He probably hadn't noticed. Jim folded his arms, and tried not to squirm as he waited for something to happen.

There was a long delay before the stationmaster appeared, long enough for Jim to start worrying that his train might arrive first. The detective glanced at the wall-clock a couple of times, and he was putting his magazine away when the stationmaster rapped on the waiting-room window. Mention of his car had the detective to the door in a moment.

"Wait here," he said to Jim, and rushed off to look at the damage.

Jim stood in the open doorway, waiting until the detective was out of sight. Then he grabbed the carrier bag with his few possessions in it, went back out onto the platform, and ran alongside the track to where the road passed underneath. The wall wasn't much more than waist-high, and when Jim looked over he saw a white Opel emerging from under the bridge and slowing to a halt. There was a steep embankment to the side; a few yards further on he'd be able to drop from the wall and scramble down the slope to the road.

Linda had opened the passenger door when he got there, scratched and panting and with his hands splashed with mud. He jumped in; the car was already moving as he closed the door.

"I only asked for the windscreen," Linda said, "but they textured the whole car."

"Please," Jim said. "I'm feeling mean enough as it is. Anyone following?"

Linda checked the mirror. "Doesn't seem to be."

Jim turned around to take a look, but there was only a yellow car some way back.

Linda said, "Any ideas on where we head from here?"

"Make for the Oberland," Jim said, facing front again. "I'll be able to say better when I've seen something I can recognise."

Linda was blank. "What's in the Oberland?"

"Memories," Jim said.

THIRTY-ONE

A couple of hours later they were in the uplands south of Berne, driving slowly through a lakeside resort at the lower end of a mountain railway. It was still some weeks from the start of the winter season, and Jim said he could remember that when he'd last been here the town's roofs had been weighted with snow and horse-drawn *fiacres* had carried tourists down the cleared esplanade. For now the big hotels like the Beaurivage and the Hôtel de l'Europe were all closed, their wide approaches chained and their shutters down. The valley sides towered overhead, making darkness in daylight. They saw no more than a handful of people from one end of the resort to the other.

He'd told her that Terry Sacks was dead, and how it had happened. But he hadn't told her how he'd come to know.

She glanced at him anxiously, remembering what Peter Viveros had told her. Viveros had avoided her for several days after their one-and-only meeting, and after that he seemed to have dropped out of sight altogether. Jim was looking better than he had when she'd first known him, but there was also a certain distance that she hadn't sensed before. He had the look of someone who'd glimpsed a place that there was no language to describe and she wondered, again, if there might be some shade of truth in what Viveros had said.

She wanted to ask him, straight out. But she didn't know how.

The mountain railway's lower terminus was out at the far end of the town, in a part of the valley beyond the hotels and tearooms where old-style wooden chalets stood isolated in acres of fertile green. The parking lot was no more than a gravelled piece of ground enclosed by a rail fence. Linda pulled in alongside a high-sided Mercedes truck, and switched off the engine. In the stillness without traffic, they could hear the sound of cowbells echoing down from the slopes.

The terminus itself was housed in a tunnel dug straight into the valley side, with the steeply-angled cogwheel track climbing out through the roof at its far end. There was maintenance work going on in the tunnel, and its entrance was almost blocked by scaffolding and a yellow mechanical digger that had been crowded like dinosaur bones into a museum. They followed a striplit walkway around the working area to a platform. The ticket booth was closed, obscured by a temporary mess of planking and cable, but there were people already on the train. Jim and Linda walked through an open turnstile and climbed aboard.

The carriage was built to the angle of the track, its aisle a narrow flight of steps and its seating steeply raked. There were five people already on board apart from the driver-conductor who sold them tickets; three of these were railway workmen and the other two appeared to be farmers, sitting close to a luggage section where they'd secured some hessian sacks and a brand-new galvanised wheelbarrow. Jim and Linda sat on the upper level, away from everybody. A few more people came aboard, heard rather than seen, and then the conductor climbed past on his way to becoming their driver.

Finally Linda said, "Do I get to find out where we're going?"

"The sled dog centre," Jim said.

"But they closed it down."

"That's what I heard." A buzzer sounded, the automatic doors closed, and after a moment the train gave a jerk and then began its slow, steady ascent into daylight. "But if the company's scrapped the project and wiped all the records, then this place may be the only leverage that's left. Rochelle thinks I still don't remember where it is or what happened there, but she's wrong. I'd like to see them get stung over this, but I'll settle for survival."

"What do you count as leverage?"

"One of the corrupt pack samples. Anything. I can't beat them, I realise that now. But maybe I can work out some kind of a truce with Rochelle."

Linda said, "It may be too late, even for that."

Jim looked out of the window. "I know it," he said.

The town and the lake were dropping away as the ratchet-drive hauled them upward. They were going where no roads could lead, although there were some farm and forest tracks that could probably be managed with a lot of patience and a four-wheel drive. After a while they emerged from the valley's shadow and into unexpected sunlight, and alongside the track there began to appear sheltered pockets of snow that had been trapped and preserved in the least-exposed hollows.

"What made you remember, in the end?" she said; and as Jim looked out of the window and tried to frame his answer, their train slowed and the darkness of two hundred yards of rock-hewn tunnel closed over them.

It wouldn't be far, now.

He told her some vague stuff about when Risinger-Genoud security had loosed their dogs to run him down. They'd backed him into a corner and he'd been scared enough almost to claw his way up to hang from the ceiling, and the notion of such a shock releasing suppressed memories seemed almost plausible in a Tom-and-Jerry kind of a way; at least, she didn't question it. But it was less than the truth.

The truth was something that he'd had to find on his own, out there in the nightmare country. Having nothing left to lose had made him bolder, and a little less resistant to its call; but now he wasn't too sure whether he'd been allowed to enter for that one brief moment, or whether he'd allowed the dark territory to enter him. He'd opened his eyes after that tentative experiment to find himself surrounded by the most profound night terrors echoing from the other cells, and for the first time he'd understood a little of the power that came with the key that he'd held.

Never again, he'd told himself.

Safety lights had been strung in the tunnel, showing tarpaulin-covered fresh casting and a line of tools neatly stacked against its inside wall. Brakes came on, and the train stopped with its nose out into the open air for as long as it took the three workmen to climb down to the trackbed and stand clear. Linda's view was blocked by the one of the open avalanche doors at the tunnel's mouth, but within moments they were moving out into the light again and she could see the slopes ahead. The track went onward and upward in a long curve over ground that was patched with snow.

"It's about another half-mile," Jim said.

And as he'd predicted, half a mile further on they were climbing past an isolated complex standing some way back from the line. Linda saw two linked concrete chalets backed by the immense snowfield of a glacier-filled basin, their windows so tiny that they might have been poked-in by skewers. Dog runs to the side were empty and there were no lights, no signs of any life at all. As the train came out of its passing curve and into the straight that would lead on up to the next resort village on the line, a last look down on the centre showed that the ground behind it had been strewn with rotting garbage.

There was a scent of woodsmoke drifting across the resort as they walked along its empty main street. Being so close to the glacier they were well above the snowline now, but it would be a month or more before the falls would be deep enough or even enough to make the *pistes* worthwhile. The tackle shops were closed, the gift counters had been cleared, and there were covers over the café terraces.

Linda said, "What do you want to do now?"

"I'm going down there," he said. "But I want you to wait around near a phone." He quickly held up a hand as she started to protest. "Think about it, Linda. If they've left somebody to watch over the place and I get caught, and there's nobody on the outside who even knows, then that's it. Getting snuffed and quietly buried somewhere is the least unpleasant thing that these people are likely to do to me."

"Who would I call, if you didn't come back?"

"The local police. They don't exactly count as allies, but I *did* jump custody so they're bound to take an interest."

She didn't like it, but she knew that he was right.

Managing a smile she said, "I want you back in one piece, now."

"I'll do my best to arrange it," he promised.

The village's main street ended at a cablecar station which would link onward via a couple of lesser peaks to more runs and a mountaintop restaurant. In the shadow of the station they found the resort's only open tearooms, getting by on local trade and the occasional lost tourist. There was a pay phone just inside the doorway on a glassed-in terrace, and it was from a table by this that Linda watched Jim as he was walking away.

The owner's thirteen year-old daughter came to take her order, and when Linda looked again Jim was no longer in sight.

This was going to be the longest wait of her life.

She unwound her scarf and dropped it on the table alongside her gloves. The terrace was heated but there was a vein of cold deep inside her that wouldn't break up until

227

Jim came back, with or without his 'leverage'. She didn't really feel able to make an honest guess at his chances, here. No matter how damning the concrete evidence, a multinational outfit like Risinger-Genoud would tend to be able to limit and contain any damage. A few heads might roll, the wrong people might shoulder some blame, shareholdings might take a short-term dip; but in any real sense, the long-term effects would be zero.

Nor had she given much thought to her own prospects. She'd been getting along for the past few weeks, treading water and somehow managing to keep her sympathies to herself, but she knew that it couldn't last. She had some money saved, but it wasn't much. She'd thought about the possibility of the two of them simply dropping out of sight, changing their names and staying low in some backwater like the coastal town where they'd first met. It would be good for a while, but for how long after that?

New beginnings. It was supposed to be an encouraging thought, but it made her stomach turn with apprehension.

She glanced around some of the other tables. At the back of the terrace, two old men were sitting in an easy silence. Closer to the door, a lone lost tourist was studying a fold-out map through reading glasses. He happened to look up, and their eyes met for a moment.

It was all the excuse that he needed. "Excuse me," he said, bundling up his map and sliding out of the seat so that he could bring both the map and his difficulties over to her. "We were on the same train coming up. Is it always as quiet as this?"

Linda tried to smile, although she wasn't really feeling sociable. "They tell me it livens up in the season."

"Only," he persisted with a kind of deferential eagerness, "I was told that this was a place to see movie stars."

"You'd be better off in Gstaad."

"I tried Gstaad. Nobody there, either."

"Or Wengen," she suggested. "I know someone who saw Robert Redford at Wengen."

His face seemed to light up with discovery behind his glasses. "I didn't know that," He indicated the unoccupied chair at her table. "May I . . .?" he began, and Linda had no choice other than to complete the invitation with a gesture.

Drat my luck, she thought wearily.

He put down his map, and sat searching through his pockets for a scrap of paper and a pen. She thought that he seemed a bit old to be a star-spotter, in his late forties at least, but you could never tell. He was wearing a ski jacket unzipped over a three-colour sweatshirt, but he had a homely peasant's face with hair cropped so close that it was almost bristle. By his accent he was probably from somewhere around Marseille, but Linda couldn't be sure. Wherever he was from, she seemed to be stuck with him.

"I'm grateful to you," he said as he made a careful note. "This is my hobby."

"You collect autographs?"

"Oh, no. I couldn't ask." He stowed the paper and the pen back in one of his pockets, and took off the reading glasses. "I just like to go to the places and maybe see the stars. Last year I saw Jagger in Paris. Monaco used to be a good place, until they lost the Princess."

Linda told herself not to be so mean. After all she had nowhere else to go, and she thought that it must take a special kind of loneliness to get such a kick out of other people's highlife.

"I'm sorry," he said. "I'm annoying you."

Linda realised that she'd been staring out of the window at the spot where Jim had disappeared. "You're not annoying me," she insisted, feeling guilty because he'd only perceived the truth.

"I never thought. I'll go back to my own table."

"I told you, you're not annoying me. I just have to watch for my friend coming back."

He accepted with a smile and a shrug, and sat down again. He started to re-fold his map, properly this time. It was a glossy giveaway brochure from the railway company showing all of the area's train, cablecar and skilift routes against a relief painting of the mountains.

He said, "I was really disappointed about Gstaad. Peter Sellers lives there."

"Peter Sellers is dead," Linda said.

He looked up, and something seemed to drop away from behind his eyes. They glittered, as dead and as empty of human feeling as those of a fish on a slab.

"Yes, of course," he said.

Jim's first call was to the now-deserted railhead. Maintenance men had left tools and supplies in its shelter, and he was able to help himself to a day-glo jerkin and a shovel. With these as a disguise, he reckoned that he could probably get most of the way down to the research centre without his approach causing any kind of suspicion. All he had to do was to follow the trackbed, and look as if he had a right to be there.

The voice inside told him to turn back. It was getting harder to ignore.

The ground was springy, and the snowcover thin and uneven. In most places it was no more than a crust, and it made brittle sounds as Jim descended in the high-mountain silence. Some way ahead on the wide open slope, the track began the curve that would take it down and around by the centre. Beyond that was the unbroken white of the glacier, and beyond the glacier was a backdrop of towering peaks that were as hard and as bright as diamonds in the afternoon sun.

One time he slipped, and nearly fell. He'd been letting his mind wander, lulled by the rhythm of the descent. When he tried to recall what he'd been thinking about, he couldn't. For the last quarter-mile he moved the shovel across to his other shoulder and kept his head down. If there *was* a watcher in the centre, he didn't want to make it easy for them to recognise him.

The entire distance took him half an hour to cover.

An iron stairway led down from the track to the buildings. Snow was inch-thick and undisturbed on the handrail and on the treads. He rammed his shovel into the ground by the rail ties, and he hung the jerkin over its handle. He descended the stairway quickly, and in silence.

He'd made this approach once before, more than a year ago. Here were three doors exactly as he remembered them, the nearest leading into the tackle room. This was the way that he'd come on the day that he'd wrenched his shoulder, out on the ice.

There had been how many – seven of them? And not one of the others had even cared to remember his name. They'd been calling him *Anglais* or *teacher* all week, when they'd spoken to him at all. Rochelle's friends had included one German prince, a brewing heiress, and a chinless French kid whose father designed racing car engines; his name was Claude and he looked like Alfred E Neuman out of *Mad* magazine. Jim's credentials for being there at all were that he'd been invited over to stay with the family in order to give the junior Risinger some much-needed language practice, but the junior Risinger had opted to spend the vacation cataloguing his staggeringly comprehensive collection of pornography. The junior Risinger was fifteen years old.

Jim had been out of it from the start. They didn't mind him, they just didn't include him. It was easy to believe that they could leave for home at the end of the day and not even notice that he was no longer with them. Claude might have looked like a grade-A prize dick, but the difference between them was that Claude was on the inside and Jim Harper wasn't. During the long walk back across the glacier he'd become wise to a simple fact, that he'd been no more than a bit player in their drama while imagining that he was the star of his own.

It had really been little Risinger's fault, the brat. Why couldn't his rich sister have been born ugly?

Now he stood before the tackle room door. There was garbage here, beer cans and papers and rotting food, most of it in unsecured trash bags that had fallen or been blown over so that the contents had scattered. The bags didn't even appear to have been stacked, just slung out of the doors as far as they'd go and with nobody caring if they split where they landed.

This wasn't promising.

The doors were all locked. Jim put his ear to each, but he heard nothing. After that he took a cautious peek through some of the unshuttered windows around the side, but he saw only empty rooms. By the time that he was climbing the outside stairs to the terrace, he was already more or less convinced; the centre was deserted, and a look into the common-room confirmed it. Nobody would live in such a mess. It seemed as if someone had been throwing furniture around, and there was a litter of opened cans and broken glass on the floor.

There was no point in being furtive, not now. He went back to get his shovel so that he could break open a door.

The smell hit him as soon as he stepped inside. It would make a monkey-house seem like a perfumery, bad meat and shit and ammonia all stirred together and left to get old. It faded a little after the first impact, but for a moment Jim wondered if he could face going any further. He didn't hesitate for long, because he knew that he didn't really have any choice.

Jesus, it was getting worse. It was worst of all in the lower-level passageway that led past the treatment rooms to the dog pens, but by then Jim was hardly noticing. He was remembering the tiled walls of the corridor with its glass bricks for windows; remembering how they'd rushed him through, a dozen hands making him weightless as he struggled to scream out in a body that was like a dead cage.

He had to pause for a minute before one of the treatment room doors. At least it wasn't *the* door, the one he always saw in his nightmares; he'd expected that it might be, but it wasn't. He took a deep breath and went in.

This wasn't the one where they'd laid him out, but it was similar. The operating table was smaller and there was a lot more lab equipment. If they hadn't stripped out all the gear yet, then he might still have a chance of finding something. His 'leverage'.

What a joke. He wasn't going to find a damn thing, and he knew it. So what had he really come here to face?

But when he crossed the room for a better look at the pharmacy cupboard, he felt hope beginning to stir again. The cupboard doors had glass panels, but the glass was frosted and reinforced with wire. Through it he could see the blurred outlines of orange-labelled boxes.

He bent closer, trying to make out the lettering on one of the packs.

"I was wondering what you were after," Bruno said from the doorway.

THIRTY-TWO

Jim turned so fast that he almost lost his balance.

Bruno came into the treatment room, the electric prod in his hand. "Remember me?" he said pleasantly. "Because if you do, you'll remember this." And then he tapped the prod against the outer rail of the operating table. It made a blue spark, and a sound like a gunshot. "They make them for riot police," Bruno went on, looking at the prod as if it were a favourite toy. "Four thousand volts, but a low current. Except that I've juiced this one a bit, so the current isn't so low. Want to try it again?"

Bruno stood there with an expression of polite enquiry. He looked as if he hadn't changed his clothes or washed in more than a month; something had spilled all the way down his pullover and his pants, and he'd let it dry. His eyes were shining, as if there was nothing but a little bulb and a lot of empty space behind them.

Jim said, "No, thanks."

Bruno nodded. "If you change your mind, just try a smart move. I'll be pleased to oblige." He put a hand on the operating table, and leaned forward as if getting ready to tell a secret. "You know," he said, "I've been hoping that you'd come back. I was doing okay here until you came along."

"That makes two of us."

"Now I'm just supposed to clean shit and feed the animals and hope that someday the company will get around to forgiving me. I'm really glad you came. Let's move."

They went out into the corridor. Bruno stayed beyond reach, and he also made sure that he stayed between Jim and the way out. Jim had once had a taste of the prod and Bruno knew that he wouldn't want another, and this made him controllable. It was a simple enough principle, but it was enough to drive Jim toward the dog pens.

Jim had another reason for backing away. The stink of the untended dogs was bad enough, but the stink of Bruno was worse. The man was unhinged. One of his wrists was bandaged, and he hadn't even tried to keep the dressing clean; it was soaked from the inside out, and the wound underneath was probably infected. Stabbing and waving with the prod, he ushered Jim through the open door and into the low passageway alongside the pens.

The silence in the centre ended as soon as the dogs got sight of Bruno.

They were weakened, but it seemed that as far as Bruno was concerned they'd always have rage to spare. Bruno smiled, happily soaking up their hatred. When their energy had started to run itself down a little – it didn't take long – he said, "I thought I'd keep you in here for a while. Like the company?"

"When did you last feed them?"

"You know, I've lost track since the freezer broke. The stuff in there was bad enough even before it started to get high, which is something you've probably noticed. Wait a minute, I tell a lie. I gave them some rotten apples about two, three weeks back. That was a hell of a fight to see, fur and skin everywhere. They're going to love you."

He indicated for Jim to move on. As he moved, Jim noticed that in the second pen all of the dogs were lying dead. He tried to tell himself that his phobia was beaten, that he'd found its cause and there was no longer any reason for him to get irrationally scared. Except that there was nothing irrational about being scared to enter one of these pens; the huskies, normally so even-tempered and friendly, had been pushed to the edge and beyond. He'd be safer in a bear pit.

Bruno stopped by one of the doors, and ran a trail of lightning across the wire. The dogs inside fell over one another to get away, and Bruno unhooked the hasp and opened the door. "This one's the Siberian's pen," he said, and made a gesture of invitation.

Jim got as far as the open doorway, but he couldn't bring himself to step forward. One animal in the pen was dead, lying untouched on a shelf even though the others appeared to be starving; their fur was too long for their ribs to be showing, but their legs were like sticks and their eyes were like beads. They were all together at the far end of the stall, and all of them were staring at him. The Siberian was in the middle, smaller than the others but no less intent.

"Don't get shy, now," Bruno said, and he tapped Jim on the back with the prod.

There was a bang, and the next thing that Jim knew was that he was lying upside-down against the back wall of the pen. He felt as if he'd been punched hard in a kidney. The dogs had scattered, and now most of them were over on one of the other shelves. As Jim's vision cleared, he could see that Bruno had closed the door on him. His face appeared at the wire.

"Just one more thing," he said, "in case you get any ideas about letting yourself loose," and he held up an open padlock for Jim to see. He kept on talking as he moved out of sight, and Jim heard the sounds of the padlock being fixed on the door. "There's a clearup job that I should have seen to months ago. If I'd known you were likely to be turning up again, I wouldn't have put it off for so long. I'll call back when I'm done, just to see how things are going." His face reappeared for a moment. "They seem pretty quiet right now, but don't worry. I can always give them some encouragement."

Bruno left, whistling. The attention of the dogs turned around again and fixed on Jim.

Slowly, he drew his knees up toward his chest. He wondered how weakened the dogs were, knowing that if they'd been healthy and well fed he wouldn't have been able to fight one of them off. He wasn't even sure of his chances now. The dogs stared, not moving.

Was there any way out, other than the door? If there was, Jim couldn't see it. There was a hatch in the door itself, but it could only be raised from outside in the passageway. The walls were of inch-thick timber and the wire in the look-through was of a heavy gauge.

The Siberian jumped down to the concrete.

It didn't approach Jim, but instead it began pawing at the door. It looked at him once, and then started pawing again. It obviously expected him to let them out.

"I can't," he said.

The dog looked at him again, weighing up how best to get its message over. It pawed, pushed at the door with its nose, pawed again with more urgency.

Jim knew that he must be seeming unbelievably obtuse, but there was nothing he could do. At least the dogs didn't mean him harm – not yet, anyway – although if it had been Bruno sitting here, Jim knew that the situation would have been different.

The Siberian came across the floor. He flinched back, but he was already as far up against the wall as he could get. The dog came around by his side and nudged at his hand with her nose.

For a second, Jim's world exploded.

He knew what it was as soon as it had happened; that brief, almost devastating first spark of contact with another intelligence that had been devoured and irreversibly altered by EPL, damaged so vastly that it had then re-integrated into something almost alien to what it was before.

And it was more; it was a lonely mirror in which he saw his own, scared eyes staring back at him.

The Siberian was waiting patiently. Jim got up, feeling stiff and bruised from his fall. He knew now what they wanted. For a moment he had a strange sensation, as if his bones were put together wrong and his skin was an uncomfortable suit zipped tight over wet fur, but the feeling passed. The Siberian followed him to the door.

He looked more closely at the feeding hatch in the middle of the panel. A determined and undernourished dog could probably just about get through it. He pushed, but there was no more than about a quarter of an inch of give. Bruno had reinforced the catch with several loops of wire. It meant that the panel couldn't be put to its normal use, but that was hardly likely to be a worry to Bruno.

The Siberian moved back as Jim sat on the concrete and raised both feet to kick at the panel. He couldn't hope to break a padlock, but the wire started to unwind on the third kick and the hatch burst outward on the sixth.

The Siberian was the first through. She glanced back at Jim once before scrambling out into the corridor. The dog's eyes were blue, shading almost into violet.

Now the Greenlanders were lining up to follow. They were silent, patient, organised, moving with a single mind. He almost shuddered as he watched them squeezing through, knowing that the others would be waiting outside in the passageway until the team was assembled. He shuddered because he knew what would be coming next.

The hatch wasn't quite wide enough for Jim to do the same, but he could see across to a makeshift-looking shelf unit against the far wall of the passageway where Bruno had tossed the padlock key amongst some dried-out ointments and antiseptics. Jim tried to reach it, but the shelf was too high. But then he managed to rock the unit until it began to topple; it came crashing down against the door and emptied all of the shelf's contents within reach.

Bruno was in the treatment room. They'd told him – what had they told him? He stood by the operating table with his hand to his head and his mind in a racing panic, suddenly overcharged and almost incapable after the long, deadly months where time had slowed to a crawl and simply ambling over to the washbasin to take a pee had become a major decision of the day. They'd told him – it was something to do with the Englishman. Something to do with covering tracks and destruction of the evidence.

Now he had it.

He went over to the pharmacy cupboard, opened it wide, and started raking the contents of the shelves out so that they fell into the work surface below. Then, using the crook of his arm, he swept them along the countertop to the laboratory sink at its end, and when all of the phials and bottles and boxes were in a heap together he doubled up his fists and started to pound them down into a mush of cardboard and liquid and powder and glass. His hands started to bleed freely and so he ran cold water to wash the blood away, and then he went back to the next cupboard along and began to repeat the procedure.

This time he stopped, puzzled. Were his hands supposed to hurt like this? Was he doing it wrong?

What *was* it they'd told him, again?

Something roughly the size and weight of a wardrobe hit him in the back as he stood wondering. His face was driven forward into the glass of the half-open pharmacy cupboard door; and then, as the weight of the Greenlander on his shoulders bore him down with his eyes full of shards, he clipped his chin on the edge of the counter and seemed to lose all power so that his grab to reach out and catch himself came to nothing.

Time seemed to slow down again.

They had a hold of him all over now, and they dragged him out into the middle of the floor; the Greenlander was still on his shoulders and another of them had bitten clean through the web of his hand and was shaking it like a rag. The Greenlander seemed to be messing around at the back of his neck, mouthing him gently but not biting, but then with a hot, bowel-emptying spasm of terror Bruno realised the dog's intentions just as its jaws closed with steam-hammer precision and its teeth slid like knives between his cervical vertebrae and severed his spinal cord.

His body became a dead thing, but his mind lived on. He had limited, bloody vision in his left eye, and he could see the meat and the skin as it started to fly.

Someone was screaming like a baby. He wondered who it might be.

What was it they'd told him?

It was as he was picking out the key that Jim heard Bruno beginning to scream.

It went on as he fumbled the key up into the padlock, and the noise was still going on as he made several unsuccessful attempts to turn it. He'd had to put his wrist at an angle which made it so that he couldn't get any leverage, but he took a moment's rest and then tried again. Bruno was still screaming as Jim got the padlock undone, but he'd stopped by the time that Jim had opened the door.

The dogs were leaving the treatment room as Jim arrived. They came out in neat order, blood-flecked and satisfied, and he stepped aside to let them pass.

He tried not to look at Bruno, but it wasn't easy. Pieces of Bruno were everywhere. The tiles were splashed red, and there was hair and skin all over the floor. The prod was where Bruno had left it, on the end of the operating table; he wouldn't have been able to reach it from the sink when the dogs had made their attack, and without it his power over them was gone.

The taps were still running. Jim stayed long enough to make sure of what he'd suspected, and then he got out. He'd had as much as he could take. He squatted against the wall in the corridor outside, and tried to breathe deeply so that he wouldn't throw up.

Bruno had gone straight to the pharmacy cupboard and taken out everything, not just the few remaining Epheteline packs but every other Risinger-Genoud preparation as well. He'd smashed them down and broken every phial into the sink, washing the potent cocktail away in running water. There wasn't a single sample of anything left, just broken glass and empty boxes.

Wearily, Jim got to his feet and went to find the dogs some other food.

Micheline was reading over the draft outline for her final report when the scratching began. *Temple rats*, she thought, and she couldn't help giving a nervous shudder. She'd scared up two of them as she'd walked through the herb garden only a few days before. They'd been fat and sleek and faster than whips, and they'd disappeared into the underpinnings of the building. She'd dreamed about them twice already.

The outline covered no more than two sheets of lined paper. The message to pull out had reached her late, and it had been phrased in such ambiguous terms that she'd had to read between the lines to gather that the Oktober project was to be abandoned altogether. Why, she couldn't guess. It could be a change of policy at top level, or perhaps the venture had been compromised in some way. She couldn't say that she was sorry. In all her time here, and for all her observations, she'd got exactly nowhere. It was going to be difficult to pad out the report to look like anything at all.

She heard the scratching again. It was coming from the door.

When she opened it, Do Minh was standing there. His boy wasn't with him; he must have been picking at the door with his claws for more than a minute, trying to get her attention.

"Come, now," he said urgently, and he said nothing more.

She started to hear the sounds before they were even halfway to the EPL ward. Bedding mats had been unrolled and pitched by the walls all the way along the corridors, but hardly anyone was sleeping. Frightened faces looked up from the shadows on either side as Do Minh and Micheline hurried by, heading for the source.

Walking through the door was like hitting a wall of noise. Micheline stopped, wincing at the sudden sharp pain of it. The blind orderly didn't seem to be around, and some of the subjects were out of their beds.

Some hadn't moved because they were strapped in, and others had tried to move but had fallen. Their muscles were too wasted, their tendons too shortened. They simply lay in twisted poses on the floor by their beds, and joined in as well as they could.

A small number had done better. They were grouped down at the far end of the ward, as bent and as gnarled and as dried-out as mummies. They'd gathered around something, a messy-looking heap on the floor. Do Minh stopped, and Micheline went on alone.

The heap seemed to be rags and bones and greasy red leather. Micheline slowed, and then she knew. She didn't dare to get any closer. The heap was the orderly.

One of them turned to face her, steadying himself on his knuckles and jerking around without grace. His dead eyes seemed to be lit by a borrowed fire, his movements controlled by an unpractised master. It was her number four subject, her prize.

He drew breath, and then joined in with the others. His voice added a new harmonic to their song.

Crouched over their kill, they howled like wolves.

Only the orderly couldn't hear.

"I was with a lady," he said to the café-owner's daughter. "Where did she go?"

The girl glanced around, nervously. "She left about half an hour ago," she said. "With the French gentleman."

"What French gentleman?"

"Another tourist. They talked for a while and then left together."

"Which way?"

"Towards the railway."

As he headed for the station, Jim tried to tell himself that there was nothing to worry about. Linda must have gone along to meet him, not realising that for the last half-mile he'd cut across-country to climb at a steeper angle to the village. The Frenchman had to be a tourist as the girl had said. He couldn't be anything more.

The odd little mountain train was just pulling out as he reached the station. Jim's foot caught as he scrambled over the barrier and he nearly pitched forward but it was too late anyway, the train was clear of the stepped platform and already gathering speed in its descent.

What now? There was no other way down, and he was out of ideas.

"Over here, Jim," Linda said.

She was coming down from the top of the platform, and she was alone. The sound of the train was already growing so faint that it was being lost in the still air of the upper slopes.

"Sorry if I worried you," she said. "This overgrown star-spotter attached himself to me and I couldn't shake him off. I had to pretend that I was going to meet you down in the valley so that I could get him onto the train, and then I made a quick excuse and hopped out through the doors as they were closing. I felt mean, but he was like a limpet."

"You're sure he was just a tourist?"

She took his arm. "Absolutely. But weird, you know, uncomfortable to be around. If I was a cat I'd have stiff fur from one end to the other. You didn't find anything."

That was it, the answer to the question that she'd been talking around and trying to avoid asking.

"No," he said. "Nothing I can use, anyway."

"Oh, Jim." She gave his arm a squeeze.

"They're going to get away with it," he said. "They rolled right over me and I've got no comeback. I'll have to spend the rest of my life with my head well down, trying not to be noticed.'

"We'll think of something."

"I wouldn't like to bet on it," Jim said.

Then they went to find somewhere else to wait out the hour that it would take for their train to return.

THIRTY-THREE

Linda took him back to Basle and her apartment, mostly because they had nowhere else left to go. As the scenery outside the car changed from mountains to autoroute to city outskirts, she'd glance at Jim to check on his mood; he'd slumped low in the passenger seat as if someone had let some of the air out of him, and he hardly spoke. Most of the time he seemed to be staring either at the dash or at the rubber flooring between his feet. He didn't even seem to notice when she pulled in under the trees on the riverside lane outside her building, and she had to say his name twice after stopping the engine before he came out of it.

"Home," she said. "For a while, anyway. Until we decide how we take it from here."

He looked around him like someone coming out of a deep sleep. The riverfront block was modern-looking and the cars along the lane on either side of them all seemed to be Jaguars or Mercedes or top-of-the range Scandinavian models.

He said, "This is where you live?" And he didn't sound as if he quite believed it.

"For the moment," she said, "but I don't expect it to last. It was a reward for services not-yet-rendered."

They saw nobody on the way up, which was a relief. She'd no idea whether there were any other Risinger-Genoud employees amongst the residents, and at the moment Jim was a conspicuous sight after his tumble in the dog pens. Once inside, she put the chain on the door.

Jim stood out in the middle of the lounge, carrier-bag at his side. It wasn't a big room, but it was an almost empty one. A dining alcove led through to a designer-fitted kitchen, while on the other side two steps led up to the bedrooms and bathroom. Even with her pictures on the walls, still the place looked as if it was waiting for someone to move in.

She went over to him. "Oh, Jim," she said for the second time that day. "What are we going to do?"

"I don't know, Linda," he said. "I honestly don't know. They've taken everything. It feels like the end of the line."

She turned his face to her own, and looked him in the eyes. "Come on," she said. "They used us both, but we're still walking and breathing. I've got a few ideas."

"Like what?"

"Lawyers, affidavits, the press. We may not be able to beat the company, but at least we should protect ourselves."

"It goes beyond that," Jim said. "I've been losing my grip. I can't even trust what I see and hear any more. All the time when I was in jail . . . it's like the boundaries have gone and I just wander in and out. It even happened up in the dog pens. It's getting so I don't know what's the real world and what isn't. I don't even know that it's safe for you to be with me."

She brushed a fleck of old straw from his cheek. "I'll take my chances," she said.

"No," he said, "you don't understand. What I mean is that it doesn't just involve me any more. I could hear them

243

in the other cells, they were starting to see it too. It's like heat. I'm getting dangerous to be near."

"I told you," she said, "I'll take my chances." And then she took a step back and looked him over. "You'll feel better when you're not such a walking zoo. Why don't I show you the bathroom and then get us some hot coffee going? It'll make all the difference."

"Sure," he said. But he didn't look as if he believed it.

She led him up the steps and into the short passageway to the rest of the apartment's rooms, including the ridiculously well-appointed bathroom with its gold dolphin taps and sunken tub. She'd lived in entire flats that were smaller than this; she turned to say so as she was opening the door, but saw that Jim had stopped. He was staring at the boxroom door at the passageway's end.

She said, "What's the matter?"

Jim tried to smile, nervously. "This is going to sound strange," he said. "But could you just push that door open and show me what's on the other side?"

She looked at the door. It didn't look any different from the others to her, a six-panel internal door in the old Victorian style with a white paint finish and a porcelain handle. It led into the so-called third bedroom, the one without windows and so small that it was hardly worth the name.

She opened the door for him, and switched on the light. There was nothing in the room apart from her cardboard boxes from the move, folded flat and stacked against one wall. There wasn't even a shade on the bulb.

"That's fine. Thanks," he said, and his relief was perceptible.

"What did you think I'd be hiding in there?"

"Nothing," he said. "For a minute I had the idea that it might lead to somewhere else, that's all. I just had to see."

They moved across into the bathroom. "Quite a tub," Jim commented. "Hope there's no water shortage around here."

"Might as well make the most of it while we can. Leave the door open, and I'll bring the coffee on a tray and join you."

"Yeah," he said, brightening a little for the first time. "That ought to be good for the troops' morale."

She left him kneeling and fiddling with the dolphin taps, and headed back to the kitchen. Now that she wasn't alone in the flat, it didn't seem quite so unwelcoming any more. Their prospects might not be so great at the moment, but with effort and a little imagination she was sure that they could be turned around somehow.

She was starting to feel more positive again as she switched on the kitchen lights against the fading of the day outside.

She was jerked back against the wall behind the door by a hand that clamped over her nose and mouth. It had caught her with no breath, and as she tried to get air to scream she only tightened its seal. Strong fingers dug into the muscle and sinew around her throat, probing for pressure-points and causing her unbelievable pain.

It didn't last. The Frenchman found her switch and turned her off like a lamp.

"You didn't tell me where you keep the towels," Jim said as he reached the two steps down into the darkening lounge, and there he stopped. He could see into the lit kitchen at a narrow angle but he didn't see Linda, he saw some hunched beast with a blurred shape that he couldn't resolve until it turned and heaved itself out to face him. Then he was able to separate it into two people, one a dead weight and the other giving one-handed support.

"Switch on the room lights," the taller figure said.

Jim faltered for a moment and then looked around him. He saw a row of three switches on the wall by the steps and moved towards them.

"Slowly," the figure said.

The lights confirmed what he'd already guessed. Daniel was holding Linda easily with one hand, his spread fingers supporting her jaw so that she hung against his side like a rag doll. His other hand held a knife; it looked like the knife from the Louvre.

"Who sent you?" Jim said quietly. "Was it Risinger, or his daughter?"

"That hardly matters," Daniel said. "I'd have come looking for you anyway."

"Why?"

"Because of Paris. Because I'm a professional and you played me for a fool."

"All I did was to lend ten francs to Rochelle. I can't take any credit for the rest."

Daniel shrugged, as if he understood Jim perfectly but couldn't help him. He said, "But I can hardly punish Mademoiselle Genoud, can I?"

It came so quickly, before Daniel had even finished speaking, that Jim didn't have the chance to dive out of the way. He'd never seen a real knife-thrower outside of a circus before and wouldn't have believed that anyone could have moved with such speed and such force. It came at him as straight and as accurate as a dart and Jim, his own reactions dull and slow by comparison, could do no more than begin to raise a hand in a weak gesture of self-protection. He knew in that instant that he was already dead. Sorry, Linda. I did my best, but I was outclassed.

The knife punched squarely through his left palm, and struck.

The hilt was touching the heel of his hand, and the blade protruded for another three inches from under his knuckles. He was so neatly pierced that the blood didn't even start to run until a couple of seconds had gone by. Daniel stared across the room, disbelieving, as if a foolproof party trick had gone wrong.

Jim felt nothing. The blade had spiked him through the no-sensation area that he'd been exercising every day for more than a year. And what was he supposed to do now?

"You'll give the knife back," Daniel said, and he hefted Linda against his side to show Jim that he still had control. But he was starting to tire; Jim saw the faintest tremble in his hand with the effort of holding her up.

Jim's arm was still raised, as if pinned in the air. He said to Daniel, "Let her go. You've got no argument with her."

"If I had, she'd be dead. Others will deal with her. Now give me back the knife or they'll never get the chance."

Jim looked at his skewered hand. He was still amazed that it didn't hurt, almost as in a dream; and for a brief moment he wondered if he *was* in a dream, if the two states had merged to the extent that he could no longer discriminate between them. But his sense of shock was real, and so was the feeling of his blood as it spread down the back of his hand like a river on a map to disappear into the darkness of his sleeve.

Slowly, he lowered himself to sit on the steps.

"I'm waiting," Daniel said.

Jim was aware of him watching, his eyes like a viper's. Linda hadn't moved or made any sound at all. *Open*, Jim told his hand, relying as always on the memory of its usefulness to make it work where there was no longer any feedback. For a moment nothing happened, but then his fingers slowly began to uncurl.

He looked at Daniel. "I don't think I can do this."

"I don't think you have any choice."

The handle had been roughened so that it would be easy to grip. Jim took a hold and pulled. It wouldn't come at first, but then he was aware of a deep sucking sensation that came out of the dead area like signals from a forgotten land. The knife had slipped through the bones of his hand but his flesh was refusing to give up the blade.

It would have been bad enough if he'd had to watch it happening to someone else, but this was beyond belief. His right hand was shaking with the effort.

The point came through. "Wipe it," Daniel ordered.

Crooking his damaged hand in an attempt to prevent it dripping, Jim slowly crouched before the steps and attempted to wipe the blade on the carpet. He fumbled and dropped it, but managed it the second time.

"Now bring it to me," Daniel said. "On your knees."

Oh, Jesus. Blood wasn't enough for this guy. Burning with fear for Linda and an anger that he didn't dare to express, Jim began a slow shuffle toward Daniel. Linda made her first sound as he moved, no more than a grunt like a dream-yelp from a sleeping puppy, but at least it told Jim for certain that she was alive and that she was maybe close to coming around. He had Daniel's knife, but he didn't have any of Daniel's skill with the weapon. He had perhaps four yards to cover.

"Now hold it by the blade, and hand it to me," Daniel said.

Jim did as he was told, a dumb beast to the slaughter. Daniel took hold of his messily-wiped knife.

Jim didn't let go.

If a dog can do this, he thought, then so can I.

Daniel didn't tug, or anything. He simply stood there looking down at Jim, his eyes wide open and his mouth slack with surprise as if he'd taken hold of a live wire that he couldn't now drop. Jim slowly got to his feet, still holding onto the blade. Daniel finally lost his grip on Linda, and she slid to the floor.

"You're wondering what's happening to you, Daniel," Jim said. "Well, that's natural. I spent a year wondering and thinking that my mind was going because of it."

Daniel continued to stare at him.

"You're starting to see the world as I can see it," Jim told him. "This is what I've had to learn to handle. Most people only see things as they are, but I get to see all the shadows as well. You thought you were going to bring me death but I've got to tell you, Daniel, I've been there and it isn't so much. There's worse. Would you like to see how much worse?"

Daniel was trying to shake his head. On the floor beside him, Linda began to stir a little.

"Come on," Jim said. "We won't have to go far."

Linda came around to some of the worst pain that she'd ever felt in her neck and shoulders, as if swords had been thrust through her from every angle. Her head felt raw and hot, but her image of the seconds before her blackout was clear. Now, as she raised her eyes from the wavering trail of blood that stained the carpet before her, she glimpsed something that didn't quite fit with that image; what she thought she saw was Jim Harper leading the Frenchman by the hand like a reluctant child, taking him up the steps and into the bedroom passageway before the two of them disappeared from sight.

I'll tell you where we're going, she heard Jim saying to the Frenchman. *It's a place I can see every time I close my eyes, I've learned to live with it. The question is, can you?*

A few moments later, the screaming began.

She tried to get to her feet, but her legs folded under her. She managed to get her balance again but she had to hold onto the end of the sofa until she stopped swaying. She didn't know who was making the noise but she knew that, for the first time ever, she was getting a second-hand sample of what mortal terror could be like.

Launching herself from the sofa and stepping out with more confidence now, she made for the bedrooms.

The noise was coming from the little boxroom at the end of the passageway. The door to the room was closing slowly, as if someone inside had given it a push and then turned away to other business.

It closed, didn't catch, began to swing open again; but in the brief instant in which the room had been isolated from the passageway, all sounds from inside had stopped with the abruptness of a snapping tape.

She got to the door and pushed it all the way open.

Jim Harper stood in the middle of the room. He was alone. In his hand he held a throwing knife by the blade, and he looked up from this as Linda hesitated on the threshold.

"What happened?" she meant to say, "Where did he go?" But when she tried to speak, she found that she had almost no voice.

Jim tossed the knife down onto the floor and guided her out. In the lounge he had her sit on the sofa while he brought her towels soaked in cold water for her bruises. Somewhere in the kitchen he found a half-bottle of duty-free Scotch that she'd forgotten she had, and he persuaded her to sip some of it neat. It burned her throat, but it also took away some of the dangerous tightness that she'd been feeling in her airway.

And when she'd been tended to, he sat beside her.

"I was wrong," he said. "It's not the end of the line after all. I have to go away for a while and I don't know how long I'll be."

She tried to ask where.

"Don't talk," he said. "But we're going to be all right. When I'm finished with them, they won't be able to touch us again."

249

Afterwards he carried her through and put her to bed. She was too sore and too weak to resist. He lifted the covers and placed Mister Bear in the crook of her arm against her side.

When she woke the next morning, still bruised but feeling better, he was gone.

THIRTY-FOUR

She saw him only once in the weeks that followed. This was out on the street in the middle of town; afterwards she couldn't exactly remember where, and a few days after that she was beginning to wonder whether the sighting had ever taken place at all. There were cars between them and she couldn't get across, but she called his name over the roar of the traffic and he turned and saw her. He was looking exhausted but driven, like someone in the process of being burned out on a permanent high. She glanced around for an opportunity to cross, but then when she met his eyes again he was shaking his head. He said something that she couldn't quite hear, and his hand came up and made a small gesture as if he could somehow push her back in spite of the moving crowds and the cars and the space between them. But she wouldn't be pushed, and when the lights changed she did her best to fight her way through; but then when she reached the spot he'd gone, lost in the mass around her like something carried away on the waves.

Wait, she'd seen him say, and *Not yet*, but she hadn't actually heard him speak; and all that she'd wanted was a word from him.

Most of the time she stayed in the apartment. She felt safer in there, with the chain on the door. She'd already packed and then repacked her boxes, and she wondered how long it would be before a notice to quit came through. She'd had no further contact with the company, and nobody phoned her to find out why.

When she sat looking out over the river and allowed her mind to wander, it would stray to a seaside town of wet slate and mist and she'd get a stab inside as if for a lost garden of childhood. At night when she slept, she would dream of a door that didn't open for her.

She got by. She waited.

There were worse things than waiting.

Although the phone in the kitchen was some distance away from her bedroom, Rochelle could hear it ringing. She had a bedside extension, but she'd disconnected it before going to sleep. If I have to plug in and answer it myself, she thought, then Dieter gets fired in the morning.

It stopped after a couple of minutes, but by then Rochelle was awake. She could hear Dieter's voice, two rooms away and muffled down to a buzz. The apartment's lease had been so expensive that Werner Risinger had looked very sour as he'd authorised the cheque, but even so the interior walls seemed to have been made out of thin cardboard.

It was no use. She rolled over and checked the radio-alarm by her bedside, and the display told her that it was after four-thirty. She'd been training herself to get up at five so that she could be behind her desk at seven anyway, so she might as well fill a bath in the next room and throw in some of the expensive scented junk that Roger had given her instead of trying to sleep for another half-hour. She couldn't find the lightswitch – again – and so she threw back the quilt and groped her way across in darkness to the chair where she'd left her robe.

Dieter was standing out in the hall. He was wearing a dressing-gown over his pyjamas, and he had the uncomprehending look of the barely-awake. He was obviously on his way to wake her.

"The telephone, Mam'selle," he said. "It's from the company, for you. They say it's very urgent."

"At *this* time?" she said.

"They insisted. Somebody called Gilbert Machoud wants to speak to you."

Machoud? She knew of him, but she'd never met him.

"I'll take it in the bedroom," she said. "Bring me some coffee."

Rochelle's apartment was in an exclusive conversion on the outskirts of Dormach, only eight kilometres out of town. At various times the building had been a hospital, a convent, and a clock museum, but now it had been subdivided into eight separate suites of rooms which had been refashioned by one of the city's most imaginative design teams. It was mainly for this reason that Rochelle intended to get an interiors man over from Paris as soon as she could arrange it; the place had about as much style and character as an airport lounge or one of the newer merchant banks. And still she couldn't find half of the switches, more than four days after moving in.

She sat on the unmade bed and plugged in her phone.

"Rochelle Genoud," she said.

"This is the computer section," the voice at the other end of the line said. "We're having big problems."

"At this hour?"

"Most of us have been here all night. It's been a battle, and it isn't going well. I think we're losing the mainframe."

She frowned, not sure whether Machoud was speaking gibberish or whether she wasn't yet awake enough to understand. "How do you lose a mainframe?"

"I wish someone would tell me. But every database is being corrupted and nothing we can do seems to stop it. We've been offline for three hours and we're down to the last set of archive copies. I don't dare to make any more in case the copy routine's been compromised, as well."

"Can that happen?"

"No, it can't. None of it can, but it's happening anyway. I've been ringing around trying to alert the board, but you're the first director I've been able to find."

"I'll come in," Rochelle said. "Keep trying the others."

After she'd cradled the phone she sat for a moment with her hand on the receiver, letting the news sink in. There was no doubting its gravity; the mainframe was at the heart of all of the company's diverse and complex business transactions. But this had to be a technical problem, and such problems always had technical solutions. It was mainly a matter of finding the right experts and sending them in. If Machoud's people couldn't hack it, then Machoud and his people could look for employment elsewhere. Some of them were getting to be past their best, anyway. Or so she'd been told.

She'd skip the bath, and drive straight in. By the sound of it she'd be first on the scene. When she stood and turned there was somebody on the other side of the room; Dieter with the coffee, she assumed, creeping around like he always did, but he stepped forward and she realised that she was wrong.

"Hello, Rochelle," Jim Harper said.

She tensed. She felt her face drain white and go cold. She was in her robe, but suddenly she felt naked.

"James," she managed, with a smile that wouldn't stick. "How . . . how did you get in?"

"You can manage most things, if you're determined enough. Don't you know that? Because you're the one who taught it to me."

Couldn't Dieter hear them? She wondered if she dared to call out. Dieter had a revolver in his room.

Jim showed her his empty hands. The left one was bandaged, and not too neatly. He said, "I don't intend to harm you. All I'm looking for is safety."

You've got it," she said quickly.

But he smiled. "As easily as that?" he said, and behind the smile he looked sad and tired and rather like a man who'd seen the wrong side of one sunrise too many. With his good hand he picked up the chair from behind the door and brought it over to the end of her bed. "I don't think so, Rochelle."

"I'm on the board now," she said, trying not to show that she was nervous as he set the chair before her and lowered himself onto it. "Didn't you hear?"

"Yes," he said. "You'll have to forgive me. I meant to congratulate you, but I couldn't get away."

Rochelle glanced at the door; surely Dieter must have heard *something* by now. Jim had reached out and was absently smoothing the rumpled satin of her bedspread.

She said, "What's done is done, James. It was nothing

personal. And the company did pull the charges in the end."

"So everything's fine," Jim said quietly.

She watched him, trying to read him.

She said, "What exactly do you want, James?" And at that, he looked up at her.

"What do you suggest?" he said.

"A better deal?"

"That shouldn't be too hard. Any deal's bound to be better than the one that I got."

Rochelle forced herself to unwind, just a little, "Let's not play games at this time of the morning," she said. "I can't undo what happened and I'm not going to pretend that I didn't plan my own part in it. That's business for you. The only question we have to address is, how do we take it from here?"

"We, meaning the company?"

"Of course."

Jim leaned forward, his elbows on his knees, and he rubbed at the back of his neck. He didn't look as if he'd shaved in a couple of days or more, and from his reddened eyes it didn't look as if he'd slept much either. "There's my problem," he said. "I was wrong to trust you, but at least I knew who I was dealing with. But what *is* the company? It doesn't sleep, it doesn't breathe, it doesn't cry. It can hurt, but it can't *be* hurt. You can try to fight it, but nobody suffers except the little people who get walked on."

Rochelle glanced down at the phone. She wondered if she could ease the receiver from its cradle without him noticing. She said, "What did you do to the mainframe?"

"Just a little virus," Jim said. "It seemed kind of appropriate."

"Something designed by your friend?"

"My friend died," Jim said, and the eyes that regarded her then had the dull gleam of moonlight on still water.

She said, "I'll try to sort something out for you, James. I won't even try to pretend that I don't owe you."

He was still looking at her; but she saw no threat there, more a regretful kind of tenderness. He said, "You know, there was a time that I'd have crossed rivers and fought with sharks for you. Just to be near you and to know that you'd noticed me."

"I'm truly sorry, James. That's the one thing I didn't push you into."

He lowered his gaze.

"Yes," he said. "I know."

Rochelle was beginning to get her confidence back. The shock of the intrusion had shaken her, but she had a growing certainty that Jim had meant it when he'd said that he wouldn't lay a hand on her. *I can handle this*, she thought to herself, and she said, "So, what's it going to be? Money?"

He looked up at her again. "I already told you, I'll settle for safety."

"And I already told you, you've got it."

He rose from the chair, and moved it aside so that she was no longer penned. "I'll need a better guarantee," he said. "Just step this way and take a look at something for me, will you?"

"Of course, James," she said, trying to sound brighter than she felt. "Why not?"

He walked her over to the bathroom.

But then she didn't want to go inside with him, because suddenly she was no longer so sure of his intentions. They were three floors up, and the bathroom led nowhere. "Wait," she said. "Please. You're scaring me."

So he backed away. "I said I wouldn't harm you," he said. "You can go in alone. I'll stay right here."

So she nodded. She was thinking quickly. The bathroom had a lock on the inside and a service buzzer alongside the tub. She was almost afraid that he'd be able to read as much on her face, so she turned away. As she did this, Jim Harper was settling onto the corner of her bed from where he'd be able to watch the door.

She stepped through into the bathroom, quickly swinging the door shut behind her. He couldn't have come in this way. So what did he expect her to find?

At first she didn't understand it. Then she didn't believe it.

She wasn't in her own bathroom after all. She was somewhere else, and she wasn't alone. Heads lifted and blank eyes gazed at her, none of them showing any surprise or welcome. Werner was there. Roger was there. All of the faces that she was accustomed to seeing around the big boardroom table at the top of the company building, old men with soft bodies and hard little eyes. Nobody smiled, apart from Daniel. Daniel was grinning broadly. Daniel was also drooling down his shirt.

"I'm going to leave you here for a little while," Jim Harper said from behind her. "I haven't decided how long, yet."

It took her a moment before she turned to reply. And when she did, there was nobody to hear. A slow horror began to dawn on her.

On and off for a few weeks now, she'd been dreaming of doors.

But this room, somewhere in the nightmare country, had none.